"You aren't ⟨...⟩ where they're going because they're too stubborn to take directions from a woman, are you?"

We face forward. The doors close.

"Do I *look* like one of those guys?"

The elevator makes its descent. Our reflections stare back at us in the polished steel of the panel door. Zack's expression remains neutral.

"Looks can be deceiving. Sometimes you think you know a person, and then you realize you don't really know him at all."

He nods. "I suppose that's true." There's a hint of sadness in his tone. Zack's shoulders tense—a reaction so brief I doubt he's even aware he reacted at all. "Everyone has secrets."

He makes his way toward the exit and I wonder again what really brought him to San Diego. I wonder why he left his pack behind in South Carolina. I wonder if he's joined one here. Mostly I wonder if he's been wondering about me.

ADVANCE PRAISE
FOR *CURSED*

"One entertaining and fast-paced read. Best of all? Zack, the wildly sexy werewolf FBI agent! What better crime-fighting partner could a girl have?"
—Jennifer Ashley, *New York Times* bestselling author of *Tiger Magic*

"Cursed is the perfect blend of magic, mystery, and romance. Emma and Zack are strong, noble characters who are trying to overcome their dark pasts, and their quests for redemption will make your heart hurt. This is a series you need to read now."

—Sandy Williams, author of the Shadow Reader series

CURSED

A FALLEN SIREN NOVEL

S. J. HARPER

A ROC BOOK

ROC
Published by the Penguin Group
Penguin Group (USA) LLC, 375 Hudson Street,
New York, New York 10014

USA | Canada | UK | Ireland | Australia | New Zealand | India | South Africa | China
penguin.com
A Penguin Random House Company

First published by Roc, an imprint of New American Library,
a division of Penguin Group (USA) LLC

First Printing, October 2013

ROC REGISTERED TRADEMARK — MARCA REGISTRADA

ISBN 978-0-425-26329-7

Printed in the United States of America
10 9 8 7 6 5 4 3 2 1

From Jeanne— To the heart of the Pearl Street Critique group: Aaron, Angie, Tamra, Mario and Warren. You always have something interesting to say! To Phil, who constantly tells me I can, and Jeanette, who constantly reminds me that I have! And to my coauthor, Samantha Sommersby: if you hadn't come up with the idea of working together, this book would not be a reality.

From Samantha— To my son, Max, whose imagination and appreciation for world building holds no bounds. You've been a consistent cheerleader and a constant source of joy in my life. To my husband, Bill, my mother Beverly, and my dear friend Barb—without your support, I wouldn't have the courage to pursue my dreams. And to Jeanne, collaborating with you has been both a privilege and a pleasure. We did it!

ACKNOWLEDGMENTS

We've known each other for a long time, but it wasn't until we sat down during Comic-Con and again during DragonCon a few years ago and started kicking around ideas that the notion of working together was conceived. One thing led to another and before we knew it, we had Emma and Zack, a plot, a backstory, and a book!! Jeanne's agent, Scott Miller, liked it, sold it and the rest, as they say, is history.

To those of you out there giving *Cursed* a chance, we hope you enjoy reading it as much as we enjoyed writing it.

—Samantha & Jeanne

Siren *noun* 1. One of three sisters ejected from Mount Olympus by Zeus and cursed by Demeter for failing to prevent Hades from kidnapping Persephone. 2. An immortal goddess bound to earth who, in search of her own salvation, saves others from peril. 3. A beautiful and powerful seductress, capable of infiltrating the minds of others in order to extract truth or exert influence.

CHAPTER 1

You've seen one dark, rugged werewolf, you've seen them all.

That's what I told myself the first time I laid eyes on Zack Armstrong. I was wrong. Dead wrong. And now that presumption has come back to bite me in the ass.

I interrupt my best friend, Liz, in the middle of—something. I realize I'd lost the thread of our phone conversation the minute I spied Zack weaving his way through the maze of indistinct gray cubicles that make up the bull pen of the San Diego FBI Field Office. Save the hair and nine a.m. four o'clock shadow, the man is all spit and polish. Tailored dark blue suit, starched white shirt, blue-and-gold silk tie, and gleaming black shoes. The hair gives him a distinct edge—dark brown, slightly longer than regulation, no part. It's swept straight back, accentuating the lines of his square jaw.

I resist the urge to crawl under my desk. "I'll call you back later. New partner's here. I've got to go."

"Not until I hear the details. What's he look like?"

Liz is forever trying to play matchmaker. Ironically, I rely on her spell casting to make sure a match will never happen.

I turn around and lower my voice a notch. "Remember the guy from South Carolina I told you about? The one I was partnered with on that missing person's case in Charleston last year?"

"Really?" New interest sparks in her voice. "He looks like him?"

"It *is* him," I say. "Which you'd think Johnson would have mentioned."

"So what's the problem? I'll tell you now what I told you then. You shouldn't write off the possibility of a good romp with a guy just because he goes furry a few days every month. Weres have amazing stamina. Hey, did I ever tell you about Walter?"

You name it, Liz has dated it. Being a witch with serious magical talent puts her in contact with a wide variety of supernaturals. A strong advocate for equal opportunity love, she's currently dating a vampire.

But Walter the werewolf was decidedly *not* one of her success stories.

"Yeah, Liz. A few dozen times. The problem isn't Zack's nature."

"The FBI has rules about fraternization?"

"No." I wish they did. I wish it could be that easy. Not that getting involved with a partner is encouraged.

"What, then?"

My eyes squeeze shut. I shouldn't have given Zack Armstrong a second thought in the last thirteen months, seventeen days. But I have. I've thought of him often. Too often.

Gooseflesh appears on my arms; the hair on the back of my neck rises. A sense of dread washes over me. That's why he's here. This isn't a coincidence. It's a test the Olympians have their hands in. Or, more specifically, one particular Olympian. Demeter. I'm a Siren—one of three. We were banished by Zeus and cursed by Demeter thousands of years ago for failing to protect her daughter Persephone—for failing to rescue her before she was dragged by Hades to the Underworld. It's for this I atone. For this I pay.

And pay. And pay.

I'm tempted to make something up, but this is Liz. She deserves the truth. "I liked him. *More* than liked him."

Her tone turns serious. "You never mentioned that. This could be bad."

The understatement of the year. Guys I get into meaningful relationships with tend to end up dead, courtesy of my favorite vindictive goddess. Partnering with Zack Armstrong and risking a rekindling of whatever was between us could prove exceedingly dangerous. Even lethal.

For him.

"I've got to go."

I click off, the sound of Liz's protests ringing in my ear, and concentrate on the familiar six-foot-plus werewolf coming toward me. Deputy Director Jimmy Johnson emerges from his office. "Here's the memo I promised you about your new partner. Better late than never."

He may be chronically behind with paperwork, but otherwise Johnson's tenacious about his job, a real pit bull. And, despite being only five foot six, he's one of the toughest guys I've ever met.

I snatch the sheet from his hand and drop it on my desk. "Why didn't you tell me it was Armstrong?"

"I thought I did." His look is quizzical, but it doesn't stay that way for long. "Zack! Good to see you again."

The two men greet each other with a hearty handshake.

"Good to see you again, Deputy Director." The Southern accent is smooth; the cadence of his voice is, as I remember, low and lilting. It was the first of many things that got to me about Zack Armstrong.

Johnson dives in without preamble. "Emma Monroe's your new partner. I don't have to waste time with introductions. What's it been, a year since you worked on that case together?"

"Just over," Zack answers, flashing a sideways glance in my direction.

What Johnson couldn't possibly know is that we share more than a past case. We both have secrets—supernatural powers we've managed to keep hidden from the Bureau, the world, and, as far as Zack is concerned, each other. Unbeknownst to him, I sensed what he was the instant we met. We never discussed it. He's never revealed it. But of course he wouldn't, not to an outsider.

And then there is the other secret we share. Zack and I slept together.

Once.

It was during our last night in Charleston. We'd celebrated wrapping up the case, indulging in a good meal and too much wine. The attraction had been building for weeks, the sexual tension as thick as the South Carolina air. I wish I could say that one thing led to another. That I was impulsively swept away. But I'm not impetuous when it comes to sex. I can't afford to be. The potential consequences are too high.

We agreed that after, we'd go our separate ways. There would be no telephone calls. No texts. No emails. No contact. Period. With twenty-four hundred miles between us, it seemed safe.

Johnson startles me with a slap on the back. "Show him the ropes. He's all yours."

I offer my hand. "Good to see you again."

Zack takes it.

A woman can tell a lot about a man from his handshake. Zack's hasn't changed. It's confident, firm, and friendly. It's the handshake of a man who has nothing to apologize for and no regrets.

Johnson is already on his way back to his office. Zack doesn't seem to notice. His eyes are on me.

"I'm pleased to be working with you again, Agent Monroe."

Is he? The handshake. The demeanor. Both seem genuine. But, despite the old-world charm, I can't shake the feeling that something is off.

Maybe coming here isn't something he wanted at all. Maybe it's strictly a Bureau-initiated transfer. Maybe he's merely worried about how I'm going to react. My curiosity has gone into overdrive. The possibilities ricochet through my mind like bullets in a steel barrel. I want to know how he feels. To taste the truth, whatever that may be. And I could. All it would take is lowering the dampening spell that keeps my powers in check. But giving in to temptation like this would be uncharacteristic. Using my gift comes at a price.

"I thought we'd moved past you calling me Agent Monroe," I say finally. "Emma or Monroe will do fine."

Zack releases my hand, then subtly breathes in my scent before stepping back to continue his appraisal. His gaze, now cool and calculating, sweeps the length of my body. He's searching for a reaction, sizing me up. He sees what I want him to see, what he saw when we worked together before, a no-nonsense professional who is dedicated, capable, all about the mission. Denying my powers and disguising my beauty has become second nature to me.

Over the centuries I've become an expert at blending in. My dark hair may be long, but it's never loose. I wear sunscreen. No mascara. No lipstick. No makeup. Period. Today's suit, like all of my suits, is black and tailored. The white cotton twill blouse is classic, conservative. I don't accessorize. I don't wear jewelry. I don't wear silk where a man can see it.

Zack's eyes, an intense dark brown, ringed with gold, linger a fraction of a second too long on my collarbone. I can't help myself. For one, fleeting moment, I remember the feel of his mouth there. Suddenly I'm conscious of the rise and fall of my chest. My throat is dry. I push the memory aside. The last thing I need to be doing right now is dwelling on what happened in Charleston. I know I should say something. I just have no idea what. Zack breaks the ice.

"It's been a while," he says.

"Yeah. So, how are you?" Before he has a chance to answer, I add, "I should introduce you to the others."

Zack lifts his hand in the air and shouts out, "Zack Armstrong, new guy."

There's a collective "Hey, Zack."

He turns back to face me square-on. "I'm itching to get started. What have you got for me?"

I take a step closer and lower my voice. "That's it? You have nothing else to say to me?"

He matches my tone. "I was hoping to postpone the awkward 'what are you doing here?' conversation for as long as possible. At least until lunch?"

Since I'm not anxious to go down that road, either, I gesture to the desk facing mine. "Have a seat. This one's yours."

When he sits, I check my reflection in the window behind him. The glamour I rely on is firmly in place. The lock on my powers under control. He shouldn't be able to see through the wholesome "plain Jane" facade, to discover what's underneath, what's real. Thanks to Liz, no one should.

"You heard what the man said." He leans back in his chair and spreads his arms wide, giving me a glimpse of what I know to be a well-muscled chest under the fabric of his shirt. "I'm all yours." His look is serious, expectant. "What can I do?"

A thousand possibilities rush through my mind. Not one of them has anything to do with the case.

Focus, Emma.

I pull a sheet from the file and give Zack the rundown. "Amy Patterson has been missing for two weeks. She's thirty years old, an artist. She lives alone. We got the case this morning."

Zack pulls a pen and a small notebook from his inside coat pocket. "What kind of artist?"

I quickly scan the report. "Painter, Expressionist, mixed media mostly."

"Kidnapping gone bad?" he speculates.

"Could be. She's successful. But there's no known family and, according to her manager, no request for ransom."

Zack sets the pen and notebook down, centering them deliberately on the empty desk. "Who reported her missing?"

"The manager, Bernadette Haskell. She's known Amy

for years. Haskell owns the gallery in La Jolla where Amy's art is exclusively exhibited and handles Amy's gallery bookings and commissions worldwide. I spoke to her earlier this morning. She said Amy rarely leaves her apartment. She both lives and works there. Plus, she has a huge show coming up in New York. And before you ask, yes, she called there to see if Amy might have gone ahead to check the space out." I shake my head. "She's not in New York, either."

His brow furrows. "Why is the FBI involved in a straightforward missing person's case? Shouldn't the local police be handling this?"

I nod. "They should. They are. But Haskell has a friend in the district attorney's office and he's calling in a favor. The relationship between Haskell and Patterson was more than purely business. Over the years Patterson became like a daughter to this woman. SDPD hasn't made much progress. Officially, we're just reviewing the casework."

"Unofficially?"

"The fact that she's missing hit the papers yesterday. The story is getting a fair amount of press. The DA wants us to close the case. It's an election year and he's out to win the hearts and minds of the voters. Something with this amount of visibility, if handled right, could clinch what is sure to be a close election."

"Politics as usual. Where do you want to start?"

"SDPD already covered the usual stuff. They checked the psych wards, hospitals, and morgues. There haven't been any recent credit card charges or bank withdrawals."

"What about login access for things like email, social networks, and other accounts?"

"Nothing for a couple weeks."

"I almost hate to ask, but could this be a publicity stunt of some kind?"

I remember the sense of urgency and concern in Haskell's voice when we spoke. "My gut says no, but I don't think we should rule anything out."

Zack nods.

"According to Haskell, it's not unusual for Amy to go incommunicado when she's finishing a project. But it's highly unusual that she'd up and leave town without telling her. And Patterson's car is still in the building's parking garage."

"I assume they checked local taxi and car services?"

"Yup. That turned up zip, too."

"No signs of a struggle in her apartment?"

I push back from my desk. "Not according to the police report. I haven't personally searched the place yet. It hasn't been declared a crime scene. No sign of foul play. Haskell said she couldn't get away from the gallery this morning. She's the only one there. But she'll give us the keys so we can check the place out on our own. She's expecting us."

He rises. "Want me to drive?"

"Sure. The Haskell Gallery is on Prospect Street. I can give you directions."

Zack follows me toward the elevator. "I know where Prospect is." He punches the call button. The doors slide open instantly. He holds them and waits, allowing me to enter first.

He did most of the driving in Charleston, which made sense. We were in his territory. San Diego is mine.

"You aren't one of those guys who pretends they know where they're going because they're too stubborn to take directions from a woman, are you?"

We face forward. The doors close.

"Do I *look* like one of those guys?"

The elevator makes its descent. Our reflections stare back at us in the polished steel of the panel door. Zack's expression remains neutral.

"Looks can be deceiving. Sometimes you think you know a person, and then you realize you don't really know him at all."

He nods. "I suppose that's true." There's a hint of sadness in his tone. Zack's shoulders tense—a reaction so brief I doubt he's even aware he reacted at all. "Everyone has secrets."

He makes his way toward the exit and I wonder again what really brought him to San Diego. I wonder why he left his pack behind in South Carolina. I wonder if he's joined one here. Mostly I wonder if he's been wondering about me.

We walk through the foyer of the FBI building into the light of day. I pause, close my eyes, and tilt my face up toward the sun. How many more days will pass? How many more women will I have to save? I silently recite the same words I do every time I go out on a new case. *Redemption could be one rescue away.*

"You coming, partner?"

Zack has passed me and is waiting next to one of the Bureau's many black Chevy Suburbans parked near the entrance.

Before I can answer, a silver BMW convertible pulls into the lot. It whizzes by, making a sharp right turn and pulling up to the row of SUVs directly in front of Zack. The car's curves are sleek, its paint job gleaming. A woman steps out of the driver's side. Zack's eyes are glued to her. I can't blame him. Her long legs emerge first, toned and sporting a pair of expensive red heels that boldly accentuate her black-and-white dress. As she approaches Zack, she removes her dark designer sunglasses and the silk scarf covering her head. She's pretty, even-featured. Her makeup is meticulous. Long blond hair spills out and hangs loose in waves that brush her shoulders.

The tension in Zack's body tells me the woman is more than a stranger stopping to ask for directions. He knows who she is and he's not happy to see her. His shoulders bunch, his mouth turns down. I can't quite make out what she says to him as she approaches, but his response is clear. He shakes his head and motions her away. The gesture is understated, discreet, but it carries with it a sense of finality. He looks past the woman, at me.

Her head turns, following his line of sight. Her eyes connect with mine briefly before she dons the glasses once again. The fraction of a second is all she needs to convey a warning. All I need to determine that she, too, is Were. One intent on marking her territory? I resist the urge to let my hand slide to my hip, where my gun rests securely in its holster. I choose instead to annoy her further by smiling and waving.

"You waiting for an invitation, Monroe?" Zack calls out before climbing into the Suburban and closing the door, effectively dismissing Miss Fancy Pants.

As I approach she turns on her heel. A confident toss of her head in Zack's direction says she's gotten her message across. Now that she's seen me, now that she's convinced I'm not a threat, she doesn't bother to spare me a second glance. By the time I reach the Suburban, she's returned to her car, climbed inside, and fired up the engine. With a squeal of tires, she's gone.

But not before I notice the license plate. South Carolina. It's reflex to store the number away in the back of my mind.

I open the car door. "I get the feeling she doesn't like me."

Zack is waiting behind the wheel, hands at the ten and two o'clock position, knuckles white. He avoids looking me in the eye. "She doesn't like the fact that we slept together."

He says it casually.

"You told her we slept together?" I ask, sliding into the passenger seat.

His gaze meets me head-on. "Would you have preferred I lied?"

"She your girlfriend?"

He throws the car into reverse and steps on the gas. "Ex."

I wonder if the status came before the revelation and how long they were together. I'm guessing a few months, a year at most. The breakup seems fresh. In the month we worked together, he never mentioned being involved with anyone. There were no calls to apologize for having to work late and no women showing up at the office. But I did come to know Zack's moods well enough to interpret this one. With one single syllable, he's effectively closing the door on that subject.

It's okay.

Zack can have his secrets.

I certainly have mine.

CHAPTER 2

Zack wasn't bluffing. He gets us from our office in Kearney Mesa to the Haskell Gallery on Prospect Street in La Jolla without a single hesitation or wrong turn. We've managed to miss the early-morning rush hours on both Highways 15 and 52, so it only takes about twenty minutes.

La Jolla is an enclave of the rich and famous. Prospect Street is aptly named. It's the mother lode. A street lined with boutiques, a luxury hotel, fancy restaurants, and galleries of all sorts, the connecting artery to the center of town. Zack scores a spot right in front of the gallery.

He's been uncharacteristically quiet on the ride over. I don't recall Zack being one to hold back. I suppose he's still thinking about the unexpected visit from his ex. I am, too. What's she doing here? It's not exactly an afternoon's joy ride from South Carolina. Or he might be bracing himself for lunch and what he anticipates is going to be a major confrontation.

We sit for a minute, facing the gallery. It's located in the middle of a block built of gray cut stone, arched entryways separating one business from the next. We could be in the center of a European village, the intent of the architects who planned La Jolla's exclusive shopping areas.

The gallery is not the largest storefront. In fact, some of the businesses on either side are bigger. There's a simple banner reading HASKELL GALLERY above the door, and adding to the old-world charm, flower-filled clay pots sit on either side of the entrance.

"Ready?" Zack says.

He has a notebook and pen in his hand.

I nod and push open the car door.

We enter into an airy open space broken only by partitions displaying what I presume are Amy's works. The walls are painted dove gray, the floor is an oak hardwood, and the partitions are stark white—colors picked to emphasize the brilliant hues in Amy's paintings. They shine like jewels under the subtle lighting.

"Abstract Expressionist." It's more of a statement than a question as Zack steps to take a closer look at one of the canvases. It's about three feet by six feet and ablaze with the golds and crimsons of a fiery sunset, all intertwined until the canvas looks more like a piece of woven cloth than a painting. "Reminiscent of Jackson Pollock, only more controlled, purposeful, less chaotic, more deliberate. I like it."

Before I can react with surprise to Zack's adept appraisal, a voice calls out, "Very good."

The reply comes from just behind the partition we've paused in front of. A woman steps out. "Amy's most definitely influenced by Pollock's techniques. Incorporating her own individual style, of course. She's studied many of the Impressionists. Notice the short, intense brushstrokes." She holds out a hand. "I'm Bernadette Haskell."

Zack grasps it. "Agent Armstrong. This is Agent Monroe."

Haskell gives us both the once-over. "I'm glad to see the DA has taken me seriously."

It's not hard to understand why he might. Haskell's presence screams *no-nonsense career woman*. I'd guess her to be in her early fifties, dressed in an expensive tailored suit made of black lightweight wool. Under the jacket is an open-necked shirt of white poplin. The cuffs of the shirt are adorned with black onyx cuff links, matching her earrings. Black suede loafers and frameless glasses complete the ensemble. Her hair is silver, feathered at the sides to accentuate piercing blue eyes.

She fixes those eyes on me. "My office is in the back."

We follow her through the gallery to a door at the very back. Her office is ultramodern, all polished chrome and glass. She motions us to sit in two white leather chairs across from her desk. When we are settled, she starts right in.

"Something has happened to Amy. I know it. She would not have left town without telling me. And before you ask, she didn't have a boyfriend she ran off with, either." She opens her top desk drawer and retrieves a set of keys. "These are the keys to her apartment. I haven't touched anything since the police conducted their search."

When I take the keys from her hand, she slumps back in her chair. "The police went through everything on her computer, checked her phone records. They didn't find one single item to shed light on Amy's disappearance. But I'm certain someone's taken her."

"What makes you so certain?" asks Zack.

"Look around the gallery, Agents. Amy's career is flowering. She gets so many inquiries regarding new commissions, we have to turn some away. She has a show opening in New York in two days. Her reputation is growing. She wouldn't walk away from it. It's what she's worked for all her life." She draws a quick, sharp breath. "And, quite honestly, I can't bring myself to consider the alternative—that something worse has happened to her."

"You seem very close to Amy," Zack says.

"We are very close, Agent Armstrong." She waves a hand. "Amy is reclusive. Doesn't make friends easily. Her work really is her life. I am the only person Amy has let share that life since her parents died two years ago. I do more than manage the gallery. I am her friend, confidante, personal assistant, and, dare I say it"—she smiles here—"biggest critic. She looks to me to keep her grounded, on track."

"When did you realize Amy was missing?" I ask.

She answers without hesitation. "March twenty-ninth. She had an appointment here at three that she missed. I called her cell, her home number. There was no answer. I left messages, spent the next two hours checking my voice mail. As soon as the gallery closed, I went over to her apartment. That's when I really started to worry. Her car was there, but no Amy. By that time, my calls to her cell started to roll straight into voice mail. Either Amy had turned it off or she'd let it run out of battery. Again, uncharacteristic."

Zack leans forward, listening intently. "Is that when you called the police?"

Haskell nods. "Yes. They told me I had to come to the station if I wanted to file a report. I was torn. I wasn't sure I should."

"Did you?" he asks.

"Not that night. The police suggested I call the local

hospitals, the coroner's office, the morgue. By daylight I was frantic. I called a friend in the district attorney's office and begged her to convince the police to help. She promised she'd get SDPD to come, told me to stay put. I waited for hours. They took my statement, gave the apartment a quick once-over, then left. They've done nothing. Nothing. Someone needs to take this seriously. It's been almost two weeks. I *had* to get you involved."

To Haskell, it would appear that the police have done nothing. But we have their case records to show they had done all the requisite background checks. Small comfort, though, to someone waiting for concrete news of a missing loved one.

I let a beat go by before saying, "You mentioned Amy having missing an appointment. Do you keep her schedule?"

"I do." Haskell punches up something on her laptop, turns the screen so I can see. "Here are last week's appointments. I keep it week to week."

"Can you print it out for us?" Zack asks. "Not only the most recent entries, but for the last two months?"

Without replying, Haskell hits a key and the printer on a credenza behind her begins to whir. It spits out a dozen sheets of paper, which she takes from the printer, taps on the desktop to align, and hands to Zack. "You will see that Amy never missed an appointment before—" Her voice drops. "I've managed to put off most of what she's missed. But now that her disappearance has become public knowledge. . . ." One manicured fingernail taps a copy of the *San Diego Union-Tribune*. It's open to the Arts page where a headline reads LOCAL ARTIST MISSING.

I rise. "We'll head over to Amy's apartment." I take a

business card from my pocket and hand it to her. "We'll be in touch as soon as we finish there. We may have more questions for you."

"Anything," she replies. "Just bring Amy back."

Her telephone rings and she glances down. "I expect I'll be busy today answering this damned thing."

Zack has risen with me. "We'll leave you to it. We'd appreciate if you didn't mention our involvement just yet. Gives us a little time to work without the interruption of inquiries from reporters."

"Of course."

She reaches for the telephone and Zack and I take our leave.

"Patterson lives downtown in a high-rise at the corner of Kettner and A Street." I'm reading from the police report. I look over at Zack. "I suppose you don't need directions there, either."

Zack is back behind the wheel. He smiles. "Nope."

His manner is more relaxed. He seems to have shaken off the effects of his encounter with the woman in the parking lot.

"So, how do you know your way around San Diego so well?"

"Long story. I'll tell you about it sometime. Right now I want to know your reaction to Haskell."

"Smart. Efficient. All business. But her feelings for Amy are real. She's worried. And it goes beyond her own self-interest in a business that appears to be doing very well."

"We should look into the gallery's financials, as well as Amy's and her own."

I put in a call to the office and let Johnson know what

we need. He says he'll get the warrants and put one of our people right on it.

I disconnect. "How do you know so much about art?" I ask when I've slipped my cell back into my handbag.

"I know a little about a lot of things," he answers.

"Did you really like Amy's paintings?"

"You didn't?"

By now we're making good time. Zack has navigated his way out of La Jolla, and Interstate 5 is wide open.

"Give me Giorgione's *Sleeping Venus* or Heda's *Breakfast.*" I sigh. "That's art."

He laughs. "You realize most people our age don't even know who the Old Masters are?"

Our age? I stifle a snort.

"Age has nothing to do with preference." It's what I say, but actually, it does. I was living in Europe during the fourteenth through eighteenth centuries. While the art was magnificent, living conditions were decidedly not.

Ten minutes later we've pulled off the highway and I sit quietly with my thoughts as Zack winds through the maze of one-way streets downtown. We're not so lucky in finding a parking spot this time. It takes several turns around the block before we spy a driver pulling out of a metered space. Fortunately, we manage to snag it before anyone else.

I look up at the building while Zack feeds quarters into the meter. "Nice digs."

It's an upscale condo complex, lots of glass, very modern in design. We let ourselves in through a locked entry with one of the keys on the ring Haskell gave us. There's a concierge desk, unoccupied at the moment, so we walk straight to the elevators. Amy lives on one of the top floors, requiring use of another key to gain access.

"Secure building," I note.

"Maybe not secure enough."

The elevator opens and we realize there are only two residences on the floor. Amy's is to the left. Zack unlocks the door. We pause for a moment to don gloves, then step inside.

My first impression is that Amy *must* make a good living with her art. The layout of her apartment is open, airy, with windows overlooking the city and the bay beyond. I take mental inventory. There's a small kitchen and a dining area just to the left of the entryway. There are no dishes in the sink, nothing on the table or on the counters. I open one after another of the cupboards. A few cups and glasses. A set of dishes. No food. Not even crackers or a box of cereal. The refrigerator contains bottled water.

Zack is looking over my shoulder. "She must order in a lot."

Like me, I think.

I look for and find a trash can under the sink. It's empty with a fresh liner.

"Someone tidied up."

"Haskell?" Zack asks. "She said she hadn't touched anything."

I move on to the living room. Amy's furniture is plain, functional. A couch and a love seat arranged to take advantage of the views. No television or other electronics. I wander over to the windows. There are no curtains or screens. The bay sparkles in the distance and I watch a plane dip into position to land at the airport just visible to the right. The streets below are dotted with houses and other apartment buildings. The city lights must be spectacular at night.

Zack joins me, follows my line of sight across the street.

"You thinking what I'm thinking?" I ask him.

Zack nods. "There is one building across the way that looks into this apartment. Maybe someone saw something the day Amy disappeared."

There's a remote lying on a small table near the windows. It seems out of place since there's no television or stereo in the room. I pick it up, press a button. The window brightens, as if a shield had been lifted.

"So much for interviewing the neighbors," Zack says. "I've heard of these windows. Highly energy-efficient. And impossible to see in from the outside. Appears Amy really did value her privacy."

I step toward a closed set of doors. They open onto a bedroom. There's a queen-sized bed, dresser, walk-in closet. The top of the dresser is bare except for three pictures in silver frames. I recognize Amy in one of them—the one the police copied for her missing person's report. It's an outdoor shot, probably professional, judging from the way the background has been blurred to emphasize a pretty thirtysomething redhead with laughing green eyes and an impish smile.

The second is a picture of an older couple taken on what looks like the front porch of a comfortable suburban home. I hold the picture up to Zack. "Her parents?"

"Probably. And this one." He points to the third picture. It's an informal shot of Haskell and Patterson. They have their arms around each other's waists and are grinning into the camera. In the foreground is a birthday cake, ablaze with dozens of candles. "Seems to lend credence to what Haskell told us about the two of them being friends."

I cross the room to peek into the bathroom. Towels are hung neatly, cosmetics lined up in orderly fashion next to a toothbrush holder.

"What woman goes on a trip without her makeup or a toothbrush?" Zack asks. He's rejoined me and is looking over my shoulder into the bathroom.

From the way she looked this morning, certainly not his ex, I want to say. Instead I keep my mouth shut and shake my head.

There's one room left and we check it out together.

Amy's office is the only room that reflects more personality than orderliness. This is the room where she undoubtedly spends the bulk of her time. In it are two computers, a laptop and a desktop. Her desk is covered with unopened mail and stacks of magazines. The nearby floor-to-ceiling bookshelves contain everything from Nora Roberts to Nietzsche.

"A woman of eclectic tastes," Zack says.

There are double doors at the back of the room that I assume is a closet. When I pull the doors open, however, I reassess my opinion that her office is where she spends her time.

This is the heart of Amy Patterson's home.

It's her studio.

Zack pushes past me. "Look at this," he says with obvious appreciation. "North light, high ceiling, expansive windows. It's the perfect setup."

"For what?"

"For a studio." Zack stops in front of a large canvas spread in the middle of the floor. "The northern exposure means the space is bright, but the light is even. Not shining directly onto the canvas or in the artist's eyes."

"So you know a *little* about art, huh?"

"This must be the last project she worked on." He squats down for a closer look.

I join him. All I see is an explosion of red in a pattern that resembles poppies, intertwined with blotches of bright blue, orange, and dribbles of yellow.

"It's beautiful," Zack says. "Primitive and alive. Soulful."

"Yeah. Just what I was thinking." I stand back and let Zack continue his rapt study of the canvas. I move around the room looking for anything that might give us a clue as to what became of Amy. I stop in front of a credenza covered in plastic and topped with cans, bottles, and tubes of paint. There are brushes soaking in jars of some kind of oil. Others are standing upright in an old ceramic vase. A couple have been left to dry on the top of the workspace.

I pick one up. The bristles are stiff with red paint. The other one on the credenza is caked with orange.

Zack has come up behind me. He takes the brush from my hand. "Remember when I asked what kind of woman would go on a trip without her makeup and toothbrush?"

"Yeah."

He turns the brush slowly in his hand. "Well, what kind of artist walks out of her studio and leaves an expensive brush to dry without cleaning it first?"

"I'm guessing the answer's the same."

He returns to the painting. The canvas is stretched out on the floor, a taut plastic tarp underneath, anchored on the four corners with tacks. There's a heavy blotch of bright red paint that bleeds from the corners of the canvas onto the tarp as if in her exuberance, Amy overshot her target. It's at these places that Zack focuses his attention. I remember what Haskell said about those short, intense brushstrokes. What Zack said about Amy being controlled and deliberate.

He looks up at me. "I'm going to call Forensics. I think there might be more than paint here."

CHAPTER 3

Zack and I are seated on an outside patio in a restaurant not far from Amy's condo. Our forensics team is busy inside, and since we just seemed to be in the way, Zack and I left to grab lunch while we await their findings.

"You really think there might be blood on the floor?" I ask to break the silence that's fallen.

Zack takes a pull of his iced tea. "I think it's worth looking into. Call it a hunch."

Or a Were sensibility. Could it be Zack was able to smell two-week-old blood through the paint? If so, neat trick.

Silence descends once more. We've exhausted the subject of the case. My choices are small talk or the topic we've been avoiding all day. I suck at small talk. So I drag in a deep breath and go for the second. "It's lunchtime. Time for that awkward conversation you and I need to have."

It's hot. Zack and I have both shed our jackets. Our food has been in front of us for all of two minutes. He's gone for a double portion of slaw with his pulled pork sandwich. I've picked the corn on the cob and the onion rings. Admittedly the corn was a mistake. The kernels are shriveled like raisins from sitting in water for too long.

Zack makes a face. "I was hoping you'd forgotten." He scrunches his napkin into a ball and tosses it on the table. "Looks like it'll be an early dinner tonight. Next time, I pick the place."

"Don't change the subject. What are you doing here?"

"I'd say enjoying barbecue, but that would be a bald-faced lie." He pushes his plate back, then combs his fingers through his hair. I notice it looks a little lighter in the full sun.

I lean back in my chair and cross my arms over my chest. "You know what I mean."

He sighs. "You're pissed."

"You thought I wouldn't be?"

He takes a bite of his sandwich and chews. Since he's so eloquently expressed his opinion of the food, I know he's stalling. I'm not one of those people who feel the need to fill gaps of silence with needless chatter, so I just wait.

Finally he answers, "I guess I hoped you wouldn't be." He leans forward, forearms on the table. "I remember what you said about not being able to afford anything complicated. I've played by your rules. No cards. No flowers." There's a long pause and then he asks, "I suppose it's too much to hope for that you're pissed because I didn't send flowers?"

"Way too much to hope for. At the airport we agreed there wouldn't be any calls, any emails . . ."

He nods. "And there haven't been. Look, I didn't come here with the expectation that we'd pick up where we left off in Charleston. You made your feelings perfectly clear."

I'm not sure I believe him, but I desperately want to. "Then why are you here?"

Zack wears a ring on his right hand. It's gold and reminiscent of a wedding band, engraved with a pattern resembling a tangle of thorns. He taps it three times on the table. Then the explanation comes out in a rush. "Let's just say I've been struggling with my career path."

Not the answer I was expecting. It brings a rush of relief right along with a not so surprising flash of disappointment.

"Go on," I say.

"After the case we worked in Charleston, there was a lot of pressure for me to join the hostage rescue team. It was like at the Academy, only worse."

"I don't understand. What happened at the Academy?"

He shrugs. "My marksmanship scores were perfect. They recommended me for sniper training. Wanted me on the HRT then. It's not what I wanted."

"Because?"

"I have my reasons. Can we just leave it at that?"

I nod. "For now." The guys in HRT are a tight-knit group. It'd be tough to hide going furry three nights a month in that environment. That's reason enough for him to avoid the assignment. But I'm somehow left with the impression it's more than that.

There's a moment of silence. I can tell he's searching for the right words.

"I've been struggling to find my place. Then I bumped into your boss at Quantico a few months ago. We had a couple beers. I asked about you. He mentioned your partner was leaving. I think my place is here. You're the best field agent I've ever met. I want to work with you again, Emma."

"There are plenty of good agents." I lean forward and lower my voice. "Ones you haven't slept with."

He looks away briefly before responding. "You might find this hard to believe, but I don't generally have trouble finding sexual companionship. Finding a *partner* that makes me better than I am alone? That's far more difficult."

He says the word *partner* as though it means something special. Having worked alongside him, I don't doubt it does.

"That month in Charleston," he continues, "we were good together. Damned good. No one has closed as many cases in as little time as you. You've got one of the best clearance records in the Bureau."

I brush off the compliment. "I've had some terrific partners. I've been lucky."

"Luck doesn't have anything to do with it. I've seen you in action. The way you handled the Mason interrogation? It was magic."

He's not wrong. It was magic. In part. After all, a Siren is a Siren. Every once in a while I step over the line, help things along, insinuate myself into the mind of someone in order to extract truth or exert influence. I did it with the case I worked with Zack. It was a kidnapping. We had a suspect, Mason. We were sure he was involved. Zack and I had been tag-teaming him and coming up empty. He'd been taking a hard line with the suspect. I suggested he give me a few minutes alone to play the sympathy card. Then I did what I had to do. I unleashed my gift and discovered the truth, the location of the missing child.

Risky? Yes. I never know when Demeter might be watching. She frowns on any use of my gift that might draw attention to an Immortal on Earth. Having power is a burden. Not using it, a constant struggle. Though each use of my magic risks Demeter's wrath, finding one of the missing, saving them, tips the scales in my direction. A justified risk for the greater good. Necessary so that I can continue with the mission, so that I can bring another victim home, so that maybe, someday, I can go home.

"Yes, you've discovered my deep, dark secret, Zack." When they get too close, tell the truth. It's too absurd for anyone, even a werewolf, to believe. "I'm really a goddess with special powers. You may now throw away your lucky rabbit's foot. Stick with me and your next promotion is most certainly right around the corner." I punctuate my special brand of sarcasm with a very noisy slurp of tea.

Zack's not deterred in the least. "I'm not looking to get promoted, Emma. I belong in the field. I want to stay in the field."

"Seriously?"

He nods solemnly. "Seriously."

Strange as it might seem to some, I understand that. Promotion is the furthest thing from my mind. Since joining the Bureau as Emma Monroe, I've been fortunate enough to be paired with ambitious partners. Unlike them, I haven't wanted to move up. My clearance record has benefited all of them as they climbed the Bureau ladder.

Zack may have alpha in him, but there's something else there, too. He's ambitious and driven, but not for power or control. For what? I have no idea. Zack Armstrong is one complicated man.

I take another slurp of tea. "So, how recently did you break up with your ex?"

I can't tell if it's the fact that I changed the subject or

the question itself that's surprised him. Just as I reach the conclusion he's going to tell me to mind my own business, he comes out with her name.

"Sarah. Her name is Sarah. Referring to her as an ex makes . . . whatever we had . . . seem more significant than it was. It was a thing. It was casual. It's over. End of story."

End of Zack's version. If she followed him from South Carolina, it couldn't have been that casual.

"Okay. You want to work with me, find yourself a girl-friend." I gather up my plate and Zack's, stroll over to a nearby trash can, and toss it all in.

Zack's risen from his chair. "Girlfriend? I haven't had one of those since I was seventeen."

Somehow I find that hard to believe. "It's a condition."

He frowns. "It's a stupid condition."

I respond with a show of my hands, palms up to the universe in a take-it-or-leave-it gesture.

"So, have I found myself a partner?" He slides on his sports coat. "We good?"

"We're good."

For now.

I make a quick stop in the break room and pour myself a cup of coffee. When I return to my desk, I find Zack looking happier than a kid on Christmas morning.

"Check this out. They delivered everything on the supply list I sent." He is brandishing a pack of red gel pens in one hand and a pack of black in the other. There's a pile of various-colored Post-its in front of him.

I slide into the chair at the desk across from his. "Pens. Post-its. Very exciting."

"You think that's exciting? Look at this."

Zack's fingers fly across the keyboard, and his computer comes alive. "I'm all hooked up."

I leave Zack fiddling with his computer and settle in to review the printout of Amy's appointment calendar. From the way it's laid out, Amy spent most days doing what she loved, painting. From time to time she'd have a personal appointment in the afternoon. On occasion she'd spend an hour or two meeting with someone at the gallery. Thanks to Haskell's meticulous notes, we have not only a record of who Amy met with, but a summary of the meeting and what, if any, follow-up was needed. Haskell also added an addendum if a commission was accepted that specified details of the contract such as price to be paid, deadlines, and when that contract was filed.

I whistle softly.

Zack looks up. "What?"

"You should see what Amy gets paid for some of her paintings. Twenty, twenty-five thousand. Apiece."

"Told you she was good," Zack says. "And she's just getting started."

I meet Zack's eyes. "I just remembered something. A case I read about a few years back. An up-and-coming artist was murdered. The killer did it to increase the value of his own collection."

"Can't rule anything out. I'm thinking if that was the motive, though, we'd have found a body." He turns back to his computer. "The PD stored copies of Patterson's hard drives. I've got her emails, browsing history, years' worth of documents." He strikes a few more keys. "And here are the financials on Amy, Haskell, and the gallery."

"That was fast."

He talks as he scrolls. "The gallery looks to be turning a nice profit. No red flags. Taxes collected and paid. Amy paid cash for her condo and a bundle to have the second unit converted for the studio. Otherwise, she lives pretty simply. There are some statements for a few personal investments, an IRA with a very nice balance, a smaller rainy-day savings account. Nothing unusual or out of proportion to what she's bringing in from her artwork. Haskell's accounts are healthy, but again, not out of proportion to what she earns."

"What about email? Browsing history?"

"There's been a series of recent email discussions with Haskell about the New York exhibit. There's a lot here to go through."

"Send me the link. You take the documents. I'll take the emails and browsing history."

He nods. Fueled with caffeine, I go to work. The job is tedious. I spend two hours scanning emails, then another reviewing a long list of Web sites. I finally land on hers. There's a link to her official Facebook page. There are hundreds of posts from worried "friends."

By the time I look up, most of the other agents have left for the day. "I've gone back a full month. There's nothing remarkable in her emails or her browsing history."

"I have no idea why I wanted to work with you," Zack says, stretching his arms over his head. "Clearly, you suck."

I wad up a scrap of paper that's on my desk and chuck it at him. He doesn't bother ducking. He just casually reaches up and plucks it out of the air. With Were reflexes, he probably could have done it with his eyes closed.

"So, what have you got, hotshot?"

"Nothing concrete so far. I'm going to put in a request for her cell records."

I nod. "Good idea. I'll dig deeper into her calendar, put together a more comprehensive background check tonight."

"So, how often do cases like this end up on your desk? People disappearing with no overt signs of foul play, no enemies, no ransom request, no apparent motive . . . ?"

"You know the drill. It's not a crime to go missing. There are fewer than two hundred reports filed in San Diego County each month. Seventy percent of those resolve with little to no effort within seventy-two hours. Run-of-the-mill cases barely get investigated by SDPD, never mind our unit."

"So practically never?"

"Practically never."

Zack climbs to his feet. "Well, I have to start someplace. Let's hope this Amy Patterson doesn't show up in two days with a hangover and a new husband."

"And the blood in her apartment?"

He pauses. "Might not be a waste of time. . . ." He grabs up his mug. "Time for another cup of coffee. Want one?"

"No, thanks."

Zack heads for the break room. I go back to perusing Amy's Facebook page. It's after six. I pull up the photo tab and stare at an image of Patterson's smiling face. "Where are you?" I ask, wishing I could compel the all-knowing Internet to reveal the answer.

I live in a converted carriage house in one of the oldest sections of town. I use the term *house* loosely. At less than four hundred and fifty square feet, the tiny structure is smaller than the hotel room Liz and I stayed in when we went to Dana Point on her last birthday for a spa weekend. Over the years I've lived in many apartments this size in buildings that came with noisy and nosy neighbors.

The carriage house is in back of a larger estate in Mission Hills. The owners alternate between their homes in San Diego, Santa Fe, and Honolulu. When they're absent, which is most of the time, I pick up their mail and water their plants. They love the idea that I'm a federal agent. It makes them feel as though they have personal security on the grounds. I put on a show of walking the perimeter once a day, checking the inside when they're absent. They let me occupy the carriage house for free.

No neighbors, noisy or nosy.

It's a sweet deal.

The first thing I do when I get home is fire up my laptop, which is currently on the dining room table. I have no designated workspace. I work anywhere and everywhere. The dining room, which is approximately ten by ten, is a stone's throw to the kitchen, which is smaller. I make a beeline for the fridge, where there's a cold bottle of chardonnay waiting. After pouring myself a glass, I call Expressly Gourmet. They're a local delivery service that will pick up from more than a dozen restaurants. I have them on speed dial. Tonight Hector is taking orders. He recognizes my voice.

"Emma! What's up?"

"Not much. What's the wait time for China Express?"

"We can pick up in twenty, have it to you ten minutes after that. Things are slow tonight. Hey, did you hear about that artist who's missing? Are you working the case?"

Hector started as a delivery boy a couple of years ago, fresh out of high school. His first day on the job, I answered the door with my gun still clipped to my belt and made the mistake of explaining what I did for a living. I don't have to watch or read the news to keep up with the local crime scene. I just have to check in with Hector.

"Yes."

"Really?" His voice goes up a notch. It occurs to me he always asks me if I'm involved in the story of the day and it's the first time I've said yes. "That *pendejo* on Fox is saying it's all probably some scam to make money. I guess artists fake their own death all the time so that the demand for their stuff skyrockets. What do you think?"

All the time? Quality journalism at its finest.

"I can't talk about an ongoing investigation, but I agree wholeheartedly the guy on Fox is a *pendejo*. I'll take an order of spring rolls, pork fried rice, and the black pepper chicken."

"Got it. Wait till I tell my mama you're working on the case. She's gonna flip. Talk to you later."

"Talk to you later." I always wonder if Hector ends every conversation that way, or if he reserves that close for customers who order practically every night, like me.

Like Amy.

A long shot but—"Hector?"

"Still here."

"Amy Patterson wasn't—"

He sighs. "A customer? No. I checked. Just out of curiosity." He sounds disappointed.

"Okay, Hector. Thanks."

I take my wine back to the dining room. French doors open onto a small deck where I have potted plants. I open them and take a moment to enjoy the evening's breeze. My thoughts drift to Zack. And how much—or how little—I *really* know about him. A temporary assignment is one thing. Now that he's my partner, the stakes are higher. Seconds later I'm in front of my laptop poking around in his past, using the multitude of resources at my disposal to find out what I can about the Were I'm going to be joined at the hip with for who knows how long.

There are the usual stats: he's thirty-two years old, six foot three, two hundred and ten pounds. His most recent fitness scores are off the charts. Not surprising. While in the Academy he achieved a perfect marksmanship score. Nothing I didn't already know. What I really want to know about is what he did before the Academy. He'd previously made reference to being a soldier. I'd been under the impression he'd served in the marines. But I can't find a matching service record. Maybe it was the Army? I go back to check out his SF-86, knowing it will be there from when he applied to the FBI Academy. There isn't one on record. There's always an SF-86 on record. Something in it must be highly classified. But what?

Out of curiosity, I run his ex's plate. Sarah Marie Louis. Also thirty-two. Born and raised in Hilton Head, South Carolina. No arrests. No warrants. Not even a traffic ticket. I check employment records and come up empty. The address on her driver's license is the same today as it was when she first got her permit at fifteen. I pull up an image of the house on satellite. It's a sprawling beachfront estate a stone's throw from the Atlantic. A quick title search reveals it to be in the name of Charles Louis, the colorful and notoriously conservative Republican senator from South Carolina—Sarah's father.

Just as I'm about to enter Zack's last-known address into the satellite search, my doorbell rings. It's time for dinner and time to get back to work on the other background check. The clock is ticking for Amy Patterson. She's already been gone two weeks. The odds of finding her alive decrease with time, so the mystery of Zack Armstrong will have to wait for now.

I'll unravel it eventually.

I always do.

CHAPTER 4

Day Two: Wednesday, April 11

I'm at the office early—but evidently not early enough. Zack has beaten me in. He is engrossed in what he's reading but that doesn't stop him from noticing my arrival.

"Morning, Monroe," he says as I approach, not bothering to look up.

Pesky Were senses.

He lays down the folder he'd been studying and zeroes in on the file I'm carrying. He raises an eyebrow and holds out a hand. "Homework?"

I place it on his palm. "Amy Patterson in word and deed."

He turns the folder around. "What's this?" he asks, pointing to a stain on the cover.

I shrug. "Looks like the sweet red sauce that came with the spring rolls. Did you make coffee?"

Zack waves a hand toward the break room. "The pot's fresh."

I pick up his empty cup, then find my own buried under another stack of old cases and head for the break room.

I return with two steaming mugs.

Zack accepts his and then holds up the page he's been perusing. "Good work." He takes a tentative sip. "You remembered how I take my coffee? I'm impressed."

"Don't be. I'm a trained observer. I remember lots of things."

Zack grins and turns back to the file. "This was an excellent idea—listing Amy's appointments for the last month. If we work backward—"

"We might be able to better pinpoint the exact time of her disappearance."

The cell sitting on his desk rings. "Armstrong." He listens intently, then scribbles something on a bright pink sticky note. When he hangs up, he looks at me, eyes shining. "Armstrong: two for two," he says. "There was blood mixed in with the paint scrapings from the floor of the studio. It will take a little longer to determine whose, but it's a good guess it will be Amy's. And we have a hit on the fingerprint from the paintbrush."

He sits down, and seconds later there's an old arrest record on the screen.

I look over his shoulder. "Michael Dexter. He was arrested for a DUI five years ago. Anything since?"

Zack shakes his head. "Not even a parking ticket." He turns to look at me. "What do you think?"

"I think we question him." I make a mental note of his current address. "I'll drive."

Michael Dexter lives on Crown Point Drive in Pacific Beach. The street is wide and lined with palm trees. Every other house is a newly constructed two-story minimansion squeezed into a lot sized for the Craftsman bungalows originally built here. Most have been scrapped to pay homage to the god of greed. It breaks my heart because I remember what the neighborhood was like when it was new. In the nineteen thirties—I didn't live here then, but I had a friend who did. That friend, like so many others, is long dead. I struggle for a moment, trying to remember the details of her face, the sound of her voice. They're lost to me now. Peggy? Patsy? Penelope. I called her Penny. We met at the opening of the San Diego Yacht Club in 'twenty-eight and shared a love for sunset sails, bathtub gin, and a man named Jacob—in another life.

"Looks like Dexter's place is up there on the left. The one with the red Prius in the driveway," says Zack.

I pull in behind it. We both climb out of the Suburban and head for the front door. Turns out Dexter lives in one of the original cottages, a block away from Penny's old place. The architecture is almost identical. Memories long buried threaten to stay my hand, but I push them down and ring the bell. After a short wait, I ring again. No one comes to answer.

Zack backs down the steps. "Sounds like there's a compressor running in the back."

I hadn't noticed initially. Now I hear a low, rhythmic hum. We follow the brick walkway to the side of the house, where a wooden gate set in a stucco wall stands open.

"Hello?" I call out.

I see a man, his back to me, covered in a leather apron, welder's mask down over his face, working on what looks like a free-form bronze sculpture. It's while I watch him that I realize I recognize his work. I know who he is. I've seen his sculptures in galleries both downtown and in La Jolla, read about him in the Arts section of the local paper. Michael Dexter is a young artist of some local renown, his works commanding five and six figures.

I circle to approach him from the front. Don't want to startle someone with a blowtorch in his hand. It takes a moment, but he does finally see me. The blowtorch is extinguished. The welder's mask is pushed up and back.

"Can I help you?"

"Agent Emma Monroe." I flash my badge and introduce myself. "This is my partner, Agent Armstrong. We have a few questions about Amy Patterson."

"Amy? Why on earth would the FBI be interested in Amy?" he asks.

Zack doesn't answer. Instead he asks another question. "We need to know about the last time you saw her in as much detail as you can remember."

Dexter sets the blowtorch he's been using on a stand, removes the mask, pulls off his gloves and apron. "That would have been a couple weeks ago." He squints up at the sun. "It's hot. Mind if we go inside?"

"I bet it's even hotter under that mask," I say.

He wipes his brow with the back of his hand. "Usually the climate is perfect for this kind of work. Today it's been torture. Honestly, I wouldn't be working this afternoon if I wasn't under deadline."

Dexter leads us through a pair of ornate wrought-iron doors. I finger the intricate pattern of leaves and vines. "Did you make these? They're beautiful."

He nods, pausing again to wipe his forehead before climbing the steps to the cottage. "I did. Thanks. Can I get either of you some iced tea? I could sure use some."

"That would be terrific," Zack says.

We follow as he crosses a living room and dining room complete with what looks like the original Craftsman sideboards, built-ins of mahogany against buttercream walls. The furnishings, elegant Arts and Crafts pieces, and even the artwork, watercolor landscapes, reflect the period.

"Who's the Craftsman expert?" I ask Dexter.

He smiles. "Too much?"

"Not at all. I wish everyone who bought into this neighborhood appreciated the beauty of these bungalows the way you obviously do."

Dexter frowns. "Yeah. You've noticed some of the monstrosities that have gone up."

"Hard not to."

He pushes through a door and it's like being thrust from the past back into the twenty-first century. Granite countertops, slate flooring, and stainless steel, luxury appliances that would do a small restaurant proud.

He reads my expression and laughs. "Had to make some concessions to modern living."

Dexter's tall, over six feet, and thirty years old, according to the police report. On a better day I would have described him as handsome in a bohemian way — long, dark hair worn in a ponytail, full lips, eyes a pale blue, hooded and intense. But something seems off and I'm starting to realize it's more than just the long hours and the warmth of the day. He runs cold water in the sink and cups his hands under the stream. They're shaking.

He splashes his face, washes his hands, then leans on the counter. "Sorry. I'm feeling a little light-headed. Could I impose on one of you to serve the tea? There's a pitcher in the fridge. Glasses in that cabinet." He nods toward the one to the right of the sink.

"Maybe you should sit down," suggests Zack, who moves with concern to Dexter's side.

I pull the pitcher from the refrigerator and pour the

tea. By that time Zack's helped Dexter into the living room. I spy a tray on the counter and use it to carry in filled glasses. The two men are sitting next to each other on a well-worn overstuffed sofa, speaking in hushed tones. Their voices quiet the moment I enter.

"Do you mind switching on the ceiling fan?" He points to the controller on the far wall. I set the tray down on the coffee table in front of the sofa, then oblige. The hum of the fan's motor and the *thwack, thwack, thwack* of its unbalanced blades fill the momentary silence. I take a chair opposite the sofa.

"Michael was just telling me this will likely be his last piece," says Zack, his expression grave. "He's extremely ill."

"Liver failure," he adds with a worn half smile. "I'll tell you what I can about my visit to Amy's. I'm afraid thoughts, details, well . . . they're slipping my mind these days."

"Do you recall what day it was that you last saw her?" I ask.

He pauses, thinks for a minute. "The twenty-eighth of March? Maybe the twenty-ninth. I think it was a Tuesday. We could probably check my phone. I rang her before going over. She didn't answer at first, but then she returned the call. Left a voice mail. I went right over to her studio. Took a cab. I don't drive myself anymore. I'd guess I was there within thirty, forty minutes of getting her voice mail."

Remembering that SDPD's check of local taxi and car services showed no record of a pickup at Amy's address, I follow up with "Did you return by taxi as well?"

Dexter nods. "I had the driver wait for me. We made a couple stops on the way back. The pharmacy. Then the corner market for some ice cream. I'm eating whatever I want for dinner these days. I figure I'm dying, so fuck it." He pauses. "What's this about?"

"Amy has been reported missing," I reveal.

A shadow crosses his face but quickly passes. He shakes his head. "She has a showing in New York. I think it started two days ago. There's an invitation on the desk over there." He gestures toward an old rolltop in the corner. "Have you spoken with her manager?"

Obviously Dexter hasn't seen the news in the last couple of days.

Before I have a chance to respond, Zack fires off another question. "Can you tell us what happened when you went to see Amy?"

Dexter leans forward, his expression earnest. "Sure. Sure. She said on the voice mail she'd be in the studio, to let myself in. So I did."

"Did she often leave her apartment unlocked?" I ask.

He shrugs. "I couldn't tell you. It was that day. Amy was trying to finish a major piece for the show. She'd been up all night working on it, and was running on pure adrenaline. Music was blaring in the studio. I'm afraid I scared the shit out of her. I wasn't there long. There just wasn't any way she could do what I asked. I understood. I left. Wished her luck with the show."

As unlikely as it is that someone in Dexter's condition would overpower a healthy woman on his own, get rid of the body, and tidy up a crime scene, that doesn't explain how his fingerprints got on the brush.

"What is it you wanted?" Zack takes a sip of his tea.

I've finished mine and set the glass on the coffee table between us on a coaster.

"The piece I'm working on out back is for charity. I was

hoping she might be able to donate something for the same auction. I'd contacted her gallery manager a week or so prior. Haskell suggested I speak with Amy directly. It was a few days before I felt up to calling her. It turned out everything in her studio was spoken for. We chatted for a few minutes." He sits back, sinking into the sofa. "She was excited about some new techniques she was experimenting with. She was planning a series incorporating gouache."

"What's that?" Zack asks him.

He points to a painting on the wall. "Think watercolor, only far more vibrant, bright. She'd just purchased a few series seven Kolinsky sable brushes, very expensive."

Zack pulls out his phone. "Is this one of them?" He shares the image from evidence with Dexter.

For the first time he's hesitant. "I think so."

"You handled it?" I ask.

"Yes. Should I call a lawyer? Am I under suspicion again?"

Again? Zack and I glance at each other.

"When I first saw you, I thought maybe you had news of Isabella," Dexter says.

Zack asks Dexter the question that's sprung to both of our minds. "Who is Isabella?"

Dexter looks confused. "So you're not here because you think my knowing two missing women was too much of a coincidence?" His eyes are drawn to a photograph on the end table next to where he's sitting. It's of an attractive brunette. She's barefoot on the beach, hair blowing in the breeze, smile radiant. He reaches out and touches the frame. "Isabella Mancini, I reported her missing about two months ago. I'm afraid the police have given up on her."

Zack pulls out his notepad and pen. "What is the relationship between you and Isabella?" He writes something down.

"She lived here. We've known each other since we were kids. Grew up in the same neighborhood."

"Where was that?"

"Central Los Angeles. Times were tough back then, for both of us. I got lucky. After graduation, I went to art school in New York on a scholarship."

"And Isabella?"

He smiles. "That girl's a fighter. For seven years she worked nights and attended classes during the day. It took her a while to get her psychology degree, but she stuck with it. When she got accepted to grad school at San Diego State, she was so excited. It was a dream come true. I had room for her here in the house, so I invited her to move in."

He stops to draw a ragged breath. "Is it too much to hope you could look into her case, too? The police aren't doing a damned thing. I'm beginning to think the PI I have on retainer isn't, either."

"We'll definitely be looking into Isabella's case. What's the PI's name?" Zack asks.

Dexter opens a drawer to the end table and withdraws a card. "His card."

Zack jots the name and number in his notebook and returns it and the pen to his inside pocket. "Will you tell us what you told the police?"

"Absolutely. I'll be happy to go over it again, anything to help you." Dexter takes a moment to compose himself. "The night before Isabella disappeared, everything seemed normal. She came home after finishing her shift at the detox center. We had dinner, watched a movie. When I woke the following morning she was already gone, presumably to class. But that night she didn't come home."

"She was employed at a detox center?" Zack asks.

The questioning is taking its toll on Dexter. He looks utterly exhausted.

"Do you want to take a break?" I ask.

He shakes his head. "No. I'm fine. Isabella was doing her internship at the Alcohol Detoxification Center on Island Street for part of her master's program. That's over now. They said they couldn't hold the position open any longer."

I'm familiar with the place. "Tough neighborhood and tougher population." The downtown facility has been the location of the county detoxification center for decades. It mostly houses chronic alcoholics who have been picked up by the police. "Did she ever have a run-in with any of the patients?"

"Not that she mentioned," he says.

"What about any of the teachers at State? Another student perhaps?" I ask.

Dexter smiles. "When I said she was a fighter, I didn't mean it literally. Isabella wasn't dealt an easy hand in life. Her father left when she was a kid. Her mother climbed into the bottle. She had dreams. We both did. But, despite a boatload of hard knocks, Isabella never quit."

Zack puts his glass down on the coffee table.

Michael leans forward and not so discreetly slips a coaster under it; then he chuckles. "It's strange, the things I worry about. I may eat ice cream for dinner these days, but my boyfriend's a neat freak, so I still worry about rings on the table. It's new. We just bought it a week ago."

The reference to a boyfriend catches me off guard. "You and Isabella weren't involved?"

Now Dexter laughs in earnest. "God, no. She knew I was gay before I did."

"Did your boyfriend live here the same time as Isabella?"

"No. He moved in about a month ago. He met her once or twice before . . ." He pauses, closes his eyes an instant. "Before she disappeared."

"Do you know if Isabella knew Amy?"

He considers my question for a long moment. "No. I don't think so. At least I don't recall ever introducing them. Amy and I weren't all that close. She kept mostly to herself."

"Can we ask you to check your cell? See if we can nail down the time and date you went to see her?" I ask.

"Of course." Dexter stands with effort, then slowly walks over to the desk where the phone is. A few touches later he answers, "It was the twenty-eighth. She called me around four. I'd guess I was there by four thirty, four forty-five."

Zack's followed him, looks over his shoulder and verifies. "Do you have the number of the taxi service?"

There's a nod from Dexter. "It would be the very next one."

Zack pulls the notebook back out and makes another quick note.

I pull out one of my cards and join them.

I'm tempted to ask to see Isabella's room, to ask if it's been disturbed. This revelation has my head spinning as a thousand follow-up questions take form in my mind. Before we jump in further, I want to pull the case files, look at them side by side, and consider the possibilities.

"Call me if you think of anything else that might help us," I say, offering Dexter my card.

He takes it, his expression hopeful. "You'll really look into Isabella's case?"

"We will," I promise.

Dexter shows us to the door, holds out his hand. Zack grasps it first, then me. "Thank you," he says.

I leave with the usual stock reassurances that I will stay in touch. After all this time, it would be a miracle if we found Isabella alive, or Amy for that matter.

We came here looking for information on one missing woman. Now suddenly we have two, and I can't shake the feeling they're somehow connected.

"Now what?" Zack asks as I pull out of the driveway.

"I say we head back to the office and pull Isabella Mancini's file."

I call ahead and request Isabella's case file from the SDPD. By the time we get to the office, it's waiting on my desk along with another. The second is for a twenty-three-year-old male named Adam Markham.

"Someone waiting for the Markham file?" I call out.

Garner, one of the older agents, raises his hand. "That would be me."

I stroll over and drop it on his desk. "Another homeless person?"

He nods. "His conservator says he hasn't cashed his check for three months. Who knows how long he's been gone? This one makes eleven. How's your case coming?"

I hold up Isabella's file. "I'm hoping for a break."

By the time I return to my desk, Zack's perusing the information I put together on Amy. He runs his finger down the list of appointments I'd prepared. "I don't see an appointment with Dexter on the list."

"No, but . . ."

He looks up, catching my hesitation. "What?"

"Another connection." I remove a sheet of paper from Isabella's file and hand it to him. "Check this out."

"What am I looking at?"

"There. Middle of the page. The transcript of Isabella Mancini's voice mail messages."

His eyes scan the page, then go back to the list of Amy's appointments. "Dr. Alexander Barakov. Amy had an appointment scheduled with Barakov five days before she went missing." He looks again at the sheet I handed him. "And Isabella had an appointment reminder from the same Barakov. For the day she disappeared."

"That's quite a coincidence."

Zack continues to read from Isabella's police report. "According to this, she never made it. Barakov was questioned but not considered a person of interest."

"Until now." The excitement of the chase starts to build. "I don't know about you, but I just became *very* interested. I think we should pay Barakov a visit. I wonder why Dexter didn't mention Barakov. Think that's odd?"

Zack shrugs. "Maybe he didn't know about it?" The voice mail came from her cell phone dump. My guess is the police didn't share the information with him. Zack picks up his desk phone and dials, then listens. "The office is closed for the next hour for lunch. Let's grab some ourselves."

He's already reaching for his keys.

I grab my purse. "It's your pick. Where are we going?"

"Hodad's. There's one on Tenth Avenue, not far from Barakov's."

I raise my eyebrows. "How do you know about Hodad's? You've been in town less than a week."

He glances in my direction as we wait for the elevator. "Are you kidding? I've been on a quest for the perfect burger since I was nine. Red meat and I have enjoyed a long and deeply satisfying relationship. My last partner was a vegetarian. After the first week we decided to split up for lunch. He couldn't be within ten feet of meat without unleashing a lecture. Don't get me wrong, I have nothing against veggies but—"

"You're a carnivore to the core, huh?" I say. It takes me a second to realize how true that statement is. Zack doesn't seem to catch any hidden meaning. Why would he? He doesn't know that I know of his other nature.

He checks the time on his cell. "It's going to be crowded this time of day and I bet parking is hell downtown. I'll drop you so you can order. I'd like to try to catch Barakov before he starts seeing his afternoon patients."

"What do you want?" I ask. We step into the elevator. The doors close.

"Order me a double bacon cheeseburger, rare."

Double bacon cheeseburger? Rare?

Oh yeah. Carnivore.

CHAPTER 5

As Zack feared, there's a line in front of Hodad's when he lets me out. Thankfully, most are employees from nearby offices who have come for to-go orders. The wait for a table turns out to be much shorter than I expected. In fact, it takes Zack longer to find a parking spot. I've just finished ordering when he finally walks in. He spots me and heads for the table.

"Have you ordered?"

Service at Hodad's is quick—the faster you get your food, the faster the table turns over. Before I have a chance to answer, a waitress appears with our drinks, a combo basket of fries and rings, and a beaming smile.

"Can I get you anything else?" she asks, turning up the wattage even further for Zack.

"Just the burgers," he says.

"Right!"

"Let's see how these compare to yesterday's pitiful offering," Zack says, reaching for an onion ring.

If the expression on Zack's face is any indication, he's in nirvana.

"Well?" I pick up a fry and dip it in ketchup.

"We might need more of these."

Zack continues to work on the onion rings.

I venture a question. "So, when did you live in San Diego?"

Zack doesn't acknowledge me or the question.

"Zack?" I persist, determined to get an answer out of him. "You never mentioned living in San Diego when we worked together in Charleston."

He continues dipping onion rings in ketchup as if that stalling tactic is going to work. Persistence is my middle name. I fix him with a laser beam stare. But when he finally looks up, it's to watch the approaching waitress, who arrives, burgers in hand. Zack's is so big it's almost embarrassing to be seen with it. He attacks it with both the zealousness of the true believer and the relief of a condemned man granted a reprieve.

"Oh my God." Zack's eyes roll toward the heavens.

I show a little more restraint eating my burger. But I do have to admit, in San Diego, Hodad's is by far the best burger joint. I decide to let him eat in peace before I launch the attack again. Gives me a chance to enjoy my burger, too.

We finish up and wipe the evidence from our faces. Zack relaxes back on the bench and gives his stomach a satisfied rub. "Now, that was good."

"How could you tell? You inhaled that burger."

He laughs. "And you didn't?"

"Mine was a tiny baby burger compared to your monstrosity." I stir my Coke with my straw and glance at my watch. "Now that we have a few minutes, you can tell me about your stay in San Diego. How do you know the city so well? And how come you never mentioned living here?"

Zack looks away, across the restaurant, toward the door, down at the table. Everywhere but at me. That same flash of sadness—of regret—that I felt in the elevator yesterday is back again. I fight a completely inappropriate impulse to reach for his hand.

"Seems like a lifetime ago," he says at last. "One I'd rather not revisit."

I can relate to that. It's not the same with me, of course. With me, it has literally been one new life after the other. It isn't easy to resist the urge to press. I'm crazy with curiosity to know his story. And to learn more about the woman in the parking lot, Sarah. But I know how to be patient, to wait till the time is right.

Zack crushes his napkin, tosses it onto the table. "If we want to catch the good doctor before he starts on his afternoon schedule, we'd better head out." He catches the eye of a nearby waitress. "Check please?"

I watch Zack take care of the bill, head to the car without looking back to see if I was following him or not.

I've obviously touched a nerve.

Dr. Alexander Barakov, a board-certified plastic surgeon, has his office on the third floor of a recently renovated building overlooking Petco Park downtown. When the ballpark was built, the stadium initiated a wave of regentrification in the neighborhood, but Zack and I still have to step over and around the sleeping bags and carts stored under the parking lot portico awaiting the return of the street people who make this area their home. The day is unusually hot for this time of year, and those who haven't already headed downtown to panhandle are clustered together in the shade. I feel their eyes on us as we walk past, feel a myriad of emotions in their glances. Sadness, jealousy, hunger, desperation. It casts a pall on my own emotions.

It's a relief to enter the dim coolness of Barakov's building. The foyer directory sends us to Suite 301.

The office is luxurious. The waiting area looks more like someone's living room than a holding tank for patients. There are elegantly upholstered sofas and chairs and glass cases containing fine art pieces, but not one visible patient. A woman is standing behind a desk of polished mahogany. She has a headset in her ear and looks up at us in polite interest as we approach.

"Can I help you?"

Her tone is friendly but professional. It matches the carefully coiffed hair, subtle makeup, and understated jewelry. Her features are even and without flaw, and her outfit seems designed to accentuate her perfectly symmetrical Barbie doll figure—formfitting blouse, pencil skirt. I suspect she's a walking advertisement for her employer.

There is a nameplate on the desk that reads SILVIA BARTON. Zack flashes his badge. "We'd like a moment of Dr. Barakov's time, Ms. Barton."

Barton barely spares the badge or me a glance. Her eyes linger a little longer on Zack before she sits. "Let me check the doctor's schedule for you, Agent . . ."

"Armstrong. This is Special Agent Monroe."

She consults a screen on the computer next to her. "He's in consultation now, but he will have a few moments between appointments. Would you care to wait?"

"Absolutely," I say.

Before we can take seats, she asks, "Can I get you something to drink? Coffee? Water?"

Zack requests coffee, cream, two sugars.

"A bottle of water would be nice." From me.

Barton disappears behind a door. She returns in a moment with a tray. On it there's coffee for Zack in a china cup and water for me—in a glass.

I take the glass, a little surprised. Except in restaurants, almost everyone uses bottled water these days. Or disposable cups. The thought must telegraph itself through my expression, because Barton smiles.

"Dr. Barakov is a committed environmentalist," she says. "No plastic bottles."

I've lifted the glass to my lips, but my hand stops in midair. "A *plastic* surgeon who doesn't believe in plastic?"

Barton doesn't see the irony. She frowns at me. "No plastic. No unnecessary paper products. In fact, we're almost completely paperless here."

"Admirable," I say, rolling my eyes at Zack over the rim of the glass.

Zack raises his eyebrows at me and takes his coffee over to the windows that span the far wall of the waiting room. There's a clear view of the baseball field. "It looks like the doctor's got the best seats in the house. I assume he's a Padres fan?" Before Barton can answer the question, he turns to her and shoots off another. "Is it my imagination or is the tint on this window changing?"

"They're called smart windows," she answers, giving him her full attention. "A firm that specializes in green architecture renovated the building before we moved in two years ago. Special insulation, roofing, and those windows that tint automatically to control the temperature and ensure privacy."

Like Amy's shades, I think. Going green has become a mantra in Southern California.

A door opens somewhere down the hall and Barton moves back to the desk. She pushes a button and speaks a few words into her headset before looking up.

"Dr. Barakov will see you now."

She moves ahead of us, walking gracefully down the long corridor. The sounds of her stilettos on the wooden flooring announce our approach. We pass several closed doors before she stops at one near the end of the hall and holds it open.

Barakov is seated behind another mahogany desk—this one bigger and more ornate than his receptionist's. He rises at our entrance and comes to meet us. The doctor is impeccably dressed in a well-tailored suit, most probably custom made, given that he's shorter than I am, and well-polished loafers. Carefully cut hair accents a perfectly oval face and smooth, high forehead. His stature, hair, and finely chiseled features remind me of Nero. I wonder what else he might have in common with the ruthless tyrant who foolishly burned down nearly half of Rome.

Barakov takes our proffered hands and urges us to sit.

Zack tells him why we're here. Gives me a chance to scope the place out. The office is at the front of the building. There's lots of glass here, too, but it's just as coolly comfortable as the reception area. Besides the desk and wall of windows, there are bookcases lining two walls. A couch is positioned in front of one, along with a coffee table with a fan of current news magazines. Behind the desk is the largest ego wall I've ever seen. There are well over a dozen diplomas and certificates, not to mention framed magazine articles about Barakov's work, and an impressive array of signed celebrity photos. On the desk Barakov has a computer with a flat-screen monitor, an in-box with two or three stacked files, and a set for holding clips, pens, and pencils.

There is also a door in the back of the office. For the

confidentiality of patients, I presume. A way for them to discreetly come and go, avoiding the reception area.

When Barakov hears Amy Patterson's name, a concerned frown darkens his face. "I was shocked when I read about Amy in the papers yesterday. I don't see how I can help you, though. There is an issue of privacy in terms of my consultations with her, and I certainly don't think I know anything that could shed light on her disappearance."

Zack is frowning, too. His frown doesn't reflect concern. It's deliberate, with a touch of menace thrown in. It's the disapproving frown of a hard-nosed cop, the stereotypical "bad cop" who doesn't like the answer he's getting. Or, in this case, the answer he's *not* getting. Zack clearly thinks Barakov is stonewalling. "We aren't asking you to break doctor/patient confidentiality," he says, his tone clipped, sharp. "We're asking if she kept her appointment."

Apparently it's time for Basic Interrogation 101. I assume my role of "good cop," keeping my voice soft, suppliant. "You may have been the last person to see Amy. You must understand how important it is that we establish a timeline. Any help you give us brings us one step closer to finding her."

Barakov fastens his gaze on my more sympathetic face. After a few seconds, his expression softens. "Very well."

"We really appreciate it."

I shoot Zack a subtle approving glance. He meets my eyes and winks.

Barakov has turned to his computer. He punches a few keys, and then scrolls up and down the screen. "Yes," he says finally. "She kept her appointment. She left at eleven a.m." He narrows his eyes at Zack. "That's all I can tell you."

Zack has produced a small notebook and pen from his jacket and makes a notation. Then, without the least bit of hesitation, he casually asks, "And what about Isabella Mancini?"

"Isabella Mancini?" Barakov asks, eyebrows furrowing.

I expected the same kind of rebuff we initially received when mentioning Amy, but Barakov's demeanor is decidedly different.

"Another patient," Zack replies. "You saw her about two months ago?"

The shift to irritation doesn't happen. His expression is merely perplexed. He leans back, casually, in his chair. "I'm quite good with names. I don't recognize that one."

"She's another young woman whose disappearance we're looking into," I explain. "And according to her records, she had an appointment with you, too." I gesture to the computer. "Would you mind checking your records?"

Barakov's fingers work the keyboard. "Yes," he says at last. "Here it is. Isabella Mancini made an appointment by telephone for an initial consultation." He looks at Zack and me in turn. "But she never kept the appointment. That's why the name didn't ring a bell. I never met her."

"Do you know why she wanted to see you?"

"I would assume it had something to do with my line of work, cosmetic surgery. Other than that, I have no idea."

His answers flow freely, without hesitation, yet I sense an uneasiness creeping into his manner. I am tempted to dial up my powers and press him to find out why, but at what cost? Zack would get caught in the wake. Demeter, were she to find out, would see it as reckless. Two problems I don't need.

"It's quite a coincidence," Zack says, "you having a connection to two missing women." Perhaps he feels the shift in Barakov's manner, too.

"I'd hardly call it a connection."

No missing the shift this time. Barakov is indignant. "Do you have any idea how large my practice is? How many women have plastic surgery these days? They feel the need to tweak this, enhance that, always striving for perfection. I have one of the busiest practices in Southern California. *The* busiest practice in San Diego." He leans forward. "When a woman decides to have work done, she wants the best. She wants me."

Then, in an instant, the annoyance is gone. He's turned his gaze on me. "For example, Agent Monroe, have you ever thought of getting that bump on your nose fixed?"

Suddenly both men are looking at me. Reflexively, I touch my nose, then curse myself for doing it.

Barakov laughs. "Of course, it's not a terribly noticeable flaw, but without it . . . well, we all strive for perfection."

"Not all," Zack says, his voice tight. "Some might say perfection is boring."

Barakov peers at Zack as if tallying a score, then waves a dismissive hand. "Spoken like someone who has no obvious physical flaws."

Zack's shoulders bunch. "We all have flaws, Doctor."

"Of course. That's why I made the distinction and said *physical* flaws."

The tension in the room is building and I doubt we'll get anything else from Barakov. Especially with Zack looking as though he wants to add a bump or two of his own to Barakov's perfect nose. I rise and extend my hand. "Thank you for your time."

Zack jumps to his feet. He's as anxious to get out of the doctor's office as a racehorse chafing to leave the starting gate.

Barakov motions to the door behind his desk. "You can leave this way. I hope you find Amy. She is a beautiful young woman, so vibrant."

After the door closes behind us, Zack lets out a breath. It echoes in the stairway like an explosion. "I don't like that guy."

"Really? It didn't show. He seemed quite fond of you."

Zack shakes his head. "I can't put my finger on it. There's something not right about him. I don't care how famous a plastic surgeon he is, it's too much of a coincidence that two missing women are among his patients."

"Amy was his patient," I correct. "He said he never met Isabella."

"Yeah. That's what he *said*. I'm going back three to six months, look through some unsolved cases. I'll start with women over eighteen and see if his name comes up."

I raise an eyebrow. "He also said Amy *is* a beautiful young woman, not *was*."

He concedes the point with a shrug. "Just means he's clever enough to weigh his words around cops."

I follow Zack down to the car, glancing once to look up at Barakov's office window. It's decided. If the investigation stalls, I'll come back and pay the doctor a return visit.

Without my partner.

We're pulling out of the parking lot when Zack points to a traffic camera at a stoplight across from Barakov's office.

"See that?" he asks.

"The traffic cam?"

"When we get back to the office, I'm going to get the tape from the day Isabella went missing so we can review it. The image might not be clear enough to definitively identify Isabella, but it'll be clear enough to see if a car of her model, make, and color was in the area at the time of the appointment. The one she *didn't* keep."

His sarcasm is thick enough to spread on toast. I ignore it. I'm too busy reading a text that just came in from Johnson. Apparently the district attorney is already bugging him for an update on the case. He wants me to swing by his office before the end of the day. I hate these command performances. "The DA wants to see me. How about you check the tapes? I'll call you as soon as I'm finished downtown."

CHAPTER 6

The last two hours have been a complete waste of time. Not only did District Attorney Derek Walker keep me waiting outside his office for an hour before seeing me, once I was in his office, Walker took no fewer than three phone calls. After the last, he had the gall to hit on me, suggesting we continue our debriefing over a drink. Next time he needs a debrief, I'm sending Zack.

Once back on Highway 8, I call to check in. Hopefully he's had a more productive afternoon than I did.

Zack answers with a cheery hello.

"Sounds like you had a better afternoon than I did," I grumble. "What have you got?"

"A couple of baked potatoes, a thick-cut London broil, a twelve-pack of Negro Modelo, and—wait for it— confirmation that a red 2003 PT Cruiser went through the intersection of Tenth and J fifteen minutes before Isabella's scheduled appointment." He pauses. "The one the troll said she never kept. Score one for Armstrong!"

His enthusiasm makes me smile.

"How sure are you that it's Isabella's?"

"The photo of the driver's a little fuzzy, but I could make out the license plate clear as day." He rattles off an address. "Come over. Join me for an early dinner."

Dinner at his place, just the two of us? The last time we had dinner together, we ended up in bed. Alarm bells go off. Best I hold the line. "I appreciate the offer, but when I told you to find a girlfriend earlier, I didn't mean me. I don't date my partners, Zack."

"My mother will be relieved. She thinks it's unseemly for a woman to carry a big gun. She wants me to marry Betty Crocker."

"There is no Betty Crocker. Besides, maybe I have a date."

A chuckle rolls out. "With that hideous bump on your nose? On a Wednesday night? Unlikely."

"Screw you."

I bite my lip. If I could have taken back that last response, I would have. Thankfully, Zack is still prattling on.

"Besides, this isn't a date. I have something you'll want to see."

His voice is low and lilting. It does things to me it shouldn't, conjuring images of a night I'd be better off forgetting. Zack seems to have done so. He's been nothing but professional.

"Okay, I'll bite. What have you got?" I reach for the iced tea in my cup holder and take a sip.

"The security tapes from the lobby of Barakov's building."

The cup slips out of my hand, spilling all over the passenger seat. I completely miss the turnoff to the 163.

"Shit!"

"Not the reaction I was expecting."

"I just spilled my tea. You expect me to believe Barakov just called you up and *volunteered* the security tapes?"

There's a pause. "Not exactly. I remembered seeing

cameras inside the lobby. The videos were just sitting there . . . on a secure server."

"You know how to hack into a server?"

"I can be handy that way."

My head is spinning. He sounds jubilant, talking as if he's oblivious of the implications of his actions. He has to know we'll never be able to use something illegally obtained against Barakov. I watched Zack skirt the edge when we worked together, but he never crossed the line. This most definitely crosses the line. This is major. My jaw tightens.

"You coming or aren't you?" he asks.

Damn it. "Yes."

"Are you coming now?" Again, there's an almost imperceptible lowering of his voice. I tell myself I'm reading something into it, that I should chalk it up to Southern-boy charm.

"I'm ten, maybe fifteen minutes away," I tell him before signing off and pulling onto 8 West.

The traffic is horrendous, as I get closer to the beach. I have more time than I thought to consider what to say to Zack when I see him. I understand temptation. I also understand that giving in to temptation always comes at a cost. What he did was stupid, plain and simple. We could have gotten that security footage the right way, the legal way.

Just when I think I have what I'm going to say to him all figured out, the address he gave me comes into view.

Every thought in my head flies out the window.

I have to remind myself to breathe.

I pull into the drive behind Zack's SUV, the one identical to mine. I'd assumed when Zack gave me the address that he lived in an apartment building. Or that perhaps he was renting a condo. Either of which would be pricey enough at the beach. But this is neither. It's a house. Two stories of oceanfront property.

I grab my phone and search for the address. A recent MLS listing pops up. Escrow just closed. I pull up the details. The house sold for over five million. Dollars. Five million.

Now, there are really only a few ways for an agent just over thirty to get his hands on that kind of money: marriage, inheritance, winning the lottery, or he's done something very, very wrong. Zack's cavalier attitude about getting the security tapes from Barakov's building plays over and over in my head. Maybe Zack is comfortable cutting corners, comfortable living large and taking risks. I haven't worked with him long enough to know.

But I do know I'm not.

Doing something that could jeopardize a case? That could end up shining an unwanted light on me? Definitely not something I'm comfortable with. Zack may be a liability I can ill afford.

What kind of man is Zack Armstrong really? There is one sure way to find out. This has become a matter of self-preservation.

I climb out of the SUV and pocket my cell on the way to Zack's door. I don't bother to knock. I barely even bother to take in my surroundings. The living room, dining area, and kitchen flow into one another. Zack's behind the counter, knife in hand. He's wearing a pair of red board shorts, nothing else. No shoes, no shirt. There's a towel draped around his neck and his hair is damp, as if he just came in from a swim. I remove the gun from my clip and slam it down on the cutting board alongside the sliced cucumber.

Zack jumps. The knife in his hand slips. "Crap. I almost sliced my finger off." He sets down the knife, yanks the towel from around his neck, and wraps it around his finger. "What's the matter with you?"

"For the past twenty minutes I've been thinking about what you said. The more I think about it, the more pissed off I'm getting. I figure we should not be armed for this conversation."

Zack checks his wound. Not surprisingly, the small cut has already mended itself. The bleeding has stopped. The towel is tossed aside. "I'm not armed. Talk to me." He raises both of his hands, taking a step back.

"What are you up to, Zack?"

He gestures toward the counter. "I'm making salad. Is this about your nose? You're upset because I called your bump hideous. In my own defense, I was joking. You know that, right?"

"This. Is. Not. About. My. Nose." I emphasize each and every word with a finger poke to his chest.

Zack and I are toe-to-toe. Suddenly I'm acutely aware of everything about him, his size, his strength, his power, and his almost complete lack of clothing. I try to pull away, but he reaches out for my hand and holds fast.

"What's happened?"

"I take my job seriously, Zack."

"So do I. You know that. You know me."

"Look, I thought I knew what kind of guy you are. But maybe I don't. Normally I'd say your personal life, the decisions you make are your own. I'd focus on the case, then the next one, then the one after that. I'd just go on living my quiet little life. But we're partners and that means if a shit storm comes raining down on you, I'm likely to get crap all over me. I'm clean. I want to stay that way."

He releases my hand. "And you think I'm not? You think I'm dirty?"

"Look around. Unless your mother's maiden name is Rockefeller, yes."

He looks surprised, hurt, confused. He could be all of those things. He could be none of them. One way to find out.

I lean in, lock Zack's eyes in mine, let go. This is how it begins, allowing a tiny crack in the armor that contains my powers. "You broke the law by hacking into Barakov's server. This house is worth a fortune. Your SF-86 is nowhere to be found. You agreed to no contact. Yet here you are."

As the power builds, the air around us warms, stirring an almost imperceptible perfumed breeze.

Zack's nostrils flare. His acute sense of smell detects the subtle yet complex blend of white florals layered atop citrus. A strand of hair escapes the coil at the nape of my neck and drifts in front of my eyes.

"Here I am," Zack says.

He reaches up and tucks the loose lock behind my ear, his fingers tracing the curve of my throat. His inhibitions are lowered. He feels it, the attraction, building. He steps closer, then dips his head and breathes me in.

The act is intimate, primitive. It makes me shiver.

"And here you are." He snakes one arm around my waist.

Like water pushing through the spillway of a dam, I feel the rush of pent-up magic fighting to escape. *Focus, Emma.* I squeeze my eyes shut and swallow. It isn't normally a challenge, reading someone like this. But it has been on occasion. Someone with as strong a will as mine, certain supernaturals, have a few times in the past tested my control. I know what I need to do. I need to hold steady, to ride the crest of the wave of influence, not drown in it. To stay in charge of the seduction, not get caught in it. He'll tell the truth. He has no choice.

I push myself back and away, trying to put some physical distance between us. "Are you on the take? Here under false pretences? Are you—?"

Zack, however, moves with me, placing a finger under my chin. "Look at me."

I lift my eyes and seek out his. There isn't a hint of deception. The surprise, hurt, and confusion I noticed before are all still there.

He speaks slowly. "I didn't steal evidence. I remembered seeing the camera in the lobby. Curiosity got the better of me. I didn't actually hack into the server, but I could have. Instead I made a call to Silvia Barton. I asked her to email it. Told her *you* wanted to review it, that you thought it was important to Amy's case. She checked with Dr. Barakov. Five minutes later, I had the file. I didn't commit a crime. I wouldn't do anything to jeopardize the case. You can trust me."

"I want to trust you. Why did you really come here? What is it you really want?"

As the words tumble from my lips, his eyes flash from brown to light blue, reminding me Zack is more than a human. He's also something else, and that something else is getting closer to the surface than I am comfortable with.

My heartbeat quickens.

"What do I want?" His arm tightens around my waist. He lifts me into the air and we move swiftly and silently across the kitchen. In the blink of an eye he has me pinned to the wall with his body. He's hard and ready, his breath coming faster, his control dissolving. But something prevents him from giving in, letting go.

"Zack—"

Words catch in my throat as his hands skim up the length of my body and he begins to remove the pins from my hair. The air around us is thick with desire. His lips are only an inch away from mine. He smells like sun and sand, salt and sweat. I want him to kiss me. Badly. And that petrifies me.

"Evidently the same thing you want. If I'm misreading the signals here, you better tell me fast," he says, bringing me back.

I've made a terrible mistake. Whatever is going on with Zack, whatever secrets he's hiding, I can't risk probing any further. I pull up the wall between us and slam the door shut on my powers.

The change is so sudden Zack is caught in the undertow. He distances himself quickly, shaking his head as if to clear it. I pick up the pins from the floor, then move to the sink and go about making sure every strand of hair is neatly back in place.

The silence between us drags on until it is deafening.

"I don't know what to say." He has a pin in his hand, one that I missed.

I can tell by the tone of his voice that he's shaken. He crossed a line he's not comfortable with and doesn't understand why. He's searching for some sort of explanation.

I take a deep, steadying breath to collect myself and try to give him one. "Forget about it. Emotions were high. I barged into your house, spouting off accusations." I accept the offered pin. "I did poke you in the chest."

Zack frowns. "I wouldn't normally consider that an invitation to . . ."

This is my fault. Not his. I was the one who opened Pandora's box. Zack and his beast had merely gotten caught in the wake. What Zack felt wasn't real, didn't mean anything. It was just physical. He responded to the Siren's pull, not because of any real emotion he felt for me.

"Seriously, Zack," I insist, "forget about it. I already have."

I don't lie to myself often. Deep down, I know this one is a whopper. What it felt like to have Zack's body pressed against mine again isn't something I'm going to easily forget. It brought back memories I've been trying to shake for months.

His lips purse together and he nods. "I'm gonna take a shower. Get dressed. You still up for dinner?"

"Sure." I reach for the knife. "I'll finish slicing the cucumber. I'm not a great cook, but even I can put together a simple salad."

"Help yourself to whatever," he says, before backing out of the kitchen and racing up the stairs.

"Emma Monroe, you are an idiot," I whisper to the four walls.

With Zack gone, my heartbeat returns to normal. For the first time I take in the surroundings. Zack's kitchen is palatial compared to mine. The professional-grade appliances, custom cherry cabinetry, and cream-colored marble countertops are just what you would expect in a house like this. I spend a moment taking everything in, trying to connect the home I'm standing in to the guy who is my partner. A rectangular dining table, which matches the cherry cabinets, is to my right, surrounded by cream suede chairs. A modern glass chandelier hangs above it. The living room is in front of me, on the other side of the counter, which also serves as a breakfast bar. A pair of brown suede sofas are arranged around a cozy fireplace. Above the mantel is a flat-screen television. To the left stand two gleaming guitars. To the right, a black baby grand. There are decorative pillows and throws, candles, place mats, fresh flowers, and even some artwork. But there is nothing that feels personal.

Maybe it's because he's just moved in. Maybe it's because the place is more of a designer showcase than a home. What I do know is that if I want to find out more about Zack Armstrong tonight, I'm going to have to do it the old-fashioned way—and in this case, that means asking questions. Any other way is too dangerous.

The shower comes on upstairs and I throw myself into the mission of making salad. Trouble is, the assignment doesn't take long enough. My work is soon done; the shower isn't. I look up, not because the ceiling is interesting, but because that's where my eyes are drawn. Lasting love is something I can never have. Blistering, hot sex? That is fair game and experience tells me it's just one floor away. Hot. Soapy. Shower sex. Perfectly natural. Not to mention efficient.

I pluck a cherry tomato out of the salad bowl and pop it into my mouth. "And so much more fun than interrogation." The fate of the next tomato is rescued by the ringing of my cell. It's Liz. Thank God. I push the images of Zack that have been forming—naked and wet—aside.

"Distract me."

I don't have to ask twice. Liz is in the midst of a meltdown.

"I'm in Evan's bathroom. I don't have a lot of time."

Evan Porter is a thirtysomething attorney vampire. I've met him several times. He's hardworking, earnest, loyal, and completely in love with my best friend. They've been dating for three months, which for Liz is probably some kind of record.

"Are you okay?"

"Are you kidding? I'm calling you from the friggin' bathroom. I'm a wreck!" she whispers. "We have to talk."

"We are talking," I remind her.

"Tomorrow, after Evan leaves for work. Emma, he wants me to move in."

Whoa.

"And?"

"I told him I needed to think about it."

"And?"

"And then I ran in here to call you! You know I've been staying here for a few days while my place is getting painted. Tonight we're eating dinner and he tells me he doesn't want me to leave. He wants me to put my place on the market and move in here. He's talking about putting down roots. About making a life together. That's insane. Right? Hello? Vampire. Sure, I can work some mojo, extend things a bit. But eternity? No can do. He has this vision of happily-ever-after. I'm not even sure I can commit to happily-for-now. What the hell am I going to do?"

The shower's no longer running. I'm not sure how long ago Zack turned it off.

"Let me get this straight. You're asking *me* for relationship advice?"

"See? I'm a total and complete wreck!"

This time I hear a smile in her voice.

Zack bounds down the stairs dressed in a T-shirt and

jeans, his hair still wet and slicked back from the shower. He walks straight past me into the kitchen and opens up the fridge.

"I'm free for lunch tomorrow," I tell Liz. "Can we talk about it then?"

"Yes. Come here around noon?"

"You got it. See you then."

Zack hands me a beer. "Friend having troubles?"

I don't end the call quickly enough. Liz hears his voice and before I know it, I'm being barraged with questions.

"Who is that? You're with someone? Are you out on a date?"

"It's not a date. I'm working. I'll see you tomorrow." I disconnect before she can get in another word.

Zack is leaning against the counter, eyeing me.

I wonder how much of the conversation he heard.

I hold up my phone. "My friend Liz. She has a handsome, successful, and honorable guy wanting a commitment."

"There must be something seriously wrong with him." Zack tilts the beer he's holding to his lips and takes several long swallows.

"That's what Liz is afraid of." I stroll over to the sliding glass doors that lead onto the deck. There's a grill on one side, along with a table and a few chairs. On the other, a built-in fire pit and two love seats. The entire area is surrounded by a waist-high wall. Beyond that is sand and ocean. "Tell me something, Zack. Where did the money come from?"

"For the house?"

"Yeah."

"If we're sharing secrets now, I have a question for you."

"What?" I ask.

"Your scent. It changed. I noticed earlier . . . It's different from when I first met you. How do you explain that?"

How do I explain that? The best defense is a good offense.

"Scent?" I raise my eyebrows. "What are you—part bloodhound?"

Color floods Zack's face. "Keen olfactory senses," he replies.

If there are secrets shared tonight, they aren't going to be about our supernatural origins.

I look away, shrug. "It's some new perfume. I made a detour to Nordstrom after I left the DA's to pick up something. The idiot perfume girl sprayed me before I could stop her. I think the fragrance is *finally* wearing off." I turn back around to face him. "I finished the salad. Should we light up the grill?"

Our eyes meet for one long moment. Zack seems about to say something, but then simply walks into the kitchen and picks up the salad bowl. "When are you going to tell me?" he asks without turning around.

"Tell you what?"

"Your secret. I know you have one."

I fling it back at him. "You tell me yours first. How can you afford a house, like this, on the beach? And what's the deal with your SF-86? Why is your application to the Academy missing? The only thing I can think of is that you were part of some unacknowledged Special Access Program. But you've been in the Bureau what, two years? That seems unlikely."

"You have been busy." He turns to face me. "To get that far into my file? Well, you managed to gain access to some highly classified records."

I feel the color creep up my neck. His implication is clear. I've just admitted cutting a few corners of my own. "Point taken, though I *wouldn't* do anything to jeopardize a case we're working on."

"Neither would I." He smiles. "Still, gaining unauthorized access to my records? You continue to surprise me, Agent Monroe."

"Zack, if our partnership is going to work, you need to come clean with me. I don't *want* to go digging into your past. I want to be able to trust you."

Zack puts the bowl down, then stares into it. A full minute passes before he speaks. "Before I worked for the Bureau, I worked as a kind of government mercenary. Black ops, off the books."

There can't be more than fifteen feet separating us, but the distance in his eyes makes it seem like miles. He's someplace else, reliving the past he's trying so hard to escape.

"What department?"

He shakes his head.

"You can't tell me." Or won't. "How long?"

"Too long. I spent too many years on my own, in situations where rules don't count and being morally flexible can do more than give you an advantage. It can keep you alive." Zack finishes his beer, then sets the empty bottle on the counter. "I'd like to keep the past dead and buried. It would be dangerous not to."

"Dangerous for whom?"

"For a lot of people, Emma. Let it go."

He goes back to the fridge. This time he pulls out a plastic bag. Inside is a huge London broil, soaking in marinade. "I'm gonna light the grill."

I can tell he wants to leave it at that. I open the sliding

doors and follow him out. While he fires up the grill, I lean my arms on the wall and survey the beach. It's the middle of the week, early evening, but there are still a few surfers and sunbathers out. Zack joins me. He notices my beer is empty.

"Want another?"

"Sure."

He's gone for less than a minute.

"I won't press you about this," I say when he returns. The beer is ice cold and it goes down easy.

Zack takes up the position I've left at the wall. "I appreciate that. I've done things I'm not proud of. Things I'd rather forget. Not just for the government."

We stare out at the ocean. I understand what it's like, having to live with monumental regret. "It wasn't my intention to dredge up bad memories."

"You were worried about the money for this." He waves a hand. "Whether I came by it honestly."

"Yes."

There's a long pause. I wait while he struggles to find the words. Finally he does.

"I spent more than a decade in constant danger, putting my life on the line every day." He shakes his head as if ridding himself of an unwanted memory. "What I did paid obscenely well. I've struggled with what to do with the money. Admittedly, this place is an extravagance. But it reminds me of a life I once had." He pauses. "Did I come by the money honestly? At the time, I thought what I was doing was legit—for the greater good."

"Now?"

"Now . . . I think some of it wasn't. I *know* some of it wasn't."

"That's how you paid for the house."

He closes his eyes and inhales deeply. "Yes. That's how I paid for the house."

I draw a breath, too. I can taste the salt in the air. When I open my eyes again, Zack is watching me. I look out toward the ocean. "You couldn't ask for a more beautiful view."

"I love the ocean. I grew up in Hilton Head. My family had a place right on the beach."

I remember Sarah was born and raised in Hilton Head. Perhaps they have even more of a past than I thought.

"Do your parents still live there?"

His shoulders tense. "No. They died some years ago."

Yet he spoke of his mother in the present earlier. *"My mother will be relieved. . . ."*

Zack turns his back to me, attending to the grill, a not so subtle way to close the subject.

I walk over to the wall, giving him time and space. I want to ask about his mother. I want to ask about Sarah. But it's clear he's already revealed far more to me than he ever intended to. Instead I back off, drink my beer, and watch the waves. In a moment he joins me and we stand in companionable silence, gazing out at the ocean.

"The crashing of the waves lulls me at night," he confesses. "Without it, I don't sleep."

A sense of melancholy settles over me. I, too, spend sleepless nights, being chased by past demons.

He leans in and bumps my shoulder. "I've told you my secret. Quid pro quo. You gonna come clean now and tell me yours?"

The playful tone and gesture lifts my spirits.

It doesn't, however, change how I answer. "Probably not in this lifetime."

"What happened to partners not having secrets?"

I return the shoulder bump. "Now, you and I both know you've yet to spill all of your deep, dark secrets. You just threw me a little ol' bone."

He doesn't reply. Doesn't push.

Instead he returns to his post at the grill. But the message in the look he sends back over his shoulder is clear.

I've been granted a reprieve, all right. But it's only temporary.

CHAPTER 7

"More steak?"

I lean back in my chair and shake my head. "I'm stuffed." I take another sip of wine and watch Zack as he refills his own glass. Dinner was far more comfortable than lunch. Zack filled me in on what was happening with the Mason prosecution and I filled him in on his new colleagues.

I gesture toward the now empty plates. "Everything was great. Do you cook like this often?"

Zack shrugs. "When I can. You know how it is, crazy hours. Most days I grab something on the way to work in the morning, stop someplace for a quick lunch, and then it's dinner alone at a restaurant or takeout."

"I've got a delivery service on speed dial. Hector is probably filing a missing person's report as we speak because he didn't hear from me tonight."

Zack smiles. "Hector? You're on a first-name basis with the delivery boy? Please tell me the two of you don't have a thing going."

"A *thing*? You, my friend, are watching too much porn."

"Can a guy watch too much porn?" Zack checks his watch.

He tries to be subtle, but I notice—trained observer that I am. I glance at mine, too. We probably have a little over an hour before the moon rises and our evening has to come to an end.

I stand up and start to clear the table. "I'll do the dishes."

Zack follows me into the kitchen with the salad bowl and bottle of dressing in hand. "Just leave them. I'll throw them in the dishwasher later. We've got about thirty minutes of tape to review."

"Mind if I make some coffee?"

Zack is already on his way over to the flat-screen. "Help yourself. Beans are in the container next to the coffeemaker. It'll take me a few minutes to hook this up."

I make short order of grinding the beans and within a minute or two the kitchen fills with the aroma of a dark French roast. Zack has hooked his laptop up to the flat-screen television. The display shows eight labeled views of Barakov's offices divided into blocks: Lobby, OR, Recovery, Reception, Elevator, Stairs, Break Room, Hallway.

"Mugs?" I ask.

"Next to the sink."

I pour two cups, adding the requisite cream and two sugars to Zack's, then join him on the sofa.

"All set?"

"I have this paused close to the time Isabella Mancini's car went through that light. This way we won't miss her."

I nod. "Hit it."

Zack presses PLAY and the various blocks on the screen begin to change. People walk in and out of the lobby. The OR and recovery room remain empty. We watch Silvia Barton move from her post in reception to the break room and back. Barakov walks down the hallway into what I guess is an exam room. A minute or two later he emerges and goes into his office. A woman comes out maybe a minute after him and then joins him. Her face isn't visible, but her stature and hair color are wrong for Isabella. There are two elevators, and the block showing those images alternate between the two.

"There's no view inside Barakov's office or the exam rooms," I point out.

Zack has been quietly sipping his coffee. "No. But we've got the stairwell and the hallway. If anyone were to go in or out, we'd know. Keep watching. I'll be right back."

Zack gets up suddenly and heads for a door at the far end of the living room, past the stairs. Out of the corner of my eye, I see him go through it. I reach for the mouse on the coffee table in front of me and pause the video.

"What are you doing?" I ask.

Zack is already on his way back, a set of rolled-up papers in his hand. "I picked these up from the city. They were filed at the time of the renovation of Barakov's office."

He spreads the plans out next to the laptop. "Unless you're Spider-Man, there's only two points of entry. The way we came in and the way we went out."

"So if we don't catch Isabella in the stairwell or lobby . . ."

"She didn't enter the building," Zack finishes.

We resume play. Ten minutes go by, then another ten. It's past Isabella's appointment time.

"What about the parking garage below? Any cameras there?"

"No. I swung by there after picking up the plans. There are no cameras on or in the garage, so no visual records. But there's also street parking and several nearby lots."

I reach over and click the mouse to fast-forward. Within a few minutes, the video comes to an end.

I set my cup down on the coffee table. "How do we know she wasn't late? Or maybe Barton or the doctor did something to the footage?"

"I'm the one who stipulated the start and stop times. The file was emailed to me within minutes. That kind of seamless editing would have taken longer to pull off. But I think you're onto something about the parking. Where did she park and what the hell happened to the car?"

"The police must have run the plates."

Zack's eyebrows rise, expressing his lack of confidence. "I'm gonna check myself." He looks at his watch, then gazes out at the darkening night sky.

He stands up, a flush of concern flashing in his eyes. "I have to go," he tells me. "I have an appointment."

I know what it is, so I make it easy on him. It's the second night of the full moon.

"And I should get home before I turn into a pumpkin. Thanks for dinner."

"Anytime."

I wonder where he spends those three nights a month when the beast emerges. It's curiosity, though, not alarm. I make no comment, just gather my stuff and go. Relief replaces the concern in his eyes as he shows me to the door.

I pause on the way out. I have to ask, "Do you still feel we're on the right track with Barakov?"

I get the shrug. "The dots don't seem to be connecting.

And he did volunteer the security footage. Still, where there's smoke . . ."

"There's usually fire," I finish. "You check on the plates and keep going through the evidence we've got. I'm going to do a little more digging into Barakov. Let's touch base tomorrow after lunch."

Zack agrees and I leave. I wish I had a stronger sense of whether Barakov is or isn't involved in the disappearances of Amy Patterson and Isabella Mancini. For the moment, I'm sitting squarely on the fence.

I back out of Zack's driveway and onto the road. In my rearview mirror, I catch a glimpse of a car parked down the street. Sarah's silver BMW is unmistakable. Is she here to seek refuge during the full moon or to finish her earlier conversation with Zack? Perhaps she's his *appointment* and he's expecting her. Somehow I don't believe that. Maybe I don't *want* to believe it.

Zack may consider Sarah an ex. He might consider whatever the two of them had casual. I doubt it's the same for Sarah.

By the time I get home, the sun has set. The moon, full and bright, shines down from the night sky and spills into the garden. After patrolling the house and the grounds, I perform my evening ritual: set up the coffeepot for tomorrow morning, go through the mail I picked up on the way in, pour myself a glass of wine. The wine I take with me into the bedroom, where I slip into one of a dozen Chinese silk sleeping gowns that I own. I take my hair down and shake it out, letting it fall about my shoulders and flow free. I contemplate a long soak in the bath, but I'm tired and decide against it.

Instead I wander out onto the deck. The night air is cool, but my skin is warm, my face flush. I'm tired, yet restless. I curl up in the old porch swing. Its rocking motion, like always, comforts me. I lean back, sip my wine, and breathe in the fragrant night-blooming jasmine. The motion of the swing lulls me. My thoughts drift to Zack.

I think about what might have happened if I'd let things in the kitchen continue just a few seconds longer. I think about the way he moved, the way his body felt pressed against mine. I remember the way my body responded. How my breasts felt heavy. How my nipples peaked and hardened.

I couldn't ride the sensation then, couldn't give in to it. But here, alone in the dark, there's nothing to stop me. I sense a familiar wetness between my legs.

I gulp my wine and squeeze my thighs together.

I tell myself it's been too long since I've had sex. It's release I need, plain and simple, not Zack. Anyone will do. Anyone can scratch this itch. Anyone.

I set my glass down on the deck and stretch out, letting my head fall back. I drop the walls, letting the glamour fall away, releasing my power. The air stirs around me, rustling the nearby leaves. My already warm skin becomes even more heated. I close my eyes and breathe deeply, letting the fragrance of the garden flowers fill my lungs. It triggers a memory of another place, another time—a time when everything was possible. When life was uncomplicated and pleasures existed without bounds. If I listen hard enough, I can almost hear the faraway ocean, taste the salt in the air, feel the hands on my body, strong and sure.

CHAPTER 8

Day Three: Thursday, April 12

I'd had a restless night, drifting in and out of sleep. Now as I lie in bed watching the sun filter through the windows lining the front of the carriage house, I know any possibility for real sleep is over. Stifling a yawn, I brace myself and throw back the covers. A run is the last thing I want, but my body knows it's just what I need. Within minutes I've changed into my workout clothes and am out the door heading down Sunset.

The fog is thick and the streets are wet with dew. It feels more like fall than spring. The wide, palm-lined street is silent save for the sound of my running shoes slapping against the pavement. This is one of the oldest neighborhoods in San Diego, and unlike Michael Dexter's, most of the Craftsman-style homes with their low-pitched rooflines, overhanging eaves, tapered support columns, and generous front porches have been carefully maintained. They were built in the early nineteen hundreds when I was in another town, living under another name. But I can appreciate their beauty now.

I take my normal route, merging onto Fort Stockton, then going left onto Hawk before taking another left onto West Lewis. I run past the Historic Business Center. A small coffee shop is in the process of opening. All of the other shops are still shut up tight. Back onto Fort Stockton, I continue on to Presidio Park. I wind my way through a series of paths while keeping an eye out for the homeless that sometimes occupy the area. Although I know how to defend myself, my powers don't extend to superstrength or superspeed. I've often wished they did. Hell, I don't even have superhealing, not like a vampire or a Were. Demeter didn't want to make it that easy on me. I'll heal from anything, but I do it the old-fashioned way, like a human, with time and pain.

By the time I get back to the house, the fog has lifted. I start the coffee I'd put up the night before. While I wait for it to brew, I whip up a glass of orange-mango juice with a little protein powder. Smoothie in hand, I trek out to the front of the estate's drive in search of the newspaper. I find it once again in the rosebushes instead of on the concrete. How the kid can miss twenty feet of driveway, yet manage to precisely place the paper in the center of a rosebush day after day, I'll never know. I manage to retrieve it without suffering any damage from the thorns, then tuck it under my arm and set out to check the property.

I fish the keys from the pocket of my warm-up jacket, let myself in the front door, and disable the alarm. I swallow the last of my smoothie, leaving the glass on the entryway table along with the paper and yesterday's mail before heading upstairs. It's a path I've walked hundreds of times. I check the doors and windows. I make sure there haven't been any plumbing mishaps. Twice a week I water the plants. But not today. My sweep of the downstairs goes quickly. In less than ten minutes I've done my duty, secured the house, and am on my way back to the cottage.

I scan the morning headlines on the way. The first thing I see, on page one of the *San Diego Union-Tribune*, is a picture of Amy Patterson. According to the article, Amy's disappearance is now being treated as a kidnapping. The reporter casts Haskell in an unfortunate light. She's described as being the person who was closest to Amy and in charge of all of her finances. He intimates Haskell is perhaps the person with the most to gain should a ransom be demanded and not be paid and Amy end up dead. What does Haskell have to say for herself? Apparently she failed to return the reporter's phone calls and granted him nothing more than a big fat "no comment" when he showed up at the gallery unannounced.

At that, I have to smile. I imagine he got more than a "no comment" when he showed up at the gallery. When I remember Haskell's brisk, no-nonsense style, what she really said to the reporter was most probably unprintable.

The smell of freshly brewed coffee hits me as I walk through the door. I put the paper aside and head straight into the dining area, where my laptop awaits. My job for the next few hours is to research Dr. Alexander Barakov. While my laptop powers up, I procrastinate for a few more minutes, washing out the blender and pouring myself a generous cup of coffee. I bring the pot back to the table with me. I know I'm going to need it. Where Zack seems to revel in wading through piles of paper in search of a common denominator, making color-coded notes and arranging them in neat little columns, I find research of this kind tedious, almost painful. Nevertheless, it's time to get started. I stare at the login prompt. Where to begin is the question.

Once I do, the hours pass unexpectedly fast. Dr. Alexander Barakov is a renowned and well-connected physician. There are pages of testimonials from satisfied clients. Alongside them are dozens of red-carpet photos of high-profile celebrities—their full breasts, perfect noses, and uplifted asses a testament to his skill. I find more raves and reviews on blogs, a few references to magazine articles. His patients love him. At least the ones who haven't disappeared.

Pausing to refill my coffee mug, I take a moment to review my notes.

Barakov grew up in New York. His father was a physician, his mother a member of the Junior League and the Daughters of the American Revolution. He received his undergraduate degree from Harvard in biology, then went on to Johns Hopkins Medical School, where he excelled academically. He completed his internship at Johns Hopkins Medical Center. That's where he met the first future Mrs. Alexander Barakov, nursing student Charlotte Murphy. The two married and then Barakov moved on to a coveted fellowship in plastic surgery at UCLA.

A search of birth records shows two stillbirths and one live birth for the couple. The surviving child died of SIDS at the age of four months. After the death, Charlotte attempted suicide and spent six months in a private psychiatric hospital. There would be other suicide attempts over the next twenty or so years as she struggled with bipolar disorder. Barakov always managed to keep the drama playing out on the home front separate from work.

While his reputation as a stellar physician steadily grew, Charlotte threw herself into a variety of charity projects. The *Los Angeles Times* archives hold dozens of photographs of her. There are several articles mentioning her as well. The largest spread occurred seven years ago. That's when Charlotte Barakov suddenly disappeared without a trace.

Bingo.

I bookmark the page.

About one million people go missing each year in the United States. Ninety percent turn up eventually. With over three hundred million people in the U.S., what are the chances that one man would be connected to not one, not two, but *three* missing women?

Although math has never been my strong suit, I think I can say with complete confidence that the odds fall somewhere between astronomical and fucking impossible. I smell a rat.

An alarm pops up on my computer, interrupting my chain of thought.

Crap. I'm supposed to meet Liz in an hour. There are a dozen more links in the *Times* that I need to screen. I move through them quickly, bookmarking those I want to review more thoroughly later. The last one is a wedding announcement from five years ago. Barakov remarried. Wife number two, Dr. Barbara Pierce, is ten years his junior and a surgeon. It was a small ceremony. Barakov's then long-standing secretary and Pierce's son from a prior marriage stood up for the couple, who honeymooned in Paris.

I glance at the clock. Now I'm down to forty-five minutes. I grab my cell and rush into the bathroom. I sweep aside the curtain around the old-fashioned cast-iron

claw-foot tub, turn on the taps, and then pour in a generous amount of vanilla and lavender bath salts that I
blend myself and keep on a narrow side table in an antique apothecary jar. I may be running late, but there are
some luxuries I don't deny myself. I quickly pull my top
off over my head and tie up my hair before calling Zack.
He doesn't pick up until the third ring. By that time I've
managed to divest myself of the rest of my clothes.

"The check on Isabella's plates turned up nada," he
grouses upon answering.

"Yeah? Well, what I've got will make up for that ten
times over. Guess what."

"Is that running water I hear? You're not calling me
from the ladies' room, are you? Just because you can
take a cell phone everywhere doesn't mean you should."

"I'm running late." I turn off the water, step into the
tub, and settle back against the bath pillow. "That was
the bath running."

The water is so hot that steam is rising. I close my eyes
and for a second everything melts away. I can't help
myself—a contented sigh escapes my lips.

"Emma?"

"Hmm?"

"Are you telling me you're in the bath?"

"Focus on the question, Zack."

"I'm trying," he says. Then after a beat, "I could have
focused just fine if you'd told me you were in the kitchen,
doing dishes."

"Okay, I'm in the kitchen doing dishes."

"Too late. What was the question?"

"Guess what happened to Barakov's first wife."

"The charm of being married to one of the Keebler
elves wore off and she went in search of a real boy?"

"You're making fun of him because he's short? I thought you told Barakov flaws were interesting."

"Unless you're an asshole. Then they're fair game."

"She disappeared, Zack. Went missing seven years ago without a trace."

"Ho-ly shit!"

I smile. "Knew you'd like that. Listen, I have a lunch date with a friend—"

"I'll start digging."

"You don't mind following up on the lead?"

He's already clacking away on the keyboard. "Are you kidding me? I'm *so* going to enjoy this!"

He clicks off and I settle back in the tub for a quick soak. I feel a certain sense of satisfaction that the mere mention of my being in the tub drove Zack to distraction. I wonder if he's, at this very moment, thinking of me. I shake my head as I recall the zealousness with which he began typing. Barakov is the only thing on Zack Armstrong's mind right now. And I'd bet everything I have that Zack is not picturing the doctor naked and in a bath.

CHAPTER 9

I've no sooner gotten off the phone with Zack than my cell rings again.

"What? You want a progress report on the bath?"

There is prolonged and pointed silence on the other end. I check the caller ID. It's a number I'm not familiar with. Definitely not Zack.

"Sorry," I mumble. "This is Emma Monroe."

The silence gives way to what sounds like an embarrassed cough. "I'm sorry, too, for interrupting your bath. Michael Dexter here."

I sit up straighter in the tub. "What can I do for you?"

Another pause. Then a heavy sigh. "I wasn't entirely honest with you yesterday."

"Oh?" I get the tingly feeling that comes with the possibility of finally catching a break on a tough case. I keep my voice curious yet detached when I ask, "What about?"

All I hear on the other end is breathing. He's not going to confess to playing a part in Isabella's disappearance, is he? Like Zack, I've been becoming more and more convinced that Barakov is involved in this somehow. I find myself holding my own breath.

Finally he says, "I held back something that might be

important to the case. If I tell you, will you keep it in confidence?"

"I'm not a priest, Michael. I'm a law enforcement officer, a federal agent. You know if you tell me something incriminating—"

"Oh, Jesus, no," he interrupts. "I didn't *do* anything to Isabella—" He breaks off. "This is something I can't talk about over the telephone. Can I see you this afternoon?"

"I'm free anytime after two. Do you want me to come to your place?"

"I'm having lunch with the Director of the Museum of Modern Art. I'll be finished by two. Can you meet me at the Japanese Tea Garden in Balboa Park?"

"Yes. Michael, are you sure this can wait?" I don't want him losing his courage between now and then.

"It can. And I have to see your face when I tell you this."

Now I'm *really* curious. "All right. See you at two."

I second-guess myself while I finish my bath, dress, and jump into the car to head for Evan's place. Should I go to Balboa Park and catch Dexter before his lunch date?

What good would that do? Scare him? Embarrass him?

No. Better to trust he'll show at two. And if he doesn't, I know where he lives. Liz is always there for me and she needs me now.

Evan Porter lives in the Marina District downtown. The fact that he is doing very well at his law practice is evidenced by his home. His loft is located in the old Soap Factory, one of the largest all-brick buildings on the West Coast . . . and an exclusive address. Units run close to a mil and they come with guest parking. Unfortunately, an ominous-looking black sedan with tinted windows occupies the spot Liz told me to park in. I dial her cell.

"There's a car in number twelve. You said twelve, right?"

"We just finished our meeting. He's on his way down."

Right on cue, the sedan comes to life. The engine fires and the driver steps out. With stiff precision he opens the rear passenger door, then waits at attention. He looks like a military man, close-cropped hair, compact body, dark well-tailored suit.

Who the hell has Liz been meeting with?

Before I can swivel around to look, a man walks past the driver's side of my car. Undoubtedly, it's *the* man. I never saw him coming. He's a study in black: black boots, black slacks, and black leather coat. His stride falters when he reaches the hood of my car. There's an almost imperceptible hesitation. His head turns, but only slightly. His shoulder-length dark hair, decidedly not military, masks his profile. He continues to the car and the waiting driver. The pause was so fleeting I now find myself wondering if I'd imagined it.

I still have the cell in my hand. "Who's the mystery man?"

"He's a long-standing client," Liz answers.

The man climbs into the back of the sedan. The driver slams the door. A moment later he's back behind the wheel. I put my SUV in reverse and roll back a couple of feet, giving them plenty of room to pull out.

"I assumed he was a client," I say after the sedan has pulled away. "Who is he?"

"Why do you ask?"

"He hesitated as he walked by the car. Like he might have sensed something."

Liz dismisses the idea. "Through one of my spells? Impossible. Come on up."

She clicks off and I steer into the now-vacated space.

By the time I get to Evan's door, Liz is waiting for me. I'd normally describe her as one of the most grounded, self-confident women I've ever known. And one of the most beautiful. Tall and willowy with gleaming light brown skin and a long mane of hair that's never had a bad day, she turns heads wherever she goes. Today, though, she's all wringing hands and breathless anxiety. She's wearing a pair of old flannel pajama bottoms and a T-shirt at least three sizes too big. Evan's, I imagine. And not her usual business attire.

"You saw a client looking like this?"

"It was an emergency." She pulls me inside. "There's some political unrest in the vampire community, trouble brewing. Vampire-on-vampire hate crimes are on the rise and . . . Never mind about that." She thumps her chest. "What am I going to do?"

"Well, if Evan saw you looking like this before he left for work this morning, you might not have anything to worry about now."

She runs her fingers through her hair. "I didn't sleep a wink."

I find myself looking around the loft. "So, this is Evan's place. How about a tour?"

She waves a hand. "Living room, dining room, kitchen, two bedrooms upstairs. Should we talk in the living room or maybe in the kitchen? I have lunch."

I've never seen her so upset. I reach out and attempt to smooth down her hair. "How about we start with lunch? If I know you, you probably skipped breakfast."

She leads me through a designer's showcase of a

place. Comfortable but sterile. Living room painted all white with overstuffed sofa and large media unit, dining room with whitewashed fireplace and a modern glass table, kitchen the Top Chef would feel at home in. Only here and there do I see touches that can only be Liz's—a funky black-and-white rug under the coffee table in the living room, a crystal vase on the fireplace mantel that catches the sunlight streaming in from terrace doors and reflects a rainbow of color on the wall behind it, a pot of herbs on the granite kitchen counters.

I barely have time to take it all in before Liz is pushing a plate into my hand. "Help yourself. We'll sit on the terrace. I could use some fresh air."

She's set up a salad bar on the counter separating the kitchen from the living room. I pile my plate with greens, spinach, artichoke hearts, olives, red pepper, sliced tomato. She has a tiny plate of shredded chicken breast. I know it's for me. Liz is vegan. I dump it on top of the other stuff. The only dressing I see is some kind of raspberry vinaigrette.

Vinaigrette? Liz knows me better.

"Where's the good stuff?" I ask, holding up the offending bottle.

She lets out an exaggerated sigh that telegraphs the level of her impatience, tromps to the fridge, and pulls out a bottle of ranch dressing. "Sorry. I meant to put it out."

Much better. It's my favorite. I get it at a local farmers' market. I try to be subtle as I check the expiration date.

I'm not subtle enough.

"It's still good," Liz huffs. "I bought it for you the last time you ate at my place."

I shake the bottle. "How'd it end up here?"

"I brought the perishables from my fridge so they wouldn't spoil. They had to unplug and move it to paint. Jeez. Has it only been a couple of days?"

My salad is ready. I pick up a napkin and fork. "Aren't you eating?"

"I can't. I'm too upset."

She's across the floor and out the terrace doors before I draw another breath.

I settle into a wrought-iron chair at the glass table facing Liz. I resist the urge to scold her for not eating. What she needs me to do now is listen. I'll have to remember to scold her before I leave. "I don't understand why this has you so spooked," I say between bites. "It's not as though you and Evan just met. And you *like* him, don't you?"

"Of course I like him," Liz snaps. "That's the trouble. We have fun. We understand each other. He lets me have my space and I let him have his. But there are complications, if you know what I mean."

"Of course I do. Evan is a vampire. There are naturally some things you'll never be able to share." For thousands of years vampires have lived among, but separate from, humans. Now that's changing. The boundaries are blurring, with more and more vampires like Evan blending in, holding down jobs, buying homes, and participating in all aspects of society. I make a point of looking around the spacious condo. "But he's mainstreamed pretty well, I'd say."

"He has. Evan's not the problem."

"So who is?" I ask.

"I am." She leans toward me, hands clasped on the table. "He really wants to take our relationship to the next level. These last few days have been great. And he sees that as a sign we should make this living arrangement permanent."

"And you don't?"

Her hands unclasp and fly upward. "I don't know. What if I move in and it doesn't work out? I don't want to lose Evan."

"So keep your place."

Now her hands flutter like hummingbirds' wings. I reach over and grab them. "Have you talked with Evan about how you feel?"

She shakes her head, her eyes suddenly brimming with tears. "I'm afraid."

"Of Evan?"

She gasps. "Goddess, no, not afraid like that."

"Then what?"

"I'm afraid if I don't agree to move in, he'll end our relationship."

I sit back and look at my friend. "I wish I could tell you what to do," I say at last. "But you need to talk to Evan. From what you've told me about him, he's a pretty levelheaded guy. If he respects you, he'll respect your feelings."

Liz's smile is rueful. "I just wish I knew what those feelings were."

"Well, the way I see it, you've got until your apartment is painted, a week, to decide. In the meantime, enjoy roughing it in this überluxurious condo with a man who obviously adores you. I'm sure it will be tough, but you'll muddle through."

Liz laughs. A real laugh. "Hurry up and eat. I want you to help me pick out a cocktail dress for a benefit Evan and I are attending tomorrow night at the Hotel Del."

I raise an eyebrow. "Yeah. Real tough."

While I eat, Liz asks me questions about work in general, my new partner in particular. I answer in nonspecific, noncommittal terms.

When I've finished eating, I ask in what I hope is an offhand way, "Does my dampening spell need a boost, you think?"

Liz jumps on what I'd hoped was an innocent enough query with the intensity of a witch who smells a trick question. "Why? What's going on?"

"Nothing. I just wanted to be sure I'm not giving anything away."

"Because of what happened with my client in the parking lot?"

Why not? I nod.

She tilts her head and peers at me through narrowed eyes. "Nope," she says at last. "Spell's holding just fine."

"So nothing's leaking through. The glamour and dampening spells are both solid, safe?"

"Safe as houses."

Shit. That's what I was afraid she was going to say. Zack got a zap of my powers in the kitchen, all right, but what's going on now is something else entirely.

CHAPTER 10

At one forty-five I leave Liz in a much better mood than I found her in. We didn't resolve her dilemma with Evan, but she seems calmer and ready to look at the situation through less hysterical eyes. And we picked the red Badgley Mischka for her date with Evan tomorrow night.

It's a short drive from Evan's to Balboa Park. I take an outside table in the Tea Pavilion after ordering the Spicy Green Dragon Chai from the menu. I sip it while I wait for Dexter, and consider whether I should go back inside and order a curry rice bowl with beef. I love Liz, but salad just isn't my idea of lunch.

Before I make a decision, I spy Dexter coming toward me with the determined look of a man intent on unburdening himself. He doesn't stop at the Pavilion to pick up anything to eat or drink. Instead he comes directly over and slumps into the chair across from me. He is out of breath, even paler than yesterday, and I'm alarmed at the haunted look in his eyes.

"Can I get you something to drink? To eat?" I ask.

He shakes his head, passing a hand over his face. "No. Thanks. The walk over here took more out of me than I expected. I'll be fine. Just let me catch my breath."

It takes a few minutes for Michael's breathing to return to normal, for some color to come back into his face. Still, his eyes are troubled when they meet mine. It's more now than physical illness that's clouding them. He reminds me of the way Liz looked when I first saw her, anxious, uncomfortable, uneasy in his own skin.

I take a few sips of tea while I wait. Then I gently prod him to begin. "Whatever you need to tell me, it's not going to shock me. I've heard it all before, Michael."

He closes his eyes for a moment, exhales. "I doubt you've heard this before," he mumbles.

"Want to try me?"

He breathes in, slowly, deeply, like a man about to plunge underwater. Then he lets go. His words come out in a pent-up rush.

"Isabella is a vampire. I know it sounds crazy, but hear me out. She was bitten her first week of grad school—taken by force when she wandered into the wrong place at the wrong time. She was gone two weeks. She called me once right after it happened to tell me some bullshit story about having met some old friends from her undergrad days. She didn't want me to worry, but she was going to go on a trip with them and would be gone for a little while. That's the only time I heard from her until she came back home. I knew something was wrong the minute I saw her. I kept after her until she told me the truth."

He gets all the words out without drawing a breath. Then he stops abruptly. He's waiting for me to react. He expects me to be shocked; I read it on his face. After a moment, he points out the obvious. "I just told you Isabella is a vampire. You aren't calling me crazy. Why?"

I stall by pouring another cup of tea, swirling my

spoon around in the cup, taking a sip. Gathering my thoughts. How should I answer Dexter?

I, too, know vampires exist. Their existence, like that of other supernatural creatures, is a well-guarded secret. One I wouldn't normally betray. But this cat is out of the proverbial bag. More important, I now have another angle to explore, one that might lead us to finding Isabella.

I push at my cup, edging it away, deciding the only way to find out is to be blunt with Dexter. "So she was turned just a few months before her disappearance. Do you know if Isabella had sworn fealty to any of the vampire factions?"

Dexter's shoulders wilt with relief. "You believe me? You know vampires exist? You're not trying to humor me?"

"I'm not trying to humor you. Vampires are as real as you and me."

His hand flies up to cover his mouth, and his eyes fill with tears. "I can't tell you what a relief this is."

I nod and give his hand a squeeze. He doesn't have to tell me. I know what it's like to have to hold a secret inside because you fear no one will understand or believe you.

After a few seconds he pulls himself together and continues. "Isabella never let go of her humanity. As soon as she was strong enough, she abandoned her sire. He was a junkie who could barely take care of himself, never mind show Isabella the ropes. It took time, but she came to terms with what happened. She made up her mind that she was going to finish school and she's been working toward that goal ever since."

"But she must feed to survive."

"She never feeds directly from people. She gets her supply from one of the Blood Emporiums. Or she did." He peers at me. "You know about those, too?"

I nod. Emporiums opened up a couple of decades ago, around the same time that Protectus was discovered—a drug that allows vampires to tolerate sunlight. It's these two things that really sparked the mainstream movement. It started here in California and spread east, then into Europe and other parts of the world.

Most Emporiums are located in the back of businesses catering to those who pursue alternative lifestyles, tattoo shops, and heavy metal clubs. For vampires they offer fresh blood from paid donors who, for the most part, have no idea where the blood ends up or who is paying for it. Would-be vampires and goths simply believe they are indulging in a fantasy. They never see the real vampires who come to buy their blood bags and the drugs that allow them to function during the day.

Dexter continues. "She used a drug called Protectus to be able to walk in daylight. She went back to school, held down a part-time job, lived like everyone else. Even our friends didn't know."

"So she mainstreamed."

"Totally. And as far as I know, she never had contact again with the vamp who sired her. Or any other vamp, for that matter."

"Can you tell me the address of the Blood Emporium she frequented?"

"It's somewhere downtown in the Gaslamp District." He leans toward me. "Do you think the vampire connection is important?"

"Truthfully, I'm not sure. But I'm glad you told me. It's one more lead to pursue." I read his next question in the shadow of anxiety in his expression. "Nothing we spoke of today will ever be part of the official record. It can't be."

Dexter closes his eyes for an instant, settling back in his chair. When he opens them again, the darkness is gone. "You have no idea how tied up in knots I've been about this. I love Isabella. But I just knew if I told the police what I told you, they'd ship me to Sharp Mesa Vista Hospital for a psychiatric evaluation." As quickly as the optimism has appeared, it's swallowed up by a grim frown. "Then again, if I had told them, maybe Isabella would be home instead of God knows where."

"Don't do that to yourself. You were right when you said how the police would have reacted." That, of course, is true. But what I say next sounds like cold comfort, even to my own ears. "Don't give up hope. We're not."

Dexter reaches into his pocket, pulls out a piece of paper, opens it, and slides it across the table toward me.

"What's this?" I ask.

"A receipt from the Blood Emporium. Isabella always paid cash. I found this in her room. She went there on the day she disappeared, then came home afterward. Someone there might have been the last person to see Isabella before she disappeared. Maybe she said something. Maybe someone at the Emporium saw something."

I glance at the date on the slip, refold it, and slip it into my handbag. "Thanks for this."

"You'll look into it?" he asks.

"I'll look into it," I assure him.

Yet Dexter still looks uncertain. "I feel horrible. Before now, I didn't know who to go to. Do you think this is too little too late?"

"No. Every detail is important." I push my chair away from the table and stand up. "Thank you for trusting me. I promise to be in touch."

He takes my outstretched hand but doesn't get up with me. I glance back once on the way to the exit. He's staring down at the table, as still and inanimate as one of his statues.

CHAPTER 11

It's not easy to put that last image of Dexter out of my mind as I drive to the office. It would be a miracle if we found Isabella after two months. Was it possible she didn't want to be found? Dexter seemed convinced she was taken. But maybe she'd merely decided living a double life was too hard and left to find sanctuary with her own kind. If that's the case, we'll never find her.

What I do find when I approach my cubicle is a note on my desk from Zack. *I'm in the conference room.* I stop just long enough to text Liz before trekking off to find him. I ask her to see if Evan knows anything about the Blood Emporium in the Gaslamp District.

Zack has taken over the conference room we usually use for staff meetings and potlucks. The long table is now scattered with the folders stacked in neat little piles. The whiteboard is covered with notes, some handwritten directly on it in blue or red pen, others on Post-its of various colors. Zack is sitting at the far end, hand suspended in midair as if he's forgotten the cup held halfway to his mouth. He's staring at the notes. I take a moment to observe him.

"Waiting for an invitation? Come and join the party."

Note to self: it's hard to spy on a werewolf.

He puts his cup down. "The coffee's fresh."

I shake my head. "I think I met my caffeine quota before lunch today." I look over at the board. "Anything?"

"No." The one word is spit out in disappointment and irritation. "And my research into Barakov's first wife went nowhere, either."

"Well, the board looks lovely. Very . . . colorful."

He gives me the fish-eye. "Where have you been all afternoon? Fending off attacks from the Nordstrom perfume girl?"

I ignore the gibe and close the door to the conference room.

Zack immediately perks up. "You've got something worth closing the door for? What?"

I sit down beside him. "I had a meeting with Michael Dexter."

"How did that happen?"

"He called me right after you and I hung up this morning. He asked if I could meet him." Now comes the tricky part, how to address the matter of Isabella's nature. I need to convey to Zack my knowledge of the supernatural world, without intimating that I'm part of it. I'd like to be able to do it without him feeling threatened, exposed. But after thinking it through, I don't think I can. This could be an important new lead, and whatever his reaction, I'll come up with a way to deal with it.

I draw a sharp breath. "There's something about Isabella that he wanted to tell me. Something that wasn't in the official police report."

I have his complete attention. "Oh?"

"She's a vampire, Zack." Before he can sputter that vampires don't exist and I must have had too much wine with lunch, I cut him off. "Don't waste time pretending to be shocked or telling me that I'm crazy. This isn't going to end up in any report. It won't leave the room. But we both know vampires are as real as ... well, werewolves."

Both eyebrows shoot up, but he recovers quickly. He reaches out and places a hand on my forehead. "Are you running a fever?"

I push it away, then lower my voice and lean in close. "I won't expose you, promise. But I know what you are. I've known it from the beginning. From the instant we met."

Zack's shoulders stiffen.

"This isn't about you. It's about Amy and Isabella." I stand up and walk over to where photos of them are taped to the board. "They're depending on me, on us. I feel time may be running out. We have a new angle to explore. I want to, I *need* to follow it. And I need your head in the game. I need you with me. We have to find out if any of the other kidnap victims were vampires. Can I count on you?"

I'm not only asking him to do his job; I'm asking for an admission as well.

Zack stares at me, mouth set in a hard line, fingers drumming the table. I can tell he wants to give me a firm yes, but something is holding him back, nagging at him. I'll bet it has nothing to do with the case and everything to do with me. Quid pro quo.

We're alone. I could insert a simple thought, a suggestion. He'd accept it, move on. But I can't risk using my magic with him. I know that. So I stare back at him, waiting. Hoping.

"What are you?" he asks finally. "You're not purely

human, either. What happened last night in the kitchen was *not* just emotions running wild. It was something else. Something I think you made happen. Or *encouraged* to happen. It's time for you to come clean."

"What I am is not important. What happened in the kitchen was a mistake. One we should make sure doesn't happen again."

"A mistake? Is that what you call it?" His voice has an angry edge, but there's something else in the tone, too. "Wow, and here I was, thinking it had something to do with magic. Only it wasn't like any magic I've ever felt before. So much for trust."

I swallow, resisting the urge to smooth things over.

Zack's not letting up. He takes a step closer, lowers his voice. "You get to know my secrets, but I can't know yours. Is that it, *partner*?"

His anger radiates outward like the heat from a torch. It makes me want to move away, out of range, before I get burned.

I hold my ground. "We're not here to trade secrets, Zack. We're here to solve a case. You're losing focus. You—"

"Need to keep my head in the game."

"Exactly. This isn't personal."

"Bullshit! You made this personal. Do you have any idea how many people I've shared my past with? I thought . . ." The anger vanishes. It's replaced by something else, something far more difficult to bear. Sadness. "You aren't human. Something happened between us. You made it happen. And it's something I can't stop thinking about." He moves in closer, restraint crumbling. The air between us thick with desire and tension. My breath hitches as I look up into his eyes.

"Nothing happened between us," I say. "You need to leave it alone."

At first, I think he's going to argue. He leans toward me, eyes flashing. His hands are balled into fists at his sides. Then his shoulders relax and he takes a step back. "That's the way you want to play this? Fine. I imagined everything. It's your call. Like everything else, *partner*."

I feel the sting of the last remark. It hangs in the air, like a wedge between us. I don't expect him to apologize. He's right.

Zack's eyes drift to the window, a spark of alarm registering as he catches the lengthening rays of the sun. There's less than an hour until sunset. "I've got to get home. I should be there already."

Before I can draw in a breath, he's already left the conference room. From the doorway I watch as he continues past his desk. He grabs his jacket off the back of his chair without breaking stride and heads for the elevator. He doesn't bother to look back.

I gather my things and go back to my desk. It's been a long day. It's going to be an even longer night.

I glance out the windows. Darkness will soon be descending, lights from the building across the way bite into the gloom. It's the third night of the full moon.

The elevator door opens and a delivery boy with a huge flower arrangement steps off. "Do you know Emma Monroe?"

Zack turns to face me. "I thought I did. Now I'm not so sure." He steps onto the elevator, and the door closes.

I motion the delivery boy over.

"Emma Monroe? These are for you."

I take the flowers and open the card. It's a thank-you from a grateful Michael Dexter. There's also an invitation to a fund-raiser/auction at the Hotel Del Coronado tomorrow night. The event starts at seven and there will be two tickets waiting for me at the door.

It's the same benefit Liz mentioned.

The office is nearly empty. I tuck the note and invitation in my handbag. It's time to go home. The conference room lights are still on. I wander over and scan the whiteboard. I think of Amy, of Isabella, of Zack and all the work he's been putting in trying to find them. I sink into the chair he'd occupied. My skin itches with frustration and impatience. I'll go stir-crazy if I go home to an empty house. I need to be doing something.

Amy Patterson's file is open. I peruse our notes. A bit of conversation floats to the surface.

Amy's empty cupboards.

Amy orders in a lot.

I sit up straight.

Maybe. But maybe there's another reason her cupboards and refrigerator are bare. I snatch up Amy's keys from my desk drawer and head out.

The first thing I do after letting myself into Amy's apartment is slip on latex gloves and recheck the bathroom cabinets. Nothing. Next, I look behind towels and sheets in the linen closet. Then I move things around in her closets. I methodically peer into every nook and cranny. No Protectus. No hidden cooler with blood bags. Perhaps she drinks straight from the source. Perhaps she stays cloistered behind those special tinted windows until sundown.

Perhaps I'm totally off the mark.

Back to the kitchen. Another search of the cupboards reveals no new results. I lean against the center island, eyes scanning the countertops. My gaze drops to the dishwasher. I open it. There are only four glasses in the upper rack, two wineglasses, and two juice glasses. There are lipstick smudges on the rims of the wineglasses, so the dishwasher has not been recently run. But there is no residue in the bottom of any of them, either. Amy probably rinsed them.

I pull them out. One by one I hold them up to the light, looking for a trace of what they might have held. I close my eyes, sniff the inside. Nothing. I frown at the four glasses, lined up like good little soldiers on the counter. Zack could probably tell me what each of them contained—if he were here. And speaking to me.

I withdraw a spray bottle of luminol from my handbag. Dousing the lights, I spray the glasses and stand back. A blue glow appears in the bottom and sides of each glass. The glow lasts only half a minute, but it's enough to prove my theory.

Each glass held blood.

Amy Patterson is a vampire.

CHAPTER 12

Some days it's pure pleasure to walk in my front door and close the world out behind me. Some days the stupid world follows me inside. I toss my keys, bag, and work files onto the coffee table and head for the bedroom. Now that the thrill of my earlier discovery is gone, I'm feeling restless again. In a minute, I've stripped out of the confines of my work clothes and into my favorite robe. It's silk. The living, breathing fabric is one of the oldest in the world. Being wrapped in it usually affords me a modicum of comfort. Not tonight.

I pour a glass of wine. An old-world red this time, the last remaining from a case I bought two years ago. It's complex, full-bodied, and very hard to find. Before I can take a sip, my cell phone rings.

I check the caller ID.

Liz.

I'm not ready to fill her in on the Zack situation. I'm tempted to let the call roll into voice mail. But then I remember I asked her to check with Evan about the Gaslamp's Blood Emporium.

"Have you talked to Evan?" I ask as a greeting.

A sigh. "No. He sent me a text an hour ago. He has an

important hearing tomorrow that he has to prepare for. He said not to wait up."

"So you weren't able to ask him about the Blood Emporiums?"

"Sorry. I do have someone else I could check with, though. I'll call him in the morning if I don't get a chance to ask Evan tonight."

"I'm specifically interested in the place in the Gaslamp," I remind her. Then I take a sip of my wine, taste the earthiness in the back of my throat, swallow. "Oh. I got an invitation to that benefit on Friday, too. Compliments of one of the participating artists."

Liz squeals into the phone. "Hey. I'll hook you up. We can double-date."

I almost spew out a second mouthful of wine. "No, no. I'm not bringing a date. I'm not even sure I'm going. I have nothing to wear and—"

"Don't be stupid. You can borrow something. You have to go. Keep me company. Evan will be networking all night."

There's an ominous pause. I can hear the wheels turning in Liz's brain through the phone line. Or rather, the pages of her mental Rolodex flipping from one prospect to another.

"Yes," she says triumphantly. "Walter."

"The werewolf?" The irony is almost laughable. "No, Liz."

"He's a bit of a bore, and not very bright. But he looks great in a tuxedo and he's absolutely amazing in the sack. He has this thing he does with his tongue . . ."

Once again, I have to swallow quickly to keep from choking on a mouthful of wine. "TMI, Liz. Really." I put the glass down on the dining room table. Never know what Liz is going to say next, and I really don't want to waste this wine.

"Although I'd really like to meet Zack," she says.

Shit. Did she really just say that?

"Zack?"

"Yes, Zack. Your partner. Call and ask him."

"Can't. Full moon tonight."

She's not deterred in the least. "So ask him tomorrow. Let me know what he says."

Liz hangs up.

I'm left staring dumbstruck at the phone.

Even after three glasses of wine, I can't sleep. Images from last night have been flitting through my mind off and on all day. Instead of fading, the itch seems to be growing stronger and more urgent. Try as I might to focus on something else, anything else, my thoughts are of Zack, the way he looks, the way he feels, the way he makes me feel. That moment in his kitchen last night was my doing. And yet there is more than my power sparking between us. Zack proved that this afternoon in the conference room. We agreed to keep it professional. We *need* to keep it professional. But there's something between us, not just the simple lust we felt in Charlotte. Not even the aftereffects of my powers, which I've seen drive men to distraction. Something more. And it scares me.

Why don't I just admit it?

Because I can't.

Bitterness burns the back of my throat. I lied to him. It was for a good reason. It was for the best reason. But when I think about the way I lied—so dismissive, so condescending—my gut twists. Zack deserves better. I'd like to make things right, but how can I? What would I tell him? That I'm something very old, very rare, and very dangerous? That I have been cursed by a goddess determined to bring ruin to anyone with whom I find love? That it's dangerous for both of us to even *think* of having a relationship? That he needs to forget what he knows, or what he thinks he knows?

Maybe I'll call him, apologize for being so abrupt. Keep it short. Professional. Even Demeter could find no fault with that. I dial before I lose my nerve.

His phone rings in my ear. Six. Seven. Eight rings. Then it goes to voice mail. I panic and hang up. Of course, I'd get voice mail.

I hear the howl of a coyote drifting up from the canyon at the edge of the property. Not an unusual sound. Tonight, though, it makes me feel terribly lonely. I wander out to the courtyard and look up. The moon in a cloudless sky casts shadows on the ground. Shadows that touch my feet and draw me forward into the darkness. The air is quiet and still. I am alone. Normally I would take comfort in that. Tonight, being alone simply feels . . . lonely.

I'd say my thoughts drift back to Zack. But since we had words earlier, they haven't been far from him. I wonder where he spends these changeling nights and with whom. Last night I felt confident that if Sarah came to him for shelter, he'd turn her away. Would he do so tonight? Did he make it home on time himself?

Even those who have risen through the ranks to a position of power as leader of a pack are subject to the pull of the moon. Only the absolute strongest Weres can resist. Fewer still can change at will. Whether they're Alpha, Beta, or Omega, one thing all Weres have in common is that they are fiercely loyal to one another, to their pack, and to their mates. Relocation is rare.

Why did Zack leave South Carolina? And, if his relationship to Sarah ended there, why has she followed him to San Diego? To convince him to return to his home? To his pack?

So many questions.

This is the third night. Zack will be free of the moon's hold tomorrow. The old ones used to say a waning moon is the time to eliminate negative thoughts, release all guilt.

I wish it were that easy.

Wherever Zack is, I can't reach him tonight. But tomorrow . . . I pick up the phone, dial his number again. This time I leave a message.

"I'm coming to the beach house tomorrow morning, Zack. I'll bring breakfast. See you about seven."

Demeter comes to me in a dream. She's standing in my garden, dressed in a long gown that sparkles, its fabric sheer and woven from ice crystals. Everything about her is ice—from her translucent alabaster skin to her piercing cobalt eyes to her stark white hair, flowing past her waist and tinged with frost. She holds a sword in one hand, a severed head in the other. Blood from it drips onto the pristine pile of snow that has formed at her feet, staining it.

"Do you know who this is, Ligea?" she asks, turning the head so I can see the face.

No matter what name I currently use, Demeter always calls me by the first.

My stomach knots. "Yes," I whisper, head bowed.

"His fate was in your hands. You had a choice. You made the wrong one. You betrayed him with your lust."

"Not lust," I cry, tears streaming from my eyes. "Love. He was my husband. I loved him."

"Silence! You haven't earned the right to love." Demeter's voice thunders into the night, her sparking anger splits the darkness like lightning. "You and your sisters lost that right when you lost my daughter."

"But you got Persephone back." Even as the words fall from my lips, I know I've made a mistake. We've been here before, she and I. You'd think I would have learned by now. I should never challenge Demeter.

The goddess grows still. "You'd be wise to remember who you are talking to, Ligea," she says, the soft tone of her voice more frightening than if she'd been yelling. "Or I may add another head to my trophy shelf." A cold smile turns her features into stone as a thin layer of ice and frost forms outward from the edges of her gown, covering her skin.

She holds the head up once again. She turns it so I can see the face. A scream rips out of my throat.

This time, the head she holds is Zack's.

My eyes fly open.

The moonlight coming in through the windows casts the room in an eerie glow. My heart is pounding, my breath comes hard and fast, freezing into mist on the bone-chilling night air. The doors to the garden have been thrown wide. I know I'd closed and locked them. With trepidation I slide out of bed. The normally warm wooden floor is ice-cold on my bare feet. I hardly register it or the thin layer of condensation that seems to be covering every surface. My gaze is fixated on the open doors, and the glass panes frosted now with a crackling web of ice. I move toward the door, not quite sure if I've wakened from a dream, or am in the midst of one. When I reach the threshold, I see that the deck is empty.

Except for a pool of water shining in the dark exactly where Demeter stood in my dream.

I feel as if all the air has been sucked from my body. I lean back against the wall of the house. It feels solid, real, but it's not enough to support me. My legs give way and I slide down to the ground.

CHAPTER 13

Day Four: Friday, April 13

I wake up, my face wet with tears. Demeter's warning
was clear. I can't let my feelings for Zack rage out of
control. She's watching.

My body aches. At some point last night, I'd fallen
asleep on the back deck. Again. When I awoke, my head
was pounding. I'd dragged myself back into the house
and fallen, exhausted, into bed. Still, I didn't rest well. I
couldn't. Demeter's flashing sword cut into my subcon-
scious until my early-morning dreams, like last night's
nightmares, dripped blood.

Another warning comes when I finally tumble out of
bed and look at the calendar.

Friday the thirteenth.

All the superstitions about the date flood my head,
casting even more of a pall on my already dark mood.

Ridiculous.

As ridiculous as some of the myths spun around my
sisters and me. Bird women? Mermaids? Luring men to
their death with a song? The only death we are capable
of is "le petit mort," and so far, no man has ever com-
plained about an orgasm that leaves him breathless and

panting for more. In fact, most myths were made up by men who needed a scapegoat to avoid taking responsibility for a catastrophe of their own making. Thoughts of my sisters, of the home I may never see again, fill me with melancholy. Thoughts of the possibility I'm about to make a grave mistake fill me with dread.

Demeter's visit has set my nerves on edge. Exactly her intention.

A cold shower clears my head. I know I'm here for a reason. To gain Demeter's forgiveness and earn my freedom. I need to remember that. I need to do what I keep telling Zack. Keep my head in the game. I must set Zack straight once and for all. If that means being truthful, so be it. A calculated risk for the greater good. I'll come clean. I'll make it clear our relationship is a professional one and can be nothing else. Not ever. It's a mantra I repeat a thousand times as I get dressed, shop for groceries, and drive out to the beach.

It's a little after seven when I pull up to his house. Only Zack's car is in the driveway. If Sarah was with him last night, she's already left. I curse myself for feeling relieved.

I knock on the door. Wait. Knock again. I pull out my cell. Dial. I can hear the telephone ringing somewhere just inside the door. When it goes to voice mail, I hang up. Where is he? I give the door a try. It's unlocked, which seems uncharacteristic, so I assume it's for me.

I walk inside. Just as I'm about to call out, I hear the shower running. It explains why he didn't hear me knock. This morning's newspaper is spread out on the countertop next to the coffeemaker, which is already brewing.

I flip on the kitchen light and get to work. Zack's cupboards are neatly organized. I have no trouble finding bowls, utensils, and an iron skillet. I put the pan on the stove to heat. Prepare blueberry pancake batter. Slide a dozen bacon strips into the skillet.

I figure the smell of the cooking bacon will draw him down.

In no time at all, it does.

Zack rounds the corner into the kitchen like a ninja—quick, deadly quiet, and intent. This ninja, however, carries not the traditional *tantō*, but a standard FBI-issue Glock.

When he sees me, he drops his gun hand. "Fuck, Emma. I could have shot you."

"No kidding. You just about gave me a heart attack."

He slaps his gun down on the counter. "What are you doing here?"

I point to his cell. "Didn't you get my message? I said I was coming over this morning. I thought you left the door unlocked for me."

He shakes his head.

"Oh. Sorry. I don't feel good about the way we left it yesterday. I thought this would be a better place than the office to try to sort things out."

His shoulders relax, but his expression remains unyielding. "You could have gotten yourself killed."

"With reflexes like yours? Unlikely. Besides, what kind of bad guy would break into someone's house to fix breakfast?"

Zack allows a little smile to crack the shell of his irritation and goes directly to the coffeemaker. "Wait. I know this one . . . a *cereal* killer?"

"Very funny. I'll have a cup if you're pouring," I say.

I watch as he gets a couple of mugs down from a cabinet. He's barefoot, bare-chested, dressed only in a pair of sweatpants. His hair is slicked back and wet. I realize the shower is still running upstairs. I clear my throat.

"I think you left the shower running."

He pours out the two mugs and hands me one. "The better to catch an intruder," he says. "I'll go shut it off."

When he returns he's wearing a sweatshirt and jeans. He pulls a chair out from the dining room table and slumps into it, watching me from beneath lowered eyebrows. He looks tired. I guess I'm going to have to start the conversation.

"So, where is it?" I ask, keeping my tone light.

"Where is what?"

"The cage. Where you spend the night during the full moon?" I grin. "Or do you chain yourself up? You know, some women might find that kinky."

"How do you know I didn't go rampaging through the city?"

"I listened to the news on the way over. No reports of a rampaging wolf." I take a sip of the coffee.

He does not look amused. "You shouldn't tease." His voice is rough. Not from sleep or desire, from something else. "The sun is barely up. My wolf is still restless. New area, not able to roam." He takes a gulp of coffee before skewering me with a look that's part anger, part smoldering seduction. "And it's mating season." He punctuates the last with another sip before adding, "The cage is upstairs. Right next to my bedroom. I'd invite you up to see, but I don't want to be accused of misreading your signals again."

His words send blood rushing to my face. I turn away, busy myself with finishing the pancakes. "Got any syrup?"

Zack comes into the kitchen, reaches over my head to a cabinet just above me. I smell the soap on his skin, or perhaps his aftershave. It's a blend of spice and citrus that reminds me of bay rum. I feel the heat of his body. I'm sure he feels the heat of mine. His proximity is distracting. But I can't let my resolve crumble. I close my eyes for a moment, then move away.

He follows.

I can't deny it. Something is in play here. Something I don't understand.

Demeter's face flashes in my head.

I'm kidding myself. I know exactly what this is, what's happening.

And I have to stop it.

"Damn it, Zack." I slam the plate of pancakes down on the corner and turn to face him.

"What the hell? I'm just getting the syrup."

"Your coming here was a mistake."

He's quiet for a moment. "Is that what you came to tell me?"

"Yes." Partly. I move to the dining room, sink into a chair.

He follows again, taking a seat beside me. "What are you afraid of?"

Afraid is exactly the right word. In a rare moment of honesty, I answer, "You."

He looks surprised. "Because we're attracted to each other?"

"It's not that simple."

"Then simplify it."

It takes me a minute to gather my thoughts. Zack sits quietly, his expression calm, expectant.

Okay. I can do this.

I start with the obvious. "There are so many reasons why we can't give in to this attraction, the least of which is that we are partners. Even if we're not breaking any rules, we have to work together. We have an important job to do, one that's sometimes dangerous. We can't afford to lose focus. The job has to come first."

"You're not telling me anything I haven't already told myself. But you said you were scared. Why?" he says. "Come on, Emma. Take a risk, just a little one. Trust me."

My heart beats like a jackhammer in my chest. So many years. So many secrets. Can I trust him with mine? He already suspects I'm not what I seem. For the first time, I have a partner I can be honest with. Should I be? His gaze, so steady, so patient, coaxes the words from my lips. "You were right yesterday when you said I'm not purely human."

He smiles. "I already knew that."

"How did you know? When did you know?"

He taps the side of his nose with a finger. "Everyone has their own scent. Yours changes. It's subtle, but discernible. The night before last, here in the kitchen, I've never smelled anything like it. It was . . . extremely compelling. So much so that I forgot myself and mentioned it. You deflected the question."

"And you let me."

Zack nodded. "When I was training, when I was in the field, I came across it all. But I've never crossed paths with anyone, anything that smells so intoxicating. What *are* you?"

I swallow. "There are only three of us."

"In the area?"

"In existence. I'm a Siren, Zack. I . . ." The words catch in my throat.

His expression grows skeptical. "A Siren? Like in the story about Ulysses?"

"No. That's a stupid myth," I snap. I regret the heat of my reply when Zack sits back. Goddamn Homer and his idiotic story of the Sirens' song. How I wish Leucosia, the elder of my sisters, had never met him and never scorned him. Homer was the reason we had a falling-out. The reason we decided it would be best to go our separate ways, to seek our separate redemptions. "I don't sing and I don't drive men insane. And . . . I'm *real*."

"Are you sure about the insane part? Because you do drive me just a little—"

I glare at him.

"Okay," Zack says, raising his hands as if fending off a blow. He chooses his next words carefully. "How did you become a Siren?"

"You don't *become* a Siren. I was born, of Gaia. It was very long ago—a different time, a different world."

"You're talking about the world of the Titans and Olympians? Seriously? If you tell me you're here to destroy the world or save mankind, I'm going to have to trade this coffee in for a stiff bourbon."

"I'm here for one reason: to save the innocent from peril, to find and bring home the missing."

Zack stares at me long and hard. "You expect me to believe that?"

"You change into a wolf once a month. You expect me to believe that?"

Again, just the hint of a smile ghosts his lips. "Touché."

"It's my sentence, my punishment," I continue.

I can hear the weight of emotion in my voice.

Zack must hear it, too. He stands abruptly, heads for the credenza, and splashes two fingers of bourbon into a couple of glasses and brings them back to the table. He thrusts one at me. "Punishment for what?"

I take the glass, sip. The bourbon burns, grounding me. They don't call it liquid courage for nothing. "For allowing Persephone to be taken. For not finding her quickly enough. For failing. Finding Amy Patterson and others like her may bring me one step closer to redemption."

"Then what? You go back to . . ."

"Olympus. I don't know. Maybe. I've been at this a long time. I could be at it a lot longer. One thing I do know is that this, between us, it shouldn't be happening. You shouldn't be feeling any attraction to me. My powers are suppressed and yet—"

"What powers?"

I have trouble maintaining eye contact. "I can insinuate myself into the minds of others."

"You've been reading my mind?"

I shake my head. "It's not like that. No. I can plant an idea, or a command really."

"You're *compelling* me to be attracted to you?"

"Of course not. But I can compel someone to reveal the truth."

"Like a vampire's thrall?"

"A vampire can play with memories. I can't. If I question someone, or command them, they'll remember it."

"There's more to it." His tone tells me he knows I'm holding something back. This time, he's not going to let me get away with it.

My mouth is dry. "Sirens were made to be seductresses. But I live in a mortal world. I try to live a mortal life. If I use, *when* I use my powers to get someone to reveal the truth, there are consequences—"

"And you did it to me, the other night, to find out if I was on the take."

"Yes."

"And what were the consequences?" He pauses, studying me. "You think the attraction between us is a consequence?"

"Yes. No. I don't know."

Zack reaches for my hand. "Maybe it wasn't a consequence. Maybe it was already there. From before."

"Was it?" Our eyes meet.

He nods. "Yes."

I gently pull my hand from his. "That makes pursuing a relationship even more dangerous."

"Dangerous? That's a strong word."

Shit. I don't know how to respond. I let the silence drag on too long and Zack has looked away, his eyes distant and unfocused. After a few more seconds of silence, they again find mine.

"I don't know how having a relationship with you could be dangerous. But you obviously do," he says.

I swallow. His words hang in the air. The memory of Demeter's nocturnal visit is too fresh. I'm still shaken by it. I need to do what I came here to do. Put my partnership with Zack back on course. He can be an asset. I need to *look* at him as an asset.

He knocks back the last of the bourbon. The sound the empty glass makes when he sets it down on the table has a ring of finality to it—a decision's been made.

"I could argue with you," Zack says. "Tell you we are

both adults and can handle whatever is thrown at us. Tell you that precisely because we are different from others, we could make it work. Tell you there could be something special between us and that we'll figure this out, whatever it is, together." He leans back in his chair. "But you have to want it, too. It needs to be real. And it needs to be right, for both of us." His expression is solemn, serious. "If there's going to be another move, it's going to have to come from you."

"And if that never happens?"

"We just focus on the case, then the next one, then the one after that. We go on living our quiet little lives," he says, echoing my words from two nights ago. His eyes flicker away and he nods toward the kitchen. "Think those pancakes are still warm? I'm starved."

The change of subject is like whiplash to my brain. I don't know whether to feel relieved, disappointed, or irritated. In fact, I feel them all. I jump up from the table, glad for a chance to hide my face from Zack's intent gaze. Aren't I the one who just pointed out how impossible a relationship would be? And did he not react not only like a professional, but like a gentleman?

Isn't that what I wanted?

Yes, but did he have to agree to back off so quickly? Did he have no other questions for me about my nature? I just told him something few other people in the whole world know. Even Liz had more questions when she first met me, and she'd known and been taught about me.

When I turn back around, pancakes in hand, I study Zack closely, looking for a sign of deception—some inkling that this is all part of a manipulation. I see none. The damned Were has me in knots. I place the dish of pancakes on the table, avoiding Zack's eyes.

Before I have a chance to serve myself, my cell rings. I check the caller ID. It's Liz. She's crying into the phone and it takes me a moment to get her calmed down enough to understand why she is so upset.

"Evan didn't come home last night. And he didn't show for his early-morning hearing. I've tried every spell I can think of to try to locate him. Nothing works. It's not absolute death, Emma. He hasn't been released. I can tell. He's just . . . gone."

CHAPTER 14

As soon as I disconnect, Zack is standing beside me.

"That sounded serious. Liz is the friend you were talking to the other night? The one with the guy who is ready to make a commitment?"

"The one with a *vampire* who is ready to make a commitment. Another vampire who's missing. Zack, I went back to Amy Patterson's after you left last night. I found traces of blood in the glasses in her dishwasher. She's a vampire. Isabella, Amy, now Evan? I have to go." I'm already on the move, snatching up purse and keys.

Zack raises his eyebrows, then moves to block my way. "I'm going with you. Give me five minutes to get dressed."

"Make it three."

He's on his way upstairs before the words leave my lips.

I lean against the kitchen counter. Liz's skill at casting spells is legendary in the witch community. If she can't locate Evan, there must be powerful magic working against her. If Evan's disappearance is related to Amy's and Isabella's, and supernatural elements are involved, the case just became infinitely more complicated.

Zack bounds down the steps. I told him to take three

minutes; he's taken just shy of four. I don't know how he did it, but his hair is combed, his tie knotted, his suit coat in his hand. "Let's go."

On the way over, I give Zack a quick rundown on who and what Liz is—my best friend and one of the most powerful witches west of the Rockies. He has two questions for me. "Does she know what you are?" And "How did the two of you get together?"

I feel as if I've revealed more than enough for one day, for a lifetime. So I answer yes, she knows I'm a Siren, but edit out the details of the two spells Liz works for me—the reverse glamour to hide my true appearance and the dampening spell to diminish my innate powers of seduction. As for his second question, I choose my words carefully and go for the simple truth.

"I knew her grandparents, powerful witches in themselves. They raised Liz when her own parents were killed. She's a magical mercenary of sorts, selling her services to a variety of individuals. I needed her help with—a personal problem—several years ago. We've been best friends ever since."

Sounds reasonable. No need for Zack to know the "several years" was really "a couple of decades" or that she also happens to be my touchstone when it comes to keeping my heart in line.

At Evan's, I pull into the same guest spot I occupied yesterday and lead Zack to the condo. Liz pulls the door open before I have a chance to ring. "Thank the gods you're here."

She pulls me in, barely acknowledging Zack in her panic.

Zack, however, definitely acknowledges her. I forget how beautiful Liz is until I see her reflected in the eyes of others. Zack's breath literally catches in his throat. And why shouldn't it? Liz is five feet seven inches of stunning. Her long hair is a cascade of dark waves that sets off her almond eyes. She's barefoot, dressed in jeans and a men's dress shirt, probably one of Evan's, with the sleeves rolled up. She manages to make this casual outfit look elegant enough for *Vogue*. Only the dark smudges under her eyes and worry lines pulling at the corner of her mouth mar the image.

There are other indications of her distraction. I know how Liz's mind works. If she wasn't so worried about Evan, she'd be interrogating Zack and peppering me with embarrassing questions. Her cool, appraising glance and the way she turns away from Zack after the briefest of handshakes say it all. Her attention is focused on Evan.

"This isn't like him, Emma." Liz leads us into the living room. "Not showing for a hearing? It isn't like him at all."

Liz and I take seats side by side on the couch, Zack across from us in an armchair.

I take Liz's hand. "Tell me about the last time you heard from him."

Liz bites at her lower lip. "The text I told you about last night. It said he was going to be late at the office. Preparing for an important hearing this morning. When I woke up and he wasn't home, I didn't worry. I knew he kept clothes at work for just this sort of thing—all-nighters followed by court. It's happened before."

She leans toward me. "But this morning, Sid, his assistant, called because Evan missed his court appearance. They had worked together until around midnight. After they'd finished, Sid said he asked Evan if he wanted to stop for a nightcap. There's a bar right down the street they go to. But Evan begged off. He said he had a quick note to make and then he'd be heading straight home. They were supposed to meet at the court-house this morning. When Evan didn't show, Sid got a postponement, then called me to find out what hap-pened. That's when I knew something was wrong and tried to locate Evan myself."

She gives Zack a fleeting look and whispers, "Does he know—?"

"That you're a witch? Yes."

"I've called all our friends. I've worked every locator spell I can think of. What comes up has me crazy. A void. He's yet to be released to absolute death. It's something worse. It feels as if he's trapped—on an alternative plane, or that he's in some kind of altered state. It's different than simple sleep or unconsciousness. It's dark, menacing."

She looks again at Zack, this time with trepidation, as if expecting him to make a comment about how fantasti-cal this sounds. For the moment at least, she's forgotten that fantastical applies to each of us in this room.

Zack, however, has his eyes on the coffee table. He leans forward and picks up a flyer lying there. "What's this?"

Liz glances at the brochure in his hand, shrugs. "It's a program for tonight's benefit." She looks at me. "The same one you have tickets for."

Zack is studying the logo. "Green Leaf. Where have I seen that name?" He opens the program and in the space of a heartbeat, he looks at me with grim serious-ness. "Guess who's on Green Leaf's board of directors."

He turns the page around so I can read the name he has his finger perched above. "Dr. Alexander Barakov."

"Who's that?" Liz asks.

I have to keep the eagerness out of my voice when I answer her. "Someone Zack and I recently interviewed. Evidently he's on the Green Leaf board of directors. Has Evan ever mentioned him?"

"I don't think so. I know Evan's firm represents the Green Leaf Foundation. That's why we were invited to the benefit."

I'm perusing the program. Michael Dexter's name is listed as a participating artist in the charity auction. Is that the piece he was working on the day before yesterday? No wonder he mentioned a deadline.

"Would you mind calling Evan's office to see if Dr. Barakov is a client, too?" I ask Liz, wanting a few moments alone with Zack.

"Sure." Liz stands up "My cell is in the kitchen."

When she's gone, I lean toward Zack. "Another vampire gone with a connection to Barakov?"

"When we get back to the office, I'll check the financial records for Amy and Isabella." He's quiet for a moment. "Maybe Barakov isn't the connection. Maybe this foundation is."

Liz is back in a minute. She's carrying a garment bag. Her face reflects the anxiety and fear that's been racking her mind. "No Barakov on the client list," she says. "No word from Evan."

She tosses her cell phone on the couch, passes the garment bag from her left hand to the right.

I rise to give her a hug. "We'll find him. We have a few things we need to check at the office. Will you be all right here alone?"

Liz steps reluctantly out of my arms. "Yes. Why did you have me check on Barakov?"

I don't want to alarm Liz, but I don't want to lie to her, either. "Barakov has been a common denominator in a couple missing persons' cases. But we don't have anything solid."

"He's connected to Green Leaf, and Evan has connections to Green Leaf. You think this Barakov might have done something to Evan?"

The edge in her voice is razor sharp. The last thing we need is a pissed-off witch going after the wrong guy. Zack realizes that, too, and reacts quickly. "I think we need to give Emma a few minutes alone with him so she can find out. He'll be at the party."

Liz peers at me, tossing her head in Zack's direction. "He knows about you, too?"

I nod.

She frowns. That he knows my true nature, and that he could only know it if I told him, makes our connection too intimate for her approval.

The atmosphere in the room becomes stiflingly oppressive.

Zack feels the tension between Liz and me and, once again, breaks the silence. "Let's not forget it's possible there's another explanation for why you can't locate Evan. You already mentioned an alternative reality. What else could interfere with your scrying?"

"You mean like a shield of some sort?" Liz suggests.

"Any way for you to determine if that's what's blocking you?" he asks.

I can see her wheels turning. Zack has given her something to focus on besides me . . . or Barakov. Something that not only will keep her busy, but could be a huge help.

"Maybe. A shield that strong would take a lot of energy. I'll keep trying my locator spells and start looking for pockets of unusual power." She glances down at the garment bag as if just remembering it. "Take this, before I forget."

"What is it?"

"You'll see when you get home. Trust me, you'll like it."

When she passes the bag to me, there's a rustle of fabric. This must be the dress Liz mentioned I could borrow. This is so Liz. Her world could be falling apart and she's thinking about what I'm going to wear to the party.

"I won't go if you want me to stay here with you," I tell her, pushing the bag away.

"No." Her reply is quick, adamant. "My place is here. But you go. If anyone at Green Leaf is in any way involved in Evan's disappearance, you can find out." The look she sends me telegraphs that she *knows* I can find out, that she expects me to do whatever it takes, that she's certain I will.

"Should I call the police?" she asks then.

"Wait a little while longer," Zack says. "We're doing everything possible right now. Let's see how things play out and keep one another posted."

She sighs and walks us to the door. Zack goes ahead and I pause to give Liz one last hug.

She pulls away. "Oh, I almost forgot." She turns back to the coffee table and slips a piece of paper out of a folder lying there. "A list of Blood Emporiums."

I glance at it. "Looks pretty complete. Who's your source?"

She shrugs. "A longtime client. He circled the one in the Gaslamp, the one he thought you might be interested in." Her mouth twists in a weary frown. "Ironic, isn't it, Emma? Yesterday I wasn't sure how I felt about Evan. Today I'd give my life to see him back home safe. With me."

I smile and touch her cheek. "He will be. And the good news is now you know. You have your answer."

I toss the garment bag into the backseat of the car. I can wait until I get home to see the dress. It's the piece of paper Liz handed me that has my attention—a computer-generated list of all of San Diego's Blood Emporiums with the names of each one's cover business and address.

"Check this out." I hold up the paper so Zack can see.

"Wicked Ink?" It's circled in red. The address is around Fifth and J Street.

"Michael Dexter found a receipt dated the day Isabella disappeared. He said she used to pick up her blood supply from a Blood Emporium in the Gaslamp. I think this might be it."

Zack gives the list a quick once-over. "This looks like a list of all of the Emporiums in San Diego County. Information like this isn't easy for an outsider to come by. Where did Liz get it?"

I shake my head. "I don't know. A friend of Evan's maybe? But I think it's worth paying this Wicked Ink a visit. Someone there might have been the last person to see Isabella before she disappeared."

Zack's expression clouds over with worry.

"What are you thinking?" I ask him.

"Some of the old guard have been targeting the Emporiums. They aren't happy with the number of vampires who are mainstreaming. They fear it's a sign the culture is collapsing."

"But they've been sanctioned by those in power, right?"

"That's the case here in the West. My understanding is that there's quite a bit of dissension between the four

American sovereigns. The new Southern king is vehemently opposed. He's been spewing all sorts of new rhetoric. Or should I say *old* rhetoric? He wants the Emporiums shut down."

I haven't kept up with vampire politics. "I didn't even know there was a new Southern king. When did this happen?"

"Eight, maybe nine months ago. He started by levying outrageous taxes, driving up the price of blood in his territory until it's practically unaffordable, both for those buying and selling. There's a huge propaganda machine behind the movement. The Emporiums are like a lifeline to mainstreamed vampires. They're what allow them to function and integrate into society. Shutting down the Emporiums would have the same impact on vampires that shutting down every grocery store would have on humans."

"Then why on earth is the Southern king doing it?"

"Because it's more difficult to oppressively rule people who are independent. He talks about giving control back to the vampires. Of supporting their taking what's rightfully theirs instead of lining the pockets of the elite few and kowtowing to humans. I think what he's really after is a return to the old ways. Some of the zealots have started to move into other territories. I've heard reports that Emporiums in New Mexico and Arizona have been torched. I've even heard they've gone so far as to kidnap and torture patrons. It seems they might be working their way west."

"Like here? Southern California? Do you think that's why we have three missing vampires?"

Zack shrugs. "It's something else to check out."

And something else to complicate an already complicated case. I glance at Zack. "How do you know so much about it?"

Zack avoids my eyes. "My former pack has close ties with the Southern king."

"One of the reasons you parted ways?" I ask.

I get a curt nod. Then he closes down. I see it in the set of his shoulders, the tightness of his jaw. He starts the car and pulls onto the street.

I clear my throat. "Hate crimes against vampires by other vampires. What's next?"

If Zack has an answer to that question, he keeps it to himself. We decide to split up. I'll go to the Blood Emporium alone and Zack will go back to the office to take a second look at Amy's and Isabella's financial records. When we looked the first time, we were searching for evidence that the two women were patients of Dr. Barakov. This time he's going to look for contributions to Green Leaf.

Soon I'm on my way to Wicked Ink. The first order of business will be to see if I can persuade anyone to acknowledge that an Emporium's housed there. If I get that far, I'll ask to speak to someone in charge. For obvious reasons, getting a warrant is out of the question. This is going to be up to me and my powers of persuasion.

Parking in the Gaslamp District is always a hassle. There's a road crew working on Fifth Avenue, which makes the predictably busy traffic even worse. I've been moving at a snail's pace but making progress. Until now.

Now I find myself stuck behind a black sedan that's decided to stop right in front of my destination—Wicked Ink. It's just large enough so that it blocks the lane, has tinted windows all around like so many others these days, much like the one I saw at Evan's place this morning. The light up ahead changes, but it still doesn't move. I honk. The driver gets out.

"I'll be damned."

It isn't *like* the car I saw at Evan's. It *is* the car I saw at Evan's. The driver glances back at me, not with the slightest hint of apology or even curiosity. His eyes flick my way; then he turns his back on me and holds open the rear door. The passenger gets out and heads inside. Again, there is a distinct moment of hesitation on his part. But he doesn't look back. I can't see his face. Is he the one who gave Liz the list I have in my pocket? If I can convince him to talk to me, he might have information about Isabella. He might even have a sense about whether the conflicts Zack mentioned have anything to do with the disappearances of Amy, Isabella, or Evan. They were all mainstreamed. Could it be they were all getting their blood here? Are they targets of the faction who wish to see the Emporiums closed?

The sedan is once again on the move. Traffic opens up and I luck out. There's a parking space just around the corner on J Street. I park, then hurry to catch up with the man in black.

The bell over the door rings as I walk into the shop.

It's not at all what I expected.

For a tattoo parlor, Wicked Ink has one fancy reception area. To my right is a large, round dining room table, surrounded by high-back red velvet chairs and piled high with black leather-bound books and two sterling silver candelabras. Each holds half a dozen black candles, all lit. There are more candles blazing in the standing candelabras that line the north and south walls. The walls and ceiling are padded, tufted, and covered with an elegant black on black brocade, the floors a dark polished wood. A series of ornate silver-framed floor-to-ceiling mirrors covers the east wall across from me. I see myself reflected in several of them.

It's eerily quiet, too. No heavy metal blaring from hidden speakers. Only the barely discernible hum of an air conditioner pumping refrigerated air into a room I'd guess is about sixty degrees already. A shiver races down my spine. To my left there's a sitting area. I wander over. There are two red velvet sofas facing each other. Between them is a round black velvet ottoman with silver-beaded fringe. More leather-bound volumes are stacked on it. I take a seat and flip through the first one. They're filled with designs, each one labeled and indexed.

"Can I help you?"

I turn toward the voice just in time to see a door close. It's cut into the brocade-covered wall and, once closed, is all but invisible. A touch of a button and a large flat-screen monitor that's recessed into the wall comes alive. It displays the store's highly stylized black-and-red logo. "Most of our clients prefer searching the online database." The voice belongs not to the man I was looking for, but a young woman.

More precisely, a young female vampire.

She couldn't have been more than sixteen when she was turned and looks to be completely at home in these surroundings. Her black, off-the-shoulder taffeta gown has a fitted bodice and a full skirt. I hear the rustle of silk and crinoline as she glides toward me. Her face is heart-shaped. The narrow chin and delicate cheekbones serve to further accentuate her enormous green eyes. The clothing is late Victorian, but the hair and makeup are contemporary goth. Smudged kohl eyeliner, dark red lipstick, and flawless, pale skin. Her jet-black hair is piled atop her head in an organized mess. Feather accents finish the look that must have taken hours to painstakingly create. The ink she's sporting is dramatic, an intricate pattern of black thorns and bloodred roses that start at the top of her neck and run down, disappearing into the gown. More peek out from the edges of the long sleeves of the dress and run over her hands and fingers. I wonder how much of her petite body is covered.

With the experience of one who knows exactly the reaction her image projects, she stretches out a hand. "All my work is done here. What, exactly, are you looking for? I'm sure I can point you in the right direction."

Her question is spoken in a purr. I rise from the couch, shake my head, and flash my badge. "Beautiful ink, but that's not why I'm here. Special Agent Emma Monroe."

"FBI?"

"That's right. You are?"

"Rose."

Appropriate. I slip the badge back into my pocket. "A man came in here a minute or two ago."

The vampire makes a show of looking around. "I don't think so. It appears we're quite alone, Agent Monroe."

"Perhaps he's back there?" I point to the door that she's just emerged from.

"There are three tattoo stations back there. All of them are currently empty. I was just setting up. The artists don't normally come in until late afternoon. You're welcome to look." She steps back and waves toward the door. "The man you're looking for, is he a criminal of some kind?"

"No." I don't take her up on her offer to search behind door number one. If she's so willing to have me do it, there's no point.

I decide to go for the direct approach, hoping my candor will loosen her tongue and that I won't have to resort to using my powers.

"I want to speak to someone who works the other side of the business."

"The other side?"

"Someone with the Emporium. I'm working a missing person's case. Actually, it's a missing vampire. We have reason to believe she was here the day she went missing."

At the mention of vampire, Rose allows a slow smile to form on her lips. "Missing vampire? Can I see that badge again? This is a joke, right? Max put you up to this, didn't he?"

Rose's skirt starts to ring. She turns her back on me, reaches into a pocket, and pulls out a cell phone.

"Yes?" The vampire looks up into a corner of the room where a discreet surveillance camera is positioned.

I'd bet my badge that my mystery man is watching.

"Of course, sire. Right away." She turns back to face me, the cell once again concealed in the folds of her skirt. "Follow me."

Sire? I have no time to ask the question. Rose is on the move. She crosses the room, pushing one of the tufted wall panels aside to reveal a keypad. She enters a series of numbers, and a door, like the first one she came through, swings inward. I follow her down a short hallway to a staircase. Apparently there are floors not only above, but below us. We head down. Despite the dress, Rose negotiates the steep steps rather well.

When we reach the door at the bottom, we're immediately buzzed through. I feel as if I've gone down the rabbit hole and ended up in my local grocery store. Real basements are extremely rare in Southern California. This one has a polished white floor, harsh fluorescent lights, and a long double row of industrial-grade refrigerators with glass doors.

The refrigerators are filled with blood packs. The lower shelf of one contains insulated bags that are tagged with names, dates, and times. The signs hanging on the outside that normally point shoppers to the vegetables or ice cream instead have written upon them things like A+ and B-. I pause in front of a door marked YBV.

"YBV?"

Rose walks back. "Young Blond Virgin, one of my personal favorites. We carry both male and female, of course." This time when she smiles, I see the fangs. "Come. Simon is waiting."

Rose leads the way. At the end of the first aisle, we turn right and cross several more before taking another left. I follow her up a short set of industrial stairs to what appears to be an office above. I'm not exactly sure where we are, but I'm certain we're no longer under the tattoo shop.

Rose knocks on the door before entering. "Simon?"

He's seated on a sofa, a game console in his hand and a pile of dead bodies looming on the television screen in front of him. Simon is most decidedly *not* the man I'd seen walk in. He isn't even a vampire. With his unruly bed head, rumpled T-shirt, and khakis, the twentysomething looks like a typical college student.

"Come in! Agent Monroe, is it? Have a seat."

There is an endearing and awkward nervous energy about him. I take the seat opposite the only other piece of furniture in the room, a glass and stainless steel desk. On top of the desk is a sleek, state-of-the-art desktop computer.

"I understand you're looking for a missing vampire." Simon reaches to open a small refrigerator beside the sofa and pulls out a Red Bull. "Can I offer you something?"

"I'm good." His reference to the missing vampire is stated with casual indifference, as if an FBI agent walked in every day to ask for help. As if someone is running interference.

While he pops open the drink, I look around.

His office looks like a dorm room. There's a large-screen television on one wall. In front of it is an old over-stuffed sofa and a video game console. There are shelves on the opposite wall that contain an impressive collection of manga and a variety of comic book action figures that I don't recognize. On the back of the door I entered, which is now closed, is a basketball hoop.

Simon frowns at something behind me. I turn around. Rose is standing on the other side of the door. I can see her through the glass window that gives Simon a bird's-eye view of the refrigeration system below. There are several rows like the one I just walked through. I can see now it's likely the operation stretches the entire subterranean length of the block.

Simon motions with his hand, shooing her away.

I don't particularly care if Rose overhears our conversation, so I get down to business. "I'm looking into the disappearance of someone who I believe receives her blood supply from you, Isabella Mancini."

He leans against the back of the sofa. "Does the FBI know that you're here?"

I smile. "They don't track my every move."

"They do. You just don't *know* it," he says, jabbing the air for emphasis. "They can track you using your cell phone—FBI, CIA, NSA."

"I'm here unofficially," I volunteer, hoping to get the conversation back on track.

"That's what they all say." He crosses his arms over his chest and leans back on the sofa. "What department are you with?"

"Missing Persons. San Diego Field Office."

"And *they* know about vampires? About this place?"

Whatever I say, I'll be feeding into Simon's paranoia. May as well tell him the truth. "No. This is off the books." Sort of.

I'm tempted to use my powers to ensure truthful answers, but I'm not sure it's necessary. I suspect the same person that called Rose on her cell phone already ordered Simon to cooperate with me. I wouldn't be here with him otherwise. My eyes do a quick sweep of the ceiling. There's a camera here, too. I pointedly look up at it when I add, "Time really is of the essence."

Simon follows my glance, smiles, and slides into the chair behind his desk. "Isabella Mancini." He types the name into the computer. "What do you want to know?"

"Did anything unusual happen the last day she was here?"

"She's a drive-through customer. She never actually came in."

"Drive-through?"

"We offer home delivery, drive-through, and pickup. Home delivery is more expensive and by credit card or direct withdrawal only. Pickup is the most economical, but not very convenient. Parking in this neighborhood can be a bitch."

"Tell me about it. Where is the drive-through window?"

"On the Fourth Avenue side of the building. She picked up on time, as usual, paid cash. That's all I can tell you. She hasn't been back since."

"Are there any security tapes I could review to see if perhaps she was being followed?"

"I'm sorry, no. We don't have a camera on the pickup window. For obvious reasons. Our customers demand privacy."

"Maybe I could speak to the person who worked the window that day? See if he or she remembers anything?"

"We have two people covering each shift. They rotate working the window and getting the orders prepared for pickup. Cash is picked up every hour when the supply for the next one is delivered. José was on that day. I remember him saying something about going to Baja for the weekend. I can try his cell, but you know how reception is down there."

"Please. Try."

Simon dials the number using a program on his computer. I hear it ringing, then going to voice mail. He leaves a message. "Dude, it's Simon. Listen, an Agent Monroe is going to call you and ask you a few questions about a customer. It's cool. Tell her whatever you remember."

He scribbles José's number on a Post-it and hands it to me. "The signal in Mexico totally sucks. You might not be able to reach him until Monday. Anything else I can help you with?"

I pocket the number. "I've heard there's been some trouble in other states, some political conflicts resulting in vandalism and violence against mainstreamers. Have you encountered anything like that?"

Simon shakes his head. "No, the California operation runs like clockwork. There have been a few problems in New Mexico and Arizona, but we're adding extra security at those locations."

He's sipping on his drink, answering my questions with the friendly candor of two college chums discussing one of those video games on his wall. "Simon, I have to ask. Just what do you do here?"

"My official title is Operational Director, Western Region. I was recruited from Cal Tech three years ago. Hey, you showed it to Rose, can I see your badge?"

So our mystery man isn't the only one who'd been watching. I pull my badge out and hand it to him.

"Cool." He hands it back to me. "Anything else I can tell you?"

"Amy Patterson and Evan Porter."

"What about them?"

"They're both missing. Do they get blood from you?"

His fingers fly across the keyboard. "Evan is on home delivery, and so is Amy. We deliver in Styrofoam chests containing dry ice twice a week, signature required." He frowns. "Amy missed a delivery a couple weeks ago. She hasn't contacted us since. We left several discreet messages about rescheduling. No response. Evan is scheduled for delivery today."

I lean forward. It occurs to me this might be a way to identify additional missing vampires. "Would it be possible to get a list of others who have missed deliveries or appointments?"

"Missed them in the past week?"

"How about the past six months?"

"It would take some time. We have accounts in pending status for a variety of reasons, lack of payment, people who are on vacation, et cetera."

"We only need those that don't have an explanation and haven't resumed. I'd appreciate it," I tell him. "There could be more missing. So far the common denominator in these three cases is that they are all vampires and—"

"We sourced their blood, I understand. We'll work on it. Shall I email you the file when it's ready?"

I don't bother mentioning the other common denominators, Barakov and possibly even Green Leaf, as I hand him my card. "Thank you for cooperating."

He smiles. "The order came down to give you whatever you needed."

"Order? From whom?"

Simon's desk phone rings before he can answer. He picks up the receiver, listens for a moment, then hands me the phone.

A deep baritone voice on the other end says, "We'll have the list to you within twenty-four hours. Find our missing, Agent Monroe."

The man doesn't give me a chance to respond or ask questions. I'm left listening to the dial tone. The voice wasn't one I'd heard before. It wouldn't be easily forgotten. "Who was that?" I ask, handing the phone back to Simon.

"The boss." Simon presses an intercom button and Rose appears like a genie out of a bottle. "Nice to meet you, Agent Monroe." Simon grins as if he's got a delicious secret. "We'll be in touch."

*   *   *

Zack is at his desk when I get back, working on his computer.

"Did you find anything?" I ask, slipping out of my jacket and hanging it on the desk chair. I lean over his shoulder to view the monitor.

Zack gestures to the screen. "Well, I couldn't find any checks from Isabella to Green Leaf. No automatic deductions from any of her accounts, either. But Amy supported them. I discovered five checks made out to Green Leaf in the last five months that were marked as charitable donations. She also contributed to the Red Cross, a San Diego food bank, and the Humane Society. And there's another connection. . . . Green Leaf has a special grant program that subsidizes training for contractors and laborers who promote and install the latest and greatest in green products. It looks like one of those Green Leaf crews installed the shades on Amy Patterson's windows."

"Giving them access to her apartment."

"Yup. You have any luck at Wicked Ink?"

I look around. Other agents are milling about within hearing distance. "It was . . . interesting. . . . I'll fill you in later." I take my own seat at the desk across from him. "Although they did promise to get me a list of other customers who have missed deliveries or pickups lately."

Zack lowers his voice to a whisper. "You think there might be other missing . . ." He glances around, too, regroups. "Others like Amy and Isabella that we don't know about?"

"I think it's a strong possibility," I say.

He looks over the top of his computer screen at me. "You still going to that benefit tonight?"

To myself I think, *You betcha.* Nothing's really changed.

I'm beginning to think getting Barakov alone might be the only way we'll get a break in this case. Besides, I promised Liz. To Zack, I say, "Yes."

"You have an extra ticket?"

"It's black tie. You have a tux?"

He nods. "Don't look so surprised." He pauses. "Is that all you're going to ask me?"

I smile. "Last night was the third night of the full moon. You'll be safe."

The corners of his mouth turn down. He leans forward. "Safe? Don't kid yourself. Deep down I'm dangerous, a predator. Don't ever forget it."

I can't tell if he's kidding or not. There's heat and intensity in his voice, sincerity in his eyes. But it doesn't matter. He's right. Forget that he's dangerous? Not likely. Although this afternoon proved we could work together without letting personal feelings get in the way, I don't think for a minute we're out of the woods yet.

CHAPTER 15

The Hotel Del Coronado looks as spectacular today as it did when it opened over a century ago. Since that time, the red-roofed Victorian hotel has become a favorite of presidents, royalty, and Hollywood's darlings. The beach-front resort is luxury at its finest and most elegant. There is a long line of cars sitting at the entrance. Zack veers to the left to Self Park.

"Why didn't you valet? We're never going to find a spot in here," I grumble. To say nothing of dreading the idea of hiking across the asphalt parking lot in four-inch heels.

Zack raises an eyebrow. "O ye of little faith." He pulls up to the console and pushes the big green button. The machine spits out a ticket, the gate goes up, and Zack drives into the lot. The taillights on a white Mercedes come to light as we round the corner. *Just* as we round the corner. The Mercedes pulls out, we pull in. We're within a hundred feet of the hotel entrance.

"How did you do that?" I ask, properly impressed.

Zack grins. "Another of my many talents." He springs from the car. "Let me get your door."

But I already have it open. "I know how to open a door and get out of a car. I've done it a bazillion times."

Just not in these damned heels.

The words are no sooner out of my mouth than I stumble.

Zack is there, reaching out a hand to steady me.

"Thanks."

He offers his arm. "You clean up nicely, Monroe."

I don't take it. "This isn't a date. We're working, Zack."

That's what I say. What I'm thinking is, he cleans up nicely, too. The tux is obviously tailored. The white shirt is crisply starched and the shoes, if I'm not mistaken, are Italian.

"Okay, okay. Strictly business." He touches his hand to his heart. "Just try to blend without falling."

I ignore the hint of humor in his tone. A wisp of hair escapes from my French twist. I tuck it behind my ear, then smooth down my dress. The gown is off-the-shoulder, black lace with a nude lining. It fits like a surgical glove. The shoes like a medieval torture device. I lift up the edge of my dress and start to walk. "Easier said than done. I don't know how Liz does it. These shoes are already killing me."

Zack places his hand at the small of my back as we cross the drive and go up the steps to the entrance. "Want me to carry you?"

"What I want to do is find Barakov."

Every time I walk into the Del, I'm hit by a wave of nostalgia. I feel as if I've stepped back in time—dark wooden paneling, rich fabrics, antique furnishings, and an abundance of fresh flowers all set the stage. Guests are milling about, dressed in formal attire—the men in tuxedos, the women in gowns. Except for the modern cut of the dresses and the scandalous height of our heels, we could be waiting for the Duke and Duchess of Windsor to sweep in the door.

A low whistle comes from Zack, telling me he's impressed and that he's never been here before.

"It is beautiful, isn't it?"

"You don't see woodwork like this anymore." Zack pauses a minute to take it all in before asking, "Do you know where we're going?"

I tilt my head in the direction of the Crown Room. "Michael Dexter said there would be tickets waiting for us."

There is a man at the door welcoming guests. Zack mentions my name and he checks the list in his hand. Seconds later, we're motioned through with a smile.

Once inside, Zack swipes two glasses of champagne from a passing tray and hands one to me. "We're trying to blend, remember?"

And blend he does. Zack looks as relaxed and at home in a tux as he does in T-shirt and jeans. He takes a sip from his champagne and starts to check out the room. To the casual observer, he could merely be looking for a face in the crowd, but I know he's taking in every detail, because I'm doing the same.

There are a couple of dozen ten-tops, covered in crisp white tablecloths. An extravagant buffet is set up on the far side of the room. There's a bar in the corner. Waitstaff in black slacks and white short-waist jackets with gold brocade epaulets are circulating with trays. Some, like the one that passed by earlier, hold champagne, others hors d'oeuvres. In the middle of the room is a sizable dance floor, at the back, a stage. A very retro-looking orchestra is now playing "Moonglow."

A plaque on the wall behind me catches Zack's eye and he steps closer to better read it.

"Did you know this?"

I'm too busy scanning the crowd for Barakov to pay attention to the plaque.

"Not a single nail was used in this room." Zack lifts his glass toward the ceiling. My eyes don't bother to follow. I've heard this little fact before. "Just pegs and glue. Isn't that amazing?"

"Fascinating. You take this half. I'll start my sweep from the other side," I tell him before stepping away.

I weave my way through the sea of unfamiliar faces, pausing to sample some of the appetizers and trade the champagne in my glass for ginger ale. Safer. I love champagne, and this is a good one, but tonight I want to keep a clear head.

There's no sign of Barakov. Yet.

"More champagne?" It's the third time this particular young waiter has asked me. Before I can refuse again, he leans in and smiles sheepishly. "I'm under strict orders to be generous with the booze. We were reminded that happy guests are more generous with the donations. You're making me look bad."

His Italian accent is charming, his smile disarming. I glance at his name tag—Fabrizio. What harm could come from one more glass? "Can't make you look bad." I'm placing my empty glass on his tray with the intent of taking a new one when I see Barakov at the exit, a cigar in one hand, a glass half-filled with an amber-colored liquid in the other. "Sorry. I've got to go. Excuse me."

I resist the urge to kick off my shoes and run to catch up with him. Instead I move as quickly as I can, cutting straight across the dance floor. Once outside the doors, I spy Barakov heading into the deserted courtyard. There's no one with him. He's alone. Perfect.

I watch from inside for a moment as he lights his cigar and enjoys a few leisurely puffs.

Then I take a deep breath, step outside, and let the dampening spell fall away. I say a silent prayer that Demeter isn't watching. The air stirs around me as I approach Barakov. The power begins to build, unleashing a warm, perfumed mist, unseen but felt by anyone in its sphere of influence. My hair loosens, a strand curling over my right eye. I move closer.

The courtyard is not deserted as I first thought. There's a young couple standing off to the side. They look at me, startled by my sudden appearance, caught up in the wake of my power. "Enjoy your drinks in your room," I say to them as I pass.

A casual remark, delivered softly, a whisper into the air.

The suggestion, however, is anything but casual.

The couple turns, moves toward the door, and disappears inside. Instantly.

"Dr. Barakov?"

About to take a drag on the cigar, he pauses. Stares. "Agent Monroe?"

It takes no effort at all. Once our eyes lock, I have him. "Follow me."

For a moment, his eyes go blank. Without knowing why, without even questioning, he follows. To him, it merely seems like a good idea.

I lead him to a corner where there's a cluster of trees and shrubs.

Once he adjusts to my presence, his eyes clear. "You're beautiful tonight, my dear." His whisper is reverent as he reaches out and tilts my face up into the light. "What have you done? That bump, it's—"

I push his hand away. "A little makeup can do wonders. No touching. And I'm asking the questions."

"Whatever you want."

The adoration in his eyes is nauseating. I could have Barakov on his knees in seconds, begging, with the way he worships beauty. Such games no longer bring me satisfaction. I barely remember when they did.

I get right to the point. "Where is Amy Patterson?"

"I'm afraid I don't have the faintest idea." He takes another puff on his cigar.

It's not the answer I expected. I lower the barriers further, allowing my mind to penetrate Barakov's. The temperature around us rises. The wind subtly picks up, rustling the leaves on the trees. "A man like you, so connected, so smart. You must have some idea what happened to Amy Patterson and Isabella Mancini." My voice is soft, slow, steady.

Barakov sets his drink down on a nearby table, then removes his coat. Sweat is beginning to bead on his forehead.

Is it from the warmth of my powers or from anxiety?

I hold my breath.

"No." He pulls a silk handkerchief from his pocket and mops his brow. "I already answered your questions about Amy and Isabella." The cigar falls unnoticed from his hand. His eyes glaze and his focus turns inward, as if he's trying to understand how I can exert such influence.

He would never be able to fathom it. I push on.

"What about your wife Charlotte?"

At that question, he becomes instantly tearful. He reaches for the drink and takes a fortifying sip. "You think I had something to do with Charlotte's disappearance?"

"Did you?"

"Of course not."

His answer is not only truthful; it's full of reproach. He's shocked that I could even think such a thing.

I stir restlessly. I haven't much more time. Using power like this always comes with risk. I could easily draw unwanted attention . . . from both innocent passersby and Demeter. She has spies everywhere.

There's only one other angle to explore. "Do you know of Amy's and Isabella's nature?"

His eyes narrow. "Nature?"

"You know what I mean."

Does he?

He looks about surreptitiously. "You know about"— Barakov swallows, then lowers his voice before finishing— "vampires?"

I avoid outright validation by ignoring his question and asking another of my own. "Why were you seeing them?"

For the first time, a smile. "So that I could give them eternal beauty."

"How?"

His demeanor shifts immediately. Barakov now bursts with pride as he launches into an explanation. "Although I don't know what Isabella Mancini had hoped to accomplish, Amy had inherited her father's rather unfortunate nose. The surgery wasn't going to be extensive. But it was going to be expensive." He finishes off the remains in his glass. "And under the table, of course. I accept only cash from special customers who are of a special *nature*, shall we say? The income never has to be reported that way. It's my little nest egg, tucked safely away in an offshore account."

I don't bother to ask where. Just make a mental note to see if Zack thinks we should alert the IRS when we're done with Barakov. "So you're telling me that vampires get nose jobs? Why?"

"An eternity is a very long time, Agent Monroe — nose jobs, breast and cheek implants, chin implants . . ."

"Chin implants?"

"Very popular with the men. Imagine having all that strength and speed, a physique you can hone to perfection. Then the overall effect is completely undermined by a weak chin or pitiful cheekbones. I surround the implant with a little microlayer of silver, providing a casing that can't be assimilated, and voilà."

It occurs to me grudgingly that this is a medical miracle of sorts. In some ways it explains his arrogance. Even to the immortals, he must appear a god.

"Was Evan Porter one of your patients, too?"

Puzzlement clouds his face. "The Greenleaf lawyer? Why would you ask — ?" His expression clears. "You mean Evan is a vampire, too?"

Shit.

"Am I interrupting?"

Zack is suddenly standing a few feet behind Barakov. I never heard him approach. His shoulders are drawn up, his hands fisted, every muscle taut. His eyes lock on mine. The undisguised need in them momentarily takes my breath away. He is feeling the effects of my unguarded power, getting another glimpse of my true self. I wonder how long he's been standing there.

"Go back to the party, Doctor. Enjoy the rest of your evening." Even as I say the words, I start reining the power in, bringing up the walls, locking down what I look upon as both a gift and a curse.

Barakov prepares to take his leave with a questioning glance to me. He's aware that we had a conversation and that he revealed more than he intended. As did I. Hopefully the revelation about Evan will get lost in an alcoholic haze. Before the last bit of my ability to exert influence is contained, I take pity on him. "Don't worry about what we've talked about. Chalk it up to the scotch. You'll have more than you should tonight. In fact, it looks like you could use a refill."

After a quick glance at his empty glass, he heads for the bar.

"You should go back to the party, too," I tell Zack.

I expect him to follow my suggestion. He was exposed, after all.

Instead Zack loosens his bow tie and unfastens the top button of his shirt as he watches Barakov go. "I take it Barakov didn't confess?"

Zack's question seems straightforward enough and yet . . . I try to remember the last time someone was able to exhibit such control around me. Zack alluded to having had special training earlier. Am I seeing the results of that? He doesn't appear to be struggling with the effects of exposure and yet he got a good dose of my power—more than in his kitchen, where I let loose a fragment of the magic. But then I look close. The way he's looking at me, the tenseness in his posture, belies his offhand return to a business-as-usual manner.

I tuck an errant strand of hair back behind my ear, affect a sense of calm I'm not really feeling. "He doesn't know anything about the disappearances. We need to look elsewhere. Within Green Leaf maybe."

"Are you sure?"

I was sure I'd read Barakov right. It's what's going on

with Zack that I'm unsure of. There's a knot the size of a fist in my stomach. "Yes. I'm sure Barakov told me the truth." *It's you I'm concerned about.* I square my shoulders. "Go back to the party, Zack. With a little time and distance between us, what you're feeling will dissipate."

He shoves his hands inside his pockets, then leans against the wall. The mask of indifference falls away. "Just out of curiosity, how long a separation are we talking about? Weeks? Months? Years?" The pose he's striking is casual. The turn our conversation is taking isn't.

"Minutes, like last time, at your house. By the time you finished showering, things were . . . back to normal."

Zack straightens. He strolls over to where I'm standing, closing the gap between us. "I'm a good actor, Emma. In fact, you may be the only lie detector I haven't been able to best."

"I'm not trying to read you, Zack."

He holds up a hand. "I know. If you were, you'd realize things have never been normal between us. I can pretend. I can keep my distance and my word. But you should know the attraction isn't going away. It's building and that has nothing to do with your mojo."

My mojo may be under wraps, but the air between us is as charged as it was that night in his kitchen.

His gaze is unwavering. We're venturing into dangerous and confusing territory. The time has come. A decision has to be made. It was good between us in Charleston, better than good. We worked well together as partners both in bed and out. What I doubt is what's happening here and now—whether we can keep things in what I'd come to think of as the *safe zone*.

Friendship.

Sex.

Not love. Never love.

Seconds pass. I can't bring myself to look away. To speak or move. A myriad of images, all depicting possible tragic endings, flit through my mind. Including the one Demeter so cleverly and callously placed there. The blood. Zack's head in her hand.

I've waited too long. Zack turns and starts to walk away. He's a man of his word. And I realize that despite the pull, the temptation, he's managed to find the strength to keep it. He's not going to push. He's going to walk away. No one's walked away. Ever. What if Zack is somehow different? What if we could make this work?

"Wait!"

He turns back to face me. "You don't want me to go back to the party?"

I shake my head.

"It's your move, Emma."

I know this is the moment that will change everything between us—a moment I *want* to happen. I push all my fears and doubts aside and rush into Zack's arms. One arm encircles my waist, the other the back of my neck as his lips cover mine.

He moves us effortlessly, the way he did that night in his kitchen. The wall is suddenly at my back. My mouth opens in surprise and his tongue slips inside. The kiss is demanding, urgent. Full of pent-up promises, of things left unsaid and desires denied. I lift my hand to his chest and grab hold of his shirt. I don't want it to stop. I can feel the hardness of his arousal pressing into me. I push back, eliciting a moan that I vow will be the first of many I coax from Zachary Armstrong tonight.

Zack whispers, "That was some move."

My skin is heated. My body burns with desire.

Footsteps. An embarrassed "Excuse me."

With a low groan in my ear, Zack pulls reluctantly away from me. "Yes?"

It's one of the men who had previously been working the door. "I . . . I'm interrupting."

Zack waves a hand. "Can we help you?"

I turn away, using the moment to smooth the desire from my expression and the wrinkles from my dress as the embarrassed party worker says, "The auction's about to start. I'm rounding up guests."

"Thanks, we'll be right in."

He leaves us with another mumbled apology for the interruption and heads quickly toward another couple standing a few feet away. It startles me because I hadn't noticed them before. They must have come out while I was busy with Barakov. But their eyes are on me. They saw it all, felt the pull of my power. They don't even look away while being shepherded toward the door.

Zack watches them watch us. When they've disappeared inside, he says, "Well, that was awkward."

I'm still breathless with the implication of what I almost let happen between Zack and me. I was as caught up in the moment as he was. I get a sudden chill—I can fool myself into thinking a fling with Zack would mean nothing, but Demeter? She who feels every emotion I try so hard to hide would know better.

The sound of applause spills into the entry. We pass through the double doors of the Crown Room just in time to hear Green Leaf's founder, Alan Pierce, make his introductions. I refocus my thoughts, ignore the fact that Zack's arm is around my shoulders, and watch.

Alan Pierce is younger than I expected. His tuxedo is

well tailored, traditional. He thanks the guests and talks briefly about the company's mission. He speaks with the passion of a man who believes in what he is doing, and his delivery is smooth and polished. Alan ends by publicly recognizing the members of the board of directors who are present.

First, he points out Dr. Alexander Barakov and Dr. Barbara Pierce. His parents.

Zack leans down and whispers, "There's an interesting connection."

"Yes, it is."

He moves on, introducing Taylor Cummings. The former soap opera actress is lapping up the applause. In fact, I get the distinct impression that's why she came. Cummings gave up a not so promising career a couple of years ago to marry Southern California construction magnate Jack Reynolds. I remember some talk a few years ago about her having a drinking problem. Tonight, not only is Cummings quite tipsy, she's quite conspicuously alone.

The final introduction is of Gordon Jacobs. I recognize the name and the connection. I tug on Zack's sleeve to get his attention. "Jacobs is a partner at the same firm as Evan. What if Polk and Wagner is involved with whatever is going on at Green Leaf and Evan stumbled upon it?"

"There's one sure way you can find out," Zack says. "Can you do it?"

Each use of my powers ensures Demeter's disapproval and places me further from the possibility of forgiveness. But we're at a dead end. Lives are at stake, one of them Evan's.

"Yes, I can do it."

Although an auctioneer is managing the bidding process, Alan Pierce is reading the item descriptions. The one currently up for bid is being "modeled" by an attractive young woman. It's a colorful tote bag made from brightly colored recycled candy wrappers.

"Should I take Taylor Cummings or Barbara Pierce?" Zack asks.

I look around. Drs. Pierce and Barakov are nowhere to be seen. "I think Pierce and Barakov left." Was he uneasy over the conversation we had? Perhaps he was afraid of running into me again.

Zack checks his watch. "Taylor Cummings it is," he says. "Let's meet back at the car in thirty minutes?"

I nod.

Zack grabs two glasses of champagne from a passing tray, then heads off. I see Jacobs making a beeline for the bar and follow. The man is in his mid to late fifties, overweight, red-faced. He orders a scotch, neat. I do the same. The smell coming off him confirms this scotch is not his first.

"It's a little warm in here." I fan myself, then offer him my hand. "Emma Monroe."

"Gordon Jacobs. How are you connected to Green Leaf?"

"I'm not, really." Michael Dexter's piece is about to be introduced and Alan has called him to the stage. I gesture toward Dexter. "I'm a guest of the artist."

Jacobs' eyes drift to the front of the room. The bidding has started. "Boyfriend?"

"God, no. Michael's gay. I was just going to step out for a breath of fresh air. Care to join me?" I offer him a smile filled with promise. He predictably takes the bait.

We go out the front door, circle around the side of the hotel, past some of the quaint shops that are closed, and then onto the ocean veranda. The entire time, Jacobs talks about himself, his illustrious career, and his passion for golf and deep-sea fishing. I feign fascination. Despite the leisurely pace, by the time we get there, Jacobs is out of breath. Thankfully, the veranda is empty. This time, I make doubly sure. The large open space ensures that I won't make the same mistake and miss another couple half-hidden by shrubbery.

The air has grown chilly. The moon is still bright enough that I can see the waves as they crash onto the shore in front of us. Since I'd rather not spend any more time with this bore than necessary, I tap into my powers and get down to business.

Jacobs succumbs to my influence even more quickly than Barakov. The alcohol in his system and my power break down any resistance he might feel to answering my questions. I spend ten, maybe fifteen minutes grilling him and get nothing of value. He thinks Evan is exceptionally talented, with the courtroom presence and breadth of knowledge rarely found in a man his age. When I ask if he's aware that Evan's missing, he thinks I mean from the party and says he's probably just running a bit late—there's a very high-profile case he's in the midst of trying. Mention of Isabella and Amy elicits empty stares.

Essentially, Jacobs' connection to Green Leaf is financially motivated. Scoring Green Leaf as a client helped Polk and Wagner lure in Evan and gave the firm an entrée into what's become a very lucrative niche. As a senior member of the firm, he's more than happy to attend a few board meetings a year in order to keep that highly visible cash cow happy. Privately, Jacobs thinks global warming is a bunch of hooey. He couldn't care less about the mission.

There's only one thing on Jacobs' mind tonight and it

has nothing to do with charity. Finally tiring of his feeble attempts at seduction, and with a silent apology to the other women at the party, I send him back inside.

I hope Zack is doing better than I am.

When I reach the parking lot, Zack is already in the car, waiting for me. My first thought is that he, too, struck out. Not only did he beat me back to the car, but his jacket and tie are now gone, his sleeves rolled up.

"Any luck?" I ask, steeling myself for disappointment. I'd so hoped to have news of a break for Liz.

Zack pulls a cocktail napkin from his pants pocket. "I got Taylor's phone number." He dangles it in front of me. "She put it in my pocket herself. You?"

"Nothing." I climb into the passenger seat and kick off my shoes.

Zack crushes the napkin into a ball and tosses it into the backseat. "Now what? We're no closer than before. All we've got is a thin connection between Green Leaf and the disappearances."

He's staring straight ahead, into the darkness, his brow furrowed. His profile is sharp and clean, his lips turned down at the corners.

I have to steel myself to keep from giving in to an impulse. I want to turn his face toward mine, brush my lips across his.

I look away quickly. "Then the connection to Green Leaf is where we'll start," I say. "Tomorrow. Tomorrow we'll look at the case with fresh eyes."

But not tonight. Tonight, I know what I want. I want to break this spell Zack has on me. I *need* to break it. I need to stop wondering, to get him out of my system.

There's one sure way to do that. One even Demeter can't fault.

"Take me home."

Zack reaches for the seat belt. As he slides the latch home, I cover his hand with mine.

I take his chin and turn his face until his eyes meet mine. "Take me to your home."

A slow smile forms.

"Don't. Don't read anything into this, Zack. It's just for tonight. It's just sex."

He throws the car into reverse. "Right. Just tonight. Just sex."

CHAPTER 16

"I hope red is all right. I'm out of white." Zack leans casually in the doorway, a glass of wine in each hand.

"So this is it?" I give one of the steel bars a shake before accepting the wine. The cage is built solid.

"I hope you realize I don't invite just any girl up to see my cage." He smiles, but without warmth or humor. It's a smile that doesn't quite reach his eyes.

"How long ago were you turned?"

His eyes become distant. "I wasn't *turned*. My father was Were." He nods toward the cage. "This was originally his. It's mine now. But that's a story for another day."

"So you always knew you were Were?"

"I knew my father was. He was adept at hiding it from the world, but he didn't hide it from me. He wanted to prepare me for the possibility that I carried the gene. The testing that's available now wasn't then. I didn't know for sure until my freshman year in high school. That's when everything changed."

"I can't imagine what you must have gone through."

He smiles wryly. "At first it was incredible. Everything became better, more intense. I was faster, stronger. I evolved in ways you couldn't imagine and I never anticipated. I'd always been a good athlete. After my ascension I was unbeatable, and not just during the changeling times. I should have held back. I didn't. I was ambitious. I wanted to go to college. Recruiters flocked to my games. Unfortunately, not just college recruiters. I came to the attention of the wrong people."

One glance and somehow I know. "The people you worked for?"

He studies his glass, swirling the wine gently before taking a sip. "Yes."

There's no way I can let him leave it at that. Now that he's opened up, I want to hear the whole story. "Tell me the rest."

He shakes his head. "The rest of this sounds like the plot from a bad sci-fi movie. Not the average woman's idea of foreplay."

I have to smile at that. "Remember who you're talking to. What do you think the story of my life sounds like? Plus, Siren. We don't really need foreplay. I guess I could have saved you a lot of time if I'd told you that before."

He laughs. "That's okay. I like to be thorough. Take pride in my work." He closes the gate to the cage. Locks it. Starts to move away.

I take his hand, make him turn back toward me. "Please? I want to know."

He takes another pull from his glass, stares down into it. Finally he relents.

"They knew what I was. I was told they represented a special division of the U.S. military. Only it turned out they were more of a subcontracted splinter group. They said they were building a special team to carry out top secret military operations and they wanted me on board."

"Flattering."

"It was to a seventeen-year-old. The opportunity to join an army of supernatural creatures who would fight against tyranny and protect the American way was too compelling to pass up." He looks up. "I completely let go of the idea of college. Why sit in a classroom when I could be part of a real-life Justice League? I *volunteered*. For a kid with an IQ of one sixty, I was incredibly stupid and naive."

I reach out and touch his cheek. "Or incredibly brave and courageous."

"I've never spoken of it before."

"Why me? Why now?"

"Because you're unrelenting and work on me like kryptonite?"

I frown, playing with one of the buttons on his shirt so that I don't have to look him in the eye.

"I know you could find out anything you want about me at any time," he says at last, lifting my chin. "But you let me tell the story myself. Is there anything else you want to know?"

A dozen questions flit through my mind before I settle on one.

"What is it that finally made you break away, leave that life?"

He hesitates. Seconds pass. Just when I reach the conclusion he's not going to tell me, he takes a deep breath and begins.

"I was sent on a mission. It was supposed to be quick, simple. Everything had been carefully orchestrated. The research, as always, was thorough. The target was a threat to national security. He'd reportedly been responsible for the loss of many lives, could be responsible for the deaths of a great deal more. He was a monster who needed to be eliminated. At least that's what I was told, what I believed."

"You were sent to kill him."

Zack nods. "I had a custom-made long-range rifle and a clear view. The target was supposed to be alone. No one else was visible when I lined up the shot and took aim. I'm good at what I do. What I *did*. The shot was clean." He swallows. "But the target wasn't alone. She must have entered the room right after I pulled the trigger. I watched, through my scope. It was surreal, a macabre silent horror film unfolding before me. One of my own making. One that afterward I couldn't get out of my head. I still can't. She threw herself on top of the target. Crying. Screaming. Soaked in his blood. She was four. He was her father. And ... as it turned out ... I was the monster."

I place my hand on Zack's shoulder and give it a squeeze. "You are not a monster. You killed one man to save hundreds."

He smiles ruefully. "It was a lie, Emma." He turns to look at me, his eyes shadowed with regret. "The dossier was a complete fabrication. It was about money and power. It wasn't about saving lives. And it wasn't just about killing one man. It wasn't just one man. There were a lot of men over the years. Every one of them someone's son, or husband, or father. I started to dig. The more I did, the more lies I uncovered. I wasn't doing something noble, something to be proud of. I was nothing more than a very highly trained, highly paid assassin. No matter what I do, how many I manage to save, I'll never be able to give back the lives I took."

"That's why working these cases has become so important to you. You can't return that little girl's father to her, not ever. But you can find and return others."

"And I do, just like you. In so many ways, we're coming from the same place, you and I. We're seeking the same kind of salvation. That's why we make such a great team."

Zack is right. We do make a great team. We are on the same path, in search of the same thing. "The people you worked for, they just let you walk away?"

"Hardly. Suffice it to say I fixed things so that I pose more of a threat to them dead than alive. We're at a stalemate. I've accepted I can't take them down. For now. They've accepted my decision. For now."

Zack holds out his hand.

I take it.

"No more talk about sad things. Not tonight."

I let him lead me down a short hall to a door on the left. He pushes it open, giving me a clear view of the master suite.

On the far side of the room is a set of double French doors. They open onto a balcony, offering a breathtaking view of the moonlit beach and ocean beyond. Cream doupioni curtains hang over the doors, the rich silk fabric flutters in the evening breeze. There's a fire in the fireplace to the left of the bed. It fills the room with warmth, a contrast to the cool night air drifting in from outside. On the mantel is an array of candles, which he's also taken the time to light. There are more on the dark walnut nightstands, which flank the enormous king-sized sleigh bed. The lamps on the either side of the bed remain off. They aren't needed. A natural glow fills the room. The flames from the fire and candles flicker and dance, casting shadows on the wall.

I hesitate. The first time we were together was all flying clothes, insistent hands, and hot openmouthed kisses. I guess after my admission and in light of his nature, I was expecting the same. For tonight, at least, he's got that aggression thoroughly locked away.

"You're in control here."

"Honestly, I think I'd be more comfortable if we were both out of control." I take a sip of my wine. There is the aroma of sea salt and burned wood in the air, as well as a mix of vanilla and orange, cinnamon and ginger. "You always keep scented candles around?" I ask over the rim of my glass.

"I figure you've got to give a girl something if you're going to hold back on the foreplay."

I walk over to the bed and run my hand over the duvet cover. Like those downstairs, the fabrics are rich and lush. Earth tones dominate—taupe walls, cream drapes, dark brown bedding with gold accents. I move to the fireplace. There's a large mirror above it. I can see Zack's reflection as he crosses the room to join me.

He places his hands gently on my shoulders. "Listen, it's okay if you've changed your mind. You were right this morning when you said there are a lot of reasons not to do this."

My gaze lifts to meet his in the mirror. "And yet here we are."

He reaches out with one hand, brushing his fingertips down the side of my neck before tracing a painstakingly slow path along the edge of my gown's neckline— starting in front of my shoulder and ending at the zipper. "You're sure you want this?"

I've had sex with plenty of men during my lifetime. A good many of those men have been quite imaginative.

Some have even been memorable. With a few, it still hurts to think about. I've been here many times before. So what is it about *this* man that makes me ache so?

Do I want him? I shiver. I do. "In the worst possible way."

Zack encircles my waist with his left arm, then dips his head, nose at the nape of my neck. He inhales deeply, breathing me in just like before, only then it was with more subtlety. This time it feels decidedly primitive, possessive.

My own breath catches.

I feel a slight tug as he pulls down my zipper. The fabric parts, exposing my back. I close my eyes and wait. Then I feel Zack's fingers skimming down over my skin, tracing the edges of my ink. The pair of wings covers most of my back. It's not a tattoo I chose. Like so much else, Demeter chose it for me. I was marked the day I was stripped of my real wings, the day I was sent here. Because I don't see them every day, you might think I'd forget. I never forget.

"What you told me in Charleston about this tat, it was a lie, wasn't it?" Zack murmurs, almost to himself.

I turn to face him, letting the gown fall and stepping out of it. "We're not speaking of sad things tonight."

I can see he wants to know more, but I'm standing before him in four-inch pumps, breasts bare, nipples erect, wearing only black silk panties and stockings. The glamour affects my physical beauty in that my true face is hidden. But my body is untouched. Breasts, hips, legs are of a level of perfection only a Siren can possess.

The questions die on his lips. The humidity here at the beach makes my long, dark hair wave. It's loose now, past my shoulders, partially covering my breasts.

Zack reaches out and picks up a strand. "I love your hair down." He begins to curl it around his finger, reeling me in. "You should wear it like this more often. In fact, this entire outfit meets with my approval."

I can't help smiling, more comfortable in my skin than in silk and lace. "Oh yeah?"

He looks me straight in the eye. "Yeah."

I reach for his top shirt button and slide it back through the hole. "You wouldn't find it . . . distracting?"

"Me? No. You know me. I'm all about the mission. Eye on the ball."

I'm on the last button now. "You'd be more convincing if you weren't looking at my breasts."

"Which are amazing." As if to punctuate the statement, he palms one, feeling the weight of it, squeezing gently. "Why do you insist on hiding them?"

"You mean I should take a page from television and wear low-cut blouses and spike heels on the job?"

"Works for me."

I interrupt his reverie when I step back to slide his shirt off his shoulders. Before he can express disappointment that I've moved out of reach, I do two things that are guaranteed to leave a man speechless. I reach for the button on his trousers and I drop to my knees.

I give Zack a little shove and he falls back to sit on the edge of the bed, hands braced behind him. His chest is broad and well muscled. A light carpet of hair starts below his neck, fans out across his pecs, then narrows under his ribs. My eyes follow the happy trail until it disappears into the waistband of his slacks. Zack Armstrong is one gorgeous man.

I make short order of removing his shoes and socks. Then I set my hands on his knees and run them over his thighs. I subtly brush the zipper with the backs of my fingers. His hips rise off the bed.

"You're killing me here."

I deliberately take my time lowering his zipper, letting the tension build. For a moment I hold my breath. Then I draw him into my hand. He's long, hard, and surprisingly thick. I stroke him, palm open and flat. He smells of testosterone, citrus, and spice. The scent is as complicated as the man himself. Clean. Mysterious. Sexy.

"I want to feel your mouth on me," he says.

I oblige, giving him a firm squeeze before leaning forward and offering him my tongue, sliding him between my lips.

His hand goes to the back of my head. "Christ, Emma."

I take him deep. My mouth and tongue quickly develop a nice rhythm. Both his hands tangle in my hair. Zack guides me firmly yet gently. I can tell by his breathing he's getting close. His grip tightens suddenly and he gasps.

"Emma, stop!"

The request is entirely unexpected. I sit back, releasing him. The instant I do, he pulls me up. His mouth devours mine. The kiss is demanding, insistent. A growl emanates from somewhere deep within his chest, low, primal. My eyes fly open and I pull back from him. The flash of light blue I saw Wednesday night in his normally brown eyes is there again. Before I have time to even fully register it, he's stripped his trousers off and deposited me on his bed.

"Zack—" I place my hand in the center of his chest. He's hovering over me, six foot three of tall, dark, and dangerous.

"If you don't want this to happen, now would be a good time to say so."

"Your eyes, they've changed."

Zack lowers his head and nuzzles my cheek. "My wolf likes you," he whispers. I feel the pulse of his warm breath against my neck. "But don't worry. I'm in control, not the beast. I don't let it have free rein. Not ever. That's what the cage is for." As he says the words, one hand travels down, passing my hip, gliding over the top of my thigh, then snaking its way into my panties.

His fingers separate my folds and delve into the wetness. My hips lift off the mattress, wanting more.

"Take everything off." My voice is rough with want.

Zack doesn't need to be asked twice.

He peppers hot, openmouthed kisses across my collarbone, through the valley between my breasts, and over my stomach. I shiver with anticipation as he hooks his fingers into my panties and lowers them down my silk-covered legs. The shoes come off next. He tosses them over his shoulder and they land on the floor with a clunk. Then he rolls the stockings off, taking the time to shake and smooth each one out before dropping them off the edge of the bed.

He lifts one of my legs into the air and kisses the inside of my ankle. I find myself grinning.

Zack notices. "You're smiling."

"I'm happy," I confess. It's true.

"You're beautiful," he says.

I worry my glamour is fading. That in the moment I've somehow become careless. But I don't hold on to the concern very long. Zack's climbing up the length of my body. He's hard and ready and in position.

He kisses my nose, then reaches into the drawer of his nightstand and pulls out a condom.

"We don't need it. I can't conceive." As a werewolf,

Zack isn't susceptible to human disease; the process of shape-shifting cures all ills. But he can procreate. I take the condom from him and toss it aside. "Hey, didn't you say something about me being in control?"

Zack grins. "You want to take control?"

We roll.

He places his hands on my waist. "I'm all yours, baby."

I'm flying once again. As I did long ago when I had my real wings. Zack and I soar, together. Higher and higher, until the real world is far below. Until no one in it or of it can touch us.

Day Five: Saturday, April 14

I wake up in Zack's house, in Zack's bed. His arm is draped over my waist. His hand cups my breast. I feel as if I've run a marathon. My body is sore, but I'm exhilarated. Zack is as unpredictable and versatile a lover as he is a man, as skilled at hard and fast as he is at slow and easy. The clock on the nightstand says six. We can't have been asleep more than three hours.

I gently lift his arm and roll over. The lines of his face are smoothed in sleep. His beard has grown thicker during the night. I'm tempted to trace the outline of his lips, to kiss his generous mouth. A pull of desire makes me clench my thighs together and I feel myself getting wet again. But there's also the sting of rash burn from his stubble on the inside of my thighs. What I really need is a shower.

I place a soft kiss on Zack's shoulder before slipping out of bed. He stirs and I slip the pillow I'd been sleeping on under his arm. He doesn't waken, snuggling the pillow against his cheek as if still holding me.

Smiling, I pad across the thick carpet to the bathroom.

It's an homage to luxury—marble floors, expensive tile, mirrors, and glass. I stand stock-still for a moment in wonder. Zack's bathroom is about the size of my bedroom and living room combined. The sunken tub is long and deep; I imagine even Zack can stretch out in it. The shower at the far end has three showerheads and would easily accommodate a family of five. Just as I'd reached the conclusion I could spend the rest of my life living in Zack's bathroom, I catch a glimpse of myself in the long mirror lining the wall behind the sinks.

My hand is trembling as I lift it to touch my face. It's been centuries since I've seen myself like this. My skin is radiant, my hair shining like the finest lacquer. It cascades down my back and over my shoulders in soft waves. My lips are swollen, bruised red from too many kisses. My eyes, bright with lingering desire, begin to tear, clouding my vision and threatening to spill. I haven't purposefully given up the glamour. I'm not even purposefully lowering it enough to display a hint of my real self. Yet I'm effulgent, glowing.

My heart soars free for one fabulous blissful moment.

Then reality comes crashing down.

There's only one possible explanation. I'm falling in love with Zack. And he's falling in love with me. Despite words and assurances, we weren't careful enough. We weren't honest enough. Not with each other. Not even with ourselves. Last night was supposed to be about one thing—sex.

Instead . . .

I stumble, the back of my knees hitting the edge of the tub and my legs collapsing beneath me. I sit, close my eyes, focus on my breathing, on the cool marble beneath my feet, on what needs to be done. I've practiced this exercise with Liz hundreds of times, just like with her grandmother before her, with other witches over time. It's only when there are leaks that the glamour erodes. My power is escaping. I can hear their collective voices. *If you aren't doing it on purpose, there's a crack in the armor. Find it. Fix it.*

I can do this. I have to. If Demeter so much as senses what I'm, what Zack is feeling . . .

If Zack should walk in and see me, the real me . . .

It can't happen.

I blow out a breath and struggle to stay calm. I talk myself through, step by step. Check the walls. Bring them down, one by one. Concentrate. Pull the power in. Raise the wall back up.

At last, I open my eyes, stifle a sob.

Nothing has changed.

The face staring back at me is still Ligea's, and unless I take control of my feelings, deny Zack, I can't protect him.

I close my eyes. Push everything that happened last night to the back of my mind. Remind myself who and what Zack is—a werewolf. More important, my partner. This job is the only chance I have to win my freedom. He can't stand in my way. Anyone who does risks the un-imaginable. Thinking we could have sex with no conse-quences was a foolish mistake because I can't control the way Zack feels about me. I have to control the way I feel about him. I *have* to.

Concentrate, Emma. Accept the truth. You have no fu-ture with Zack. I close my eyes and patiently work through the steps again.

The change starts slowly. I feel it in the core of my

being, feel myself disappearing. I open my eyes and watch the beauty fade. Faint lines appear around my eyes and mouth, my skin dulls, my hair loses its bounce.

Another sob escapes my lips. This time because it worked.

My human persona is back.

I open the bathroom door a sliver and peek out. Zack is still sound asleep. The mere fact that I want to keep him safe proves beyond a shadow of a doubt that he's in very serious danger. At some point during the night I slipped. I let down my guard. It can't happen again. I need to have Liz check the spell, make sure there are no other leaks.

I head for the shower. *Eye on the ball, Emma. You have a job to do. You have people counting on you. Liz is counting on you.*

I just need to take this one step at a time. Concentrate. I'll make a quick stop at the vegan bakery Liz frequents on the way over to Evan's and pick up some of those almond coconut buns she likes. If I know Liz, and I do, she'll have a pot of coffee ready, but she won't have eaten. There are three vampires missing, including Evan. It's time to go to work.

Redemption could be one rescue away.

CHAPTER 17

I park in Evan's guest spot, but I don't get out of the car. Not right away. I keep checking my reflection in the rearview mirror. If I wasn't scrupulous enough in pulling back the power, Liz will see it the instant she sees me. So far, the glamour seems firmly in place. The plain Jane facade I show to the world is once again on display. And since no news from Demeter is good news, maybe my transgression went unnoticed.

I was lucky this time. But I can't let myself think about Zack or our lovemaking or how his skin felt against mine or—

Shit. I bang my hand against the steering wheel. Pain jolts up my arm.

Double shit.

Stop it. Liz needs you.

I get out of the car and head in. Liz does her thing and pulls open the door before I have a chance to knock. I hold my breath. Is she going to say something about the fact that I'm still dressed in her gown?

Normally she'd never let something like that go. This morning, she's too preoccupied and bleary-eyed to notice. Liz takes my hand and pulls me inside. She's wearing the same clothes she had on the afternoon before, too.

I toss the pastry bag on the coffee table. "Did you get any sleep at all?"

She sinks onto the couch, buries her face in her hands. "I can't sleep. I can't eat. I can't think."

"I should have stayed here with you last night." Maybe if I had . . .

She shakes her head, then drops her hands and looks up at me. "No, you had to go. You might have learned something. But you didn't. Did you? If you had—"

I take both her hands in mine and sit next to her. "I'm sorry. We're still following leads, but we don't have anything definitive. I think it's time you call the police."

"But you and Zack will keep working on the case, too, won't you? You're not giving up? Please, tell me you're not giving up!"

"Of course we won't give up. I would never give up on someone so important to you. It's just that the more people we have out looking for Evan, the better." I reach for the bag and heft it in the palm of my hand. "Come on. Let's have some breakfast."

Liz reluctantly gets to her feet and I follow her to the kitchen. Her shoulders sag with weariness and worry. She's exhausted both mentally and physically. I suppress the impulse to tell her about the other missing vampires. I can't see that doing anything but adding to her misery. If we haven't been able to find Amy and Isabella, it won't be much consolation that Evan now makes three.

Liz goes through the motions of putting on a fresh pot of coffee as if working on autopilot. I take a dish from the pantry and lay out the pastries. The silence in the condo is like a third presence—oppressive, overwhelming. It's not until we're seated at the breakfast bar, cups in front of us, that Liz breaks it.

"What are his chances, Emma?"

She's picking at one of the pastries, pulling it into small pieces, none of which make it to her mouth. She swivels to face me. "Don't the police say that if a missing person isn't found in forty-eight hours, odds are that he won't be found at all?"

"You've been watching too much *Law & Order*," I reply, keeping my tone light. "They have to say that on television because they only have an hour to tell a story. There are no hard and fast rules. We *will* find Evan. We'll bring him home. Zack and I will make sure of it."

For the first time since I walked in the door, Liz's expression shifts from worry to surprise. She's looking at me. *Really* looking at me. "Something's wrong. Emma, what are you doing?"

My stomach clenches. "I'm doing everything I can to find Evan. I promise you."

She waves the words away with the back of a hand. "That isn't what I meant and you know it. Why are you still dressed in that gown? You didn't go home last night?" Her eyes bore into mine. "But you've showered. No makeup. Your hair is still damp."

She stops, waiting for me to say something. What can I say?

When I turn my eyes away, she grabs my hand. "You and Zack? Tell me you haven't let it go too far."

Before I can think of a way to answer, she does it for me. "You're falling for him. I can see it. You're struggling to contain the glamour. He saw you. You let him see the real you, didn't you? That's why I didn't hear from you last night."

It's as if she has a laser beamed into my head. "I was with him last night, yes. But I didn't *let* him see me. I'm not even sure he did."

"You didn't let him? You're not sure?" Liz throws up her hands. "Are we going to quibble over semantics? You know the risk. The danger. Not *letting* it happen and having it happen anyway? That's even more serious. You've stayed under the radar for decades, but that doesn't mean Demeter isn't out there waiting for you to screw up. She's a vindictive bitch. And you know that better than anyone. Remember the last man you fell in love with?"

I didn't need Demeter's graphic reminder the other night. And I certainly don't need Liz's now.

"Of course I remember. I buried him three days after our wedding." Tears cloud my vision. It's my turn to cover my face with my hands.

Liz's voice softens. "It's not too late. I can give you something." She slips from the stool and disappears up the stairs.

I'm too numb to do anything but remain motionless, staring into my coffee and trying to wipe the image of a funeral on a bleak and dark December morning in Bristol from my mind.

When Liz returns, she has an envelope in her hand. She presses it into mine, holding on to me. "Grandma told me to keep this on hand, just in case something like this happened. Stir this into Zack's coffee. It will erase his memory of any intimacy you've shared. You need to get back on course. You can't fall in love with him."

"By intimacy you mean . . . ?"

"Physical intimacy."

"Zack isn't stupid, and he's not oblivious to magic. He'll notice the gaps."

"There won't be any gaps. That's part of the elegance of this particular spell. His own imagination will create alternative, plausible, and most important, *safe* scenarios. As far as he'll be concerned, you'll be platonic partners. That's it. He'll forget the night you shared. The threat will be gone."

I look up at her through eyes glazed with tears. "There was more than one night."

"What?"

"In Charleston. We slept together. After the case was over."

Liz's face pales. "Was that what you meant when you said you *more* than liked him? Emma, are you crazy? Did you know he was coming to San Diego? That he was going to be working with you?"

I shake my head, grab Liz's hand for emphasis. "No. I had no idea. Do you think I'd go along with it if I had? This scares me, Liz. Zack scares me. But—" I lower my eyes, unable, unwilling to let Liz see what I know is reflected there. "I'm not sure I want him to forget."

"You do, Emma. Of course you do. The two of you crossed a line. The kind you can't easily take back. Hearts are involved. It's the only way."

"What if he doesn't give up?"

"Listen, change the dynamic. Fool around all you want with Zack. Fuck him senseless every night. You've had hundreds of lovers. You just need to make sure he understands it's nothing serious. That it can't be anything serious. Keep your feelings hidden. The greatest sex he's ever had completely without strings? No man on earth would turn down a relationship like that. And with the potion, he'll accept it. He won't remember anything different. Just don't let him see the real you. Never let him see the real you. Do you understand?"

Like a puppet, my head bobs as if pulled by string. Liz is squeezing my hand. The glamour, the dampening spell, those were just to warm up for this particular moment. This is the one I've been paying Liz for all these years. She's doing her job. But taking care of me has become more than a job. That's why I see the compassion in her eyes.

But all I feel is numb.

I have to cut Zack loose and I don't feel anything.

Before heading to the office, I do what I should have done before going to Liz's. I stop at home to change. The detour takes me all of fifteen minutes. Then I'm on my way up the 163, the envelope she gave me weighing on my mind, a psychological brick in my handbag. Will I have the courage to use it?

I know Liz is right. It's the only thing that makes sense. Give Zack the powder this morning, before he can do anything to make me change my mind.

Like say hello.

I'm heading for the elevator when I see her. Sarah. Standing off to one side in the lobby. Today she's dressed more casually, in blue jeans, a white Georgette silk blouse, black boots, and a red brocade jacket. I resist the urge to ask her what she did with Captain Jack and the rest of the crew of the *Black Pearl*.

Partly because she's bigger than me, partly because she looks pissed, really pissed, and the lobby is empty— I shift my bag to free the hand closer to my gun. Perhaps

I'm being paranoid, but I feel better knowing it's readily accessible.

Sarah sees the move, understands the implication. She holds up her hands. "I'm not here to hurt you," she says.

We meet a few feet from the elevators. "Why are you here?"

"Not because I want to be, that's for damn sure." The woman drops her hands to her side. She looks younger than her thirty years, except for her eyes. They harbor the shadow of sadness, of disappointment, of fear. "I'm here because I need your help."

"With Zack?"

She nods. "He likes you. I can tell."

"We're partners."

She tilts her head to the side. "It's more."

"He told you that?"

"He didn't have to. I know Zack, maybe better than anyone."

"You're pack mates?"

She looks surprised. "You know our other nature?"

"Yes."

Sarah releases a breath. "Then you know he doesn't belong here. He belongs with us, his own kind, where he can be free."

"Free?"

"Free to run under the moon. To live without restrictions. To be penned up in a cage three nights every month, alone. It's . . . unacceptable."

"Unacceptable to whom? Zack has chosen a safe way to ride out the changeling times."

Sarah pauses now. She takes a step closer. "Who are you to presume to know what's safe for us?"

"I'm Zack's partner"

"I'm his lover."

Someone didn't get the "ex" memo. "I heard it was over."

Sarah's posture becomes rigid. I get the distinct impression that if we weren't in the lobby of an FBI field office, her hands would be around my throat. There had been softness in her eyes from sadness, fear. Now brittle determination makes them spark with anger. She doesn't hold on to it long. In a flash it's gone, replaced by smug indignation and a shiny new strategy.

"It didn't *feel* over when we slept together the other night."

They spent the night together? I don't believe it. Or, if they did, I'd bet they didn't have sex.

"Whatever." I turn to push the call button for the elevator.

She grabs my arm in a viselike grip. "Feign disinterest all you want. I see the way you look at him."

I slowly look down at her hand on my arm, then back up at Sarah. "You need to be talking to Zack. Not me."

Her grip on my arm tightens. "You're playing a dangerous game. You should know here and now, it's one you won't win. I cannot, will not, leave without Zack."

Regret morphs to anger. I don't take kindly to threats. Happily-ever-after may not be in the cards for Zack and me. But I'm dead certain he isn't going to find it with Sarah, either. If he could have, he wouldn't have pushed her away, wouldn't have left her behind. I shake my arm free. "Whether Zack stays or goes is up to him."

A flash of the wolf turns Sarah's eyes blue. "Perhaps the decision will be made for him," she growls. "Perhaps the reason for his staying will suddenly be taken from him."

I may not have a werewolf's strength, but my gun at this range would blow her clear across the hall. Superfast healing isn't in my repertoire, but I'm secure in the fact that no matter what happens, I will eventually heal. Demeter would never finish me off when there was pain to be dealt. I've been around a long time. And I've experienced my fair share—been up against stronger, faster, and smarter than Sarah. I'd match my cunning and determination against this werewolf's any day.

"You're threatening the wrong girl. I know what you are and I know how to stop you. You think you can take me out? Give it your best shot," I growl right back at her.

The rumble of the elevator behind us signals its approach. Half a dozen people spill out, including Kirk, the boss' admin assistant. He steps between Sarah and me, momentarily blocking her from my sight.

"Hey, Monroe, the lottery's up to thirty million. You want in? I'm going to buy tickets. You can't win if you don't play," he points out for the hundredth time.

I reach into the pocket of my slacks, pull out a buck, and hand it to him, waving him away. The rest of the crowd has already dispersed. When he steps to the side, I no longer see Sarah.

"There was a woman here," I say. "Did you see where she went?"

"Sorry," he says. "No."

I release an angry sigh. Sarah is gone.

CHAPTER 18

The confrontation with Sarah should have left me anxious. Instead, she's made me curious . . . and sore. I'm sure I'll have a glorious bruise on my arm where she grabbed me. Rubbing the spot, I decide it's time I ask Zack if she poses a real threat or if it was all posturing — the attempts of a scorned lover to scare off the competition.

If only she knew she had no need to take me out of the game. I've got an envelope of powder in my handbag to do that for her.

I'm stepping off the elevator onto our floor when my cell phone rings. A glance at the caller ID shows it's Zack. In a flash, Sarah is pushed from my mind. Instead I wonder if *he's* wondering why I left this morning without waking him up or saying good-bye. Maybe he's calling to end it. Or to set some ground rules for office etiquette. Could be he's running late because our activities last night made him oversleep.

"This is Emma," I croak through a throat suddenly gone dry.

"Where are you?" he asks without preamble. Then, "Wait. I see you. Stay there."

I look up in time to see him crossing the floor. There's

nothing intimate in his expression — no sly sideways glances, no seductive smile. And he's not peering at me as if I've suddenly sprouted a second head. Maybe the Emma he made love to last night was the Emma he's seeing now. Maybe I'm not in as much trouble as I thought.

But I remember the feeling of soaring, of giving myself to him completely, of holding nothing back.

More important, I remember the way I looked in the mirror.

That was not my imagination. Did Zack see it, too?

All this runs through my head in the time it takes Zack to close the distance between us. For him, it seems to be all business. He's got a piece of paper in his hands.

I feel my shoulders relax a bit. If he can separate what happened last night from our professional life, I certainly should be able to.

"Just got this," he says, waving the paper. "Alan Pierce moved recently." He reads off the address.

It's one I recognize. "That's the same address as Michael Dexter's."

"Bingo!"

"He's Michael Dexter's partner?" I follow Zack as we head back to our cubicle.

"Did you peg them as being together last night?"

I shake my head. "But then, Alan was constantly working the party."

"There's more." Zack hands me a cup of coffee. "When the first Mrs. Barakov disappeared, Alan Pierce was interviewed. He had been working for an architectural firm in Los Angeles. The one the Barakovs hired to renovate their home. He had a key and free rein of the house, so the police thought he might have seen something. He hadn't and they dropped him from the suspect list."

Zack pauses to take a drink from his mug. I'm reminded of the envelope in my bag. All it would take is one little sip. Thankfully, Zack doesn't give me much time to think. He has something else to tell me. I see it in the gleam of his eyes. He plunges ahead.

"So, Alan's mother, the present Mrs. Barbara Barakov, met the good doctor at Alan's office. He was there for a consultation and she dropped in to take her son for lunch. While Alan works on the renovation project, his mother works on Barakov. The affair only lasted a couple months. It's not clear what ended it. But Barakov went back to his wife. You still with me?"

I nod, recalling my research. "A month or so later, the wife mysteriously disappears."

Zack continues. "Barakov plays the concerned husband for a while. Then he starts seeing Pierce again. Not long after that, Alan gets a new stepdaddy."

"What kind of doctor is Barbara?" I ask, remembering how she was introduced last night.

"She's a surgeon. Specializes in organ transplants."

I watch Zack as he goes over the notes in his hand. Excitement is there in his expression, hopefulness that we may have uncovered the one detail that can help us break the case, determination that we'll stick at it until we do.

The one thing that's missing is any indication that we spent last night having sex—great sex.

Am I relieved or angry?

Do I even need the fucking powder Liz gave me?

Suddenly I realize Zack is peering at me. "What's the matter? You look disappointed."

I turn away, briefly, to recompose my expression. "Nothing's the matter."

"Is it about last night?" He steps close, glances around, then whispers, "I assumed you left early this morning so you'd have time to change clothes before work. Are we okay?"

Suddenly I'm back there with him—fire crackling, candles glowing, wringing torturous pleasure from Zack's body in ways that were utterly exquisite and entirely addictive.

But that was then. This is now. "We're fine."

He lowers his head so it's close to mine. "Last night was—I don't have the words."

I can feel the pulse of his breath against my ear. "Try."

"Best. Sex. Ever." He straightens and steps back. "Now, where were we?" He makes a show of shuffling the papers in his hand, but he's grinning.

For an instant, this morning's feeling of bliss is back. With all its implications. I am at the core a sexual creature, after all. And as Liz reminded me, sex is okay. As long as we leave it at that. I see him and can't help wondering, *hoping*. Could it be possible? Just sex. Am I capable of hiding my true feelings for the chance to have even the most superficial of relationships with him? Could Liz work a spell that would make Zack accept a relationship like that?

Just sex.

Just sex.

Sarah pops into my consciousness. Maybe that's the kind of relationship he has with her now. Is this the time to bring it up?

No. Now it's time to get back to business.

I clear my throat when what I want to do is clear my head. "I think I should *interview* Alan," I say.

Zack nods. "I agree." He glances at his watch. "He should be at the Green Leaf offices right about now."

"On a Saturday morning?"

"Someone called him earlier posing as a new fat-cat customer and requesting a morning meeting."

"I wonder who that might have been."

Zack shrugs. "Don't know. I do know Mr. Pierce was very accommodating. He should be waiting for us." He flutters his fingers. "I'll wait outside or something while you work your mojo."

I pick up my bag. "Let's go."

But the telephone on his desk rings. I pause while Zack answers it. He listens for a moment, then says, "Yes, sir. I'll be right there."

He replaces the receiver. "Deputy Director wants an update. I can handle it. You go on. I'll meet you at Green Leaf as soon as I can."

CHAPTER 19

The Green Leaf central office is located on Front Street. It's a converted mansion, sitting on a lot surrounded by a high hedge. The brass sign on the wrought-iron gate is in the shape of a maple leaf on which the name Green Leaf is embossed. I ring the bell outside the entrance, and a buzzer sounds immediately. No questions. The gate clicks open.

I follow the walk up to the front door, where there's another bell. This time when I ring, a voice from inside asks, "Yes?"

I look up at a surveillance camera set high and to the right. I dig my badge out of my purse and hold it up. "Agent Emma Monroe. FBI."

The door opens immediately. Alan Pierce smiles out at me. "I remember you from last night, Agent Monroe."

"I have a couple questions I'd like to ask you."

He pulls out his cell and checks the time. "I have a client meeting scheduled, but they seem to be running late. I can give you a few minutes. Come in." He stands aside and the door closes behind me.

"I hope the party was a success," I say as we walk.

He nods enthusiastically. "We exceeded our fundraising goal. Thank you for attending. And thank you for what you're doing to find Michael's friend. He's been beside himself since she went missing."

There's a bit of a nervous edge about him, one I hadn't noticed last night. Is it surprise at finding an FBI agent at his office so early on a Saturday morning? Or concern that a *client* might be surprised to find an FBI agent at his office so early on a Saturday morning?

There's no one in the reception area. He leads me through it and into what I presume is his personal office. I attempt to set him at ease by turning the conversation to familiar territory, comfortable ground.

I make a point of looking around. "I love these old buildings. It's so good to see them being renovated, to see the history preserved."

Alan nods. "It was a shambles when we bought it." He gestures to a visitor's chair and takes his own seat across a wide expanse of burled oak desk. "Restoring it to its former glory took a lot of work."

"And, I imagine, a lot of money."

"We have generous benefactors."

Generous indeed. They've managed to get all of the details right. The period wallpaper, wainscoting, molding, even the style of doorknobs are all what you would expect in a building of this age.

I think of Dexter's comment about his partner being a neat freak. It's certainly evident here. Except for a desktop phone and a computer, the only other things on his desk are a stack of spreadsheets and a pen.

"This is a beautiful office. Are those the original moldings?"

"Good eye." He beams. "Yes. This used to be the parlor." He sweeps a hand over the smooth top of the desk.

"We found this piece in the attic when we purchased the place. It's amazing what people think of as junk, isn't it?"

"Does the staff always come in on Saturdays?" I ask with a smile. Better to find out if there is anyone else around who might get caught in the undertow before I open the floodgates.

He shakes his head. "We sometimes have a small contingent on Saturdays. But I gave everyone strict orders to take today off. Last night was a late one for us all."

"But no day off for the boss, I see."

"Like I said, client meeting." He gestures to the spreadsheet. "Plus, I wanted to tally up the proceeds from last night. We did very well. Especially Michael's piece. He's such a wonderful artist." There's a wistfulness to his voice as he adds, "I'm glad he's seeing his talent appreciated."

He pauses. "Are you here about Isabella?"

That slight hint of nervousness is back. I've interrogated enough suspects, both with and without use of my special brand of lie detection, to recognize when they are hiding something. Alan is.

"Yes. Did you know her?" I ask.

He shrugs. "We met, of course. But she disappeared before I moved in."

"And how long ago did you move in?"

"About a month ago." He stands up and makes his way over to a coffeepot on the other side of the room. "Can I offer you a cup of coffee? We also have some sodas, bottled water."

"No, thank you. Do you know a woman named Amy Patterson?"

His back is to me. The coffeepot is in his hand. There's not even a moment's hesitation. "Sure, we did work for

Amy. I saw on the news she's missing, too. Michael said you stopped by and—" He turns around to face me, alarm registering on his face. "You don't think Michael has anything to do with Amy's disappearance, do you? Or Isabella's, for that matter. Michael wouldn't hurt a fly."

I shake my head. "No. Michael isn't a suspect."

His shoulders relax. He returns to his desk with the coffee. Takes a sip. Sits down. "That's a relief."

"What about Evan Porter?" I ask.

"What about him?"

"You know Evan?"

He nods. "Sure. He's my attorney. He's . . . Are you telling me Evan's missing, too?"

Our eyes meet across the desk.

The truth dawns on him. "You think *I* might have had something to do with Evan's disappearance? Or Amy's?"

I can't help noticing he didn't mention Isabella. I add her back on and wait for the reaction. "What about Isabella? You didn't forget her, did you?"

"What? No!"

But his breathing is rapid and shallow and he's focused his gaze on the cup in his hand. I think I've gotten all I'm going to get from him with normal investigative techniques. Time for the big guns.

"Alan?"

He looks up at me. I take a breath, look him directly in the eye, and lower the dampening spell. Now he can't bring himself to look away. He lowers his hand to the table, pushes the cup away. He leans forward in the chair, as if to get closer. Even a gay man is not immune to my power and beauty.

"Alan? I'm going to ask you some questions."

The air stirs around us, blowing a slip of paper from his desk. The pen rolls to the floor. Alan doesn't notice. A faint perfume fills the air.

He nods and breathes it in.

"You want to help," I continue. "So you're going to answer truthfully. Once you do, you'll feel better."

Of course he will. He has no choice.

I stand up, pushing back the chair in which I'd been sitting. The wind rises around me. The stacks of spreadsheets on his desk begin to rustle. Since his anxiety seems to rise every time I mention Isabella's name, I start there. "Did you have anything to do with Isabella Mancini's disappearance?"

A buzzer rings before he can answer.

"Is that the doorbell?" I ask Alan.

He nods toward an open window. "It's the front gate."

I look to see Zack outside. I place Alan's phone on top of the papers and then use it to dial Zack's cell. "I'm with Alan in his office. I've already started. I don't want you to be affected by what I'm doing."

"Want me to stay outside?"

"There's a waiting room. You'll be safe behind closed doors. Alan will buzz you in. Keep this line open. I'll put us on speaker. You can listen in."

Zack agrees.

I turn to Alan. "Let my friend in."

Alan reaches under his desk. The front door buzzes open. Seconds later I hear Zack's footsteps.

"Are you ready?" I ask.

"Door's closed." Zack's voice comes through the speaker. I can hear him pacing on the other side of it. "What have you got so far?"

"Not much. We're just getting started." I turn my attention back to Alan. "Did you have anything to do with Isabella Mancini's disappearance?"

"No."

"What about the disappearances of Amy Patterson or Evan Porter?"

"No. I told you."

"And yet they all have one thing in common. Green Leaf. And you."

Alan shakes his head. "I don't understand."

He doesn't. His expression is both troubled and sincere.

Zack's voice comes through the telephone's speaker. "What's going on, Emma? I thought you said he wouldn't be able to lie."

"He can't." I peer closely at Alan. "You know Michael loves Isabella. If you're holding anything back—"

"Of course I'm not holding anything back. I'd do anything for Michael. Anything."

There it is. The truth in his statement strikes me like a slap in the face. We've made a mistake. I turn off the speaker and pick up the telephone receiver. "It's not Alan."

"So what do we do now?" Zack's expression reflects the same frustration I'm feeling.

"I wish I knew." Selfishly, I think about Liz first, then Dexter. "I hate to say it. Hate to even *think* it. Could Evan, Amy, and Isabella already be dead?"

Alan stirs in his chair. "Of course Isabella's dead. She's a vampire."

I snap my attention back to him. "You know Isabella is a vampire?"

"Yes."

I immediately replace the phone, reactivate the speaker. "Michael told you?"

Alan shakes his head. "Not Michael, my mother."

"Your mother?" The revelation comes out of left field. Then I realize she probably learned of this from someone else.

Zack's thinking the same thing.

"Barakov," he spits out. "He's the one. Ask him."

"Was it your stepfather?"

I watch Alan's face. "Barakov—Alexander—didn't take them."

Alan's shoulders slump. His hands rise to cover his face.

A strange sensation washes over me. The gut instinct that the pieces are about to fall into place.

"He's not involved?" I ask.

He answers with one word. "No."

"But you know who is?"

I hold my breath.

"Yes."

"Who?"

He glances around. A sign of resistance. We're wading through territory he's kept deeply suppressed.

I realize I may already have the answer. "Your mother?"

Alan nods, his face crumpling in shame and pain. Eyes fill with tears, not just of sadness, of anger.

"What's happening?" Zack asks.

I fall back into the chair across from Alan. "He's nodding. Barbara Pierce is the one behind all of this."

"She's saving lives. The vampires—they're making a noble sacrifice." He utters the words as if they're his lifeline, a self-soothing mantra he's been relying on to justify something horrible, something heinous. He's holding on to the arms of the chair, knuckles white. "She said I had a choice. I could let Michael go, or I could save him. How could I just let him go?"

I know what it's like to stand by, watch the worst happen to someone you love, and know there's not a thing you can do about. I've been there more than once. If someone offered me an out, would I have taken it? Possibly.

"Make him explain," Zack says.

I don't need to make him. He's started to tell the truth and he's on his way to feeling better. Just as I told him he would. He'll want to get it all out now, even if that means betraying his mother and implicating himself. I feel a rush of empathy. With power comes sacrifice. Alan chose to save Michael, and in doing so, he lost a piece of himself.

Alan stares across the desk at me through haunted eyes. "I want to help. I'll tell you everything."

Of course he will. I draw my powers back in and seal the doors shut. We won't need them anymore. Not with him. I walk over to the office door and open it, surprising Zack on the other side.

"You can come in now."

Alan doesn't even wait for introductions. He begins in a barely comprehensible rush. "It's not her fault. She's been given no choice. She made a mistake, yes. But now she's having to pay and pay and pay. That horrible man. Killing all of those people. Making her . . . all for what? Money. She was going crazy. She had to find a better way. And now . . ."

Zack holds up his hand. "Slow down. Let's start with who's been killed."

"Charlotte Barakov, for one. That's where it started. When Mother hired Davis Mager to get rid of her. It was crazy and stupid, not to mention wrong." He shakes his head. "But what that man has forced her to do since . . ."

Zack takes a seat on the edge of the desk. "So your mother hired Mager to kill the first Mrs. Barakov, then what? He blackmailed her?"

Alan nods. "Yes. About a year after Mager got rid of Charlotte, he contacted Mother. His daughter was in need of a heart transplant. Only he didn't want to wait for a voluntary donor. He blackmailed Mother into helping him identify the right person, then into doing the surgery. Naively, she thought that would be the end of it. But it got her in deeper. Gave Mager the idea that they could harvest organs and sell them on the black market. He had connections. At first they targeted the homeless." He stops abruptly, his eyes darting between Zack and me.

"And?" Zack encourages him to continue with a wave of his hand.

But Alan's eyes have settled on me. "You didn't flinch when I mentioned Isabella was a vampire."

I cross my arms in front of my chest. "No, I didn't. You said at first they targeted the homeless. Are you telling us at some point Mager and your mother shifted their focus to vampires?"

He nods. "She said she couldn't live with what she was doing. But she couldn't get out of it, either. She was getting in deeper and deeper. Then the idea came to her. She knew about Alexander's experimentation, about his technique. She convinced Mager to invest, to allow her to explore the possibility of using vampires instead of humans. They're already dead. And their organs regenerate."

"Your mother and Mager are kidnapping vampires, then harvesting and selling vampire organs?" asks Zack.

"Apparently vampires are universal donors. Mother discovered a vampire organ can be transplanted into a human with no danger of rejection. Mager's doing the kidnapping." Alan's face turns red. "Although it seems Mother has looked through Alexander's patients' records from time to time to find 'prospects.' Her word, not mine."

I sit again, trying to absorb what he's telling me. "And then your mother operates on these prospects against their will?"

Even stares down at the desktop in front of him. "Healthy new organs save lives." It's repeated like a lesson he's been forced to memorize.

"Lives like Michael Dexter's?" I shake my head. "Alan, your mother has Isabella, Amy, and Evan, doesn't she?"

He meets my gaze head-on. "I don't know about Amy and Evan, I swear. Only Isabella."

My skin is crawling. The realization of what Barbara Pierce is doing is making my stomach churn. So barbaric and so *unnecessary*.

"Where is she keeping them?" asks Zack. "And how is she containing them? No human can simply take a vampire if he or she doesn't want to be taken."

"Silver. That's where Alexander's research came in handy. The way I understand it, Mager uses tranquilizer darts containing silver to capture the vampires. Then Mother stores the shells in containers where they're given silver-laced anesthesia to keep them sedated and trapped."

"The shells?"

Alan swallows. "That's what she calls them. They

don't have souls, you know. They aren't human. The shells are like . . . like incubators."

"For organs," Zack adds. "She's built a goddamned organ factory using vampires. Have you known where Isabella was this entire time?"

"Have you?" I repeat.

He shakes his head. "No. I didn't even know about Michael's illness until after she went missing. We dated for several months and he didn't breathe a word of it. After Isabella's disappearance, he went downhill fast. There was an emergency hospitalization. Isabella was his primary contact. With her gone and no family, he had the hospital call me. I went to my mother right away, of course. Michael needs a liver transplant."

Alan climbs to his feet and walks over to the window.

"And your mother offered this neat and tidy solution?" Zack asks, his voiced laced with disdain.

Alan turns to face us. "I had to do something! Michael had exhausted all normal channels. He's on a waiting list, but he's failing so fast. I told him that there might be another way—that we had money and could look for alternatives. There are always favors to be had if one is willing to pay the price. Michael wouldn't hear of it. He said he wouldn't buy his way to the top of the list at the expense of other deserving patients. He's ready to die."

"Only, you aren't ready to let him go," I say.

Alan glances at the clock on the wall above the cof-feemaker. "Michael's was supposed to be the last life Isabella saved. According to Mother, she's at the end of her period of . . . usefulness. After a while, the levels of silver necessary to control them turns the organs, spoils them."

Zack's on his feet. "How much time do we have?"

"The operation is supposed to take place this afternoon. Maybe an hour," answers Alan.

Zack fires off a series of questions, short and direct.

"Are there other vampires being held hostage?"

Alan nods. "I don't know how many."

"Is there a security system?"

"Yes."

"Do you know the code?"

"No."

"Are there guards?"

"Yes. One. Mostly just to sign visitors in and out. And to provide security after hours and during the weekends."

"Anything else we should know?"

Zack walks over to a refurbished cast-iron radiator next to the window and gives it a good yank.

Alan hesitates.

Zack turns his attention back on him. "Well?"

"There's a door," Alan continues. "It's hidden behind a bookcase in Mother's office. It's the way into the laboratory."

"Address?"

Pierce's lab is not far from Barakov's office. We should be able to get there in ten, fifteen minutes tops.

Zack reaches back, under his suit, with one hand for his handcuffs. With his other hand he grabs Alan's wrist. "We'll come back for you." After cuffing him to the radiator, Zack turns to me. "No way he can move that thing. I'll drive ahead and scope out the building. Call me when you get there."

Alan sinks to the floor. "Michael's going to die. And I'm going to jail, aren't I?"

He's come clean. The least I can do is give him the truth. But what exactly is the truth? Nothing he said to us could be used in court. And even if it could, what kind of story are we talking about? A doctor using vampire organs in transplants? Who would believe it? Once the word got around the vampire community, though, I'm afraid he'd have more to fear from them than any human court.

I heave a sigh. "I don't know, Alan. Depends entirely on your mother. If she's willing to take responsibility for the murder of Barakov's first wife and the homeless victims, you may get a break. But I think if I were you, I'd worry more about retribution from the vampires. They don't play by the same rules we do."

CHAPTER 20

Since it's early Saturday morning, it only takes me fifteen minutes to get across town. During the drive, my thoughts are as frenetic as they are fractured. This case has turned into a nightmare with ramifications that can literally shake the worlds of both humans and supernaturals. I was serious when I told Alan he may have more to fear from the vampires than any human court. And what about this Davis Mager? Will Barbara Pierce give him up? It may be her only way to win favor with the district attorney and, possibly, immunization for her son.

The address Alan gave us for his mother's office comes into view. It's a fairly new three-story luxury medical building built around a courtyard. I pull into the parking lot next to Zack's car and climb out.

Unlike in her husband's office, there is a large air-conditioning unit perched on the flat roof and signs announcing that Crown Security monitors the premises. The area around the building and adjacent parking lot is landscaped with cascading bougainvillea and large ferns, giving the appearance of a well-kept residential yard. There's a sign on the front listing Dr. Barbara Pierce's name among the other medical tenants and a telephone number to reach the security desk outside of regular business hours, including the weekend. The security gate, which leads to a courtyard, is closed and locked.

Still no Zack in sight. Before I have the chance to pull my cell from my pocket to call him, Zack appears and opens the gate from the inside.

"How'd you get in?"

"A little trick I picked up from my previous job." He pulls the gate closed behind me.

"Have any tricks up your sleeve to get us past that?" I point up ahead to the building's main entrance. A security camera hovers over the door, no doubt monitored by the guard inside.

Zack scoffs. "Amateurs. The security is unbelievably sloppy. I've already found an alternative route. Come this way."

The courtyard has a fountain in the middle. He leads me behind it and around to a side yard. Separating the side yard from the front is a six-foot stucco wall with a locked gate. Zack easily scales the wall and seconds later the gate swings open for me.

"No camera," he says, pointing to the door up ahead. "And just an old-fashioned dead bolt." The door is partially hidden by a screen of thick bushes. As we walk toward it, Zack pulls out a ballpoint pen and begins to unscrew the top. The casing is hollow and contains a variety of picks and tension tools.

I have a very bad feeling nothing we do today is going to be reportable to our superiors. This may be the first time I've partnered with someone who has Zack's "special" skills, but there are three missing vampires, people as far as the world knows, and I shake off my reservations. Human or not, the victims get my sympathies.

Zack gets right to work. "Never met a lock I couldn't pick."

"Get a lot of practice, do you?"

"You should see my collection of chains and hand-cuffs."

"Kinky."

Within seconds, there's a metallic click and he's cracked it.

We slip inside.

This side entrance takes us to the private elevator that goes directly to Dr. Pierce's suite.

"Now what?" I whisper. This door requires a key card of some kind.

He pulls something from his wallet, swipes it, and voilà—green light.

"Do I even want to know where you got that thing?"

"Probably not," he mutters, pocketing the card, then drawing his weapon.

Zack takes point. Since he's the one with super-duper healing and I'm practical, I let him.

The waiting and reception areas are empty. We quickly move into position by the entrance to the back office. Gun in hand, I pull the door open. Zack leads the way. We proceed cautiously down the hall of exam rooms. At the end, a door stands ajar. According to the placard, it's what we've been looking for, the office of Dr. Barbara Pierce. And it's empty. Once we're inside, the real chore lies ahead of us. Finding the hidden entrance to the lab.

There are floor-to-ceiling bookcases on all four walls.

"I should have asked Alan which bookcase," I whisper.

"No need," Zack answers, in a hushed tone. He crosses

to the first bookcase, leans close. He straightens and moves to the second. Then the third. He gives me a thumbs-up. "This one." Before I can ask how he determined it, he adds, "I hear the whine from a generator. It's strongest here. Labs need power. A secret lab with its own operating suite needs its own power source."

"You are so clever."

"Thank you, ma'am. Any idea where the catch or lock is that will open this puppy?"

I've already holstered my gun. With both hands free, I begin to explore the bookcase, passing my hand under and over each shelf. Nothing. I reach behind the case as far as I can. Still nothing. On either side. I turn and look at Pierce's desk. I remember Alan had the release for the front door of his office somewhere under the top of his desk.

I take a seat in Pierce's chair and let my hands explore. No catch. I open the file drawers to the left and right, shuffle papers around so I can see the entire insides of the drawers. My impatience is growing along with my fear that if this takes any longer, we're going to lose Isabella.

I sit back in the chair, sighing with frustration. The top of Pierce's desk holds a blotter, a potted plant, a metal divider tray, a pen set.

An elaborate pen set.

I look up at Zack. "Couldn't be . . ."

He shrugs. "Only one way to find out."

He reaches over my shoulder and his fingers tighten around the first pen in the rack. It lifts free. Then he tries the second. This one doesn't. He tugs at it and it levers down.

At the same time, there's a gentle sliding sound. I

spring from the chair to watch the bookcase swing forward on a well-oiled track.

Zack and I move through the door, Glocks in hand.

We find ourselves in what looks like a small laboratory. A long table holds an autoclave, a microscope, and a desktop computer, as well as racks of test tubes and blood samples. There are other machines I don't recognize on a second table. The shelves above them are filled with supplies, including towels, sheets, and a stack of fresh scrubs. To my right are two closed doors. Directly across from us is a window. Through it, we have a clear view of the operating suite. On the other side of the glass are six coffins on stainless steel biers. Zack and I exchange glances. Pierce keeps the vampires in coffins? A macabre joke? Each casket has a large tank at the end of it. A coil of plastic tubing connecting them. I surmise that's how the silver anesthesia Alan mentioned is administered. One coffin is open, but from this vantage point we can't see inside. A woman dressed in scrubs stands in front of it, blocking our view. Her back is to us, but I know it's Pierce. I recognize the upswept blond hair from last night.

We move in tandem to the adjacent door. Zack stands to the right, I, to the left. With a sweeping motion, he cracks the door open. The sound of a Rogers and Hammerstein tune spills out. Pierce is cheerfully humming along. The door opens as soundlessly as the bookcase. Pierce doesn't hear us enter, doesn't even look up as we move behind her.

She's standing over a coffin, a syringe in her hand. The lid and sides of the coffin appear to be lined with silver. There's a blanket that looks to be of spun silver pushed to the end and partially draped over the side. The coil of plastic tubing hangs disconnected from its tank at the end. From over Pierce's shoulder, I can see inside.

Isabella. It's horrifying to get my first glimpse of what has become of her. The wispy woman with the radiant smile I've been searching for is stretched out, nude, her body withering away. Her long brown hair looks like straw. Her lips are drained of color and peeling, her skin pale and pruned. Across her abdomen is a series of ghastly-looking scars that have yet to completely heal. She's moaning softly, her eyes closed.

Pierce reaches inside the coffin and lifts Isabella's arm. "This will put you to sleep for the final time. In a moment, it will all be over."

Just as she touches the syringe to Isabella's arm, I step forward, chambering a round. Zack has moved to my left, his gun trained, too, on Pierce.

"Drop the syringe," I order, struggling to keep the emotion out of my voice. "Or don't. I would *love* an excuse to shoot you."

I expect her to whirl around, be startled, yell.

She does none of those things.

To my great disappointment, Pierce obeys. The hand with the syringe drops to her side. "You don't understand," she says, still not moving, not turning around to see who has invaded her private lab. "If you did—"

"Oh, but I do understand. Better than you imagine. We've just come from your son's office."

"Alan? Is he all right?" She's staring into the coffin.

"He told us everything. Now, I want you to step away from the coffin and turn around, slowly."

"I need to give Isabella a shot," she says, remaining motionless. "She is recovering from a powerful sedative. If she is allowed to become fully conscious—"

She doesn't get the chance to complete the sentence.

Isabella's hand flies up from the coffin and fastens on Pierce's throat.

"Isabella, no!" I shout.

Zack moves to intervene.

We're both too late.

With one strong flick of her wrist, she's pulled Pierce into the coffin. The doctor flails, trying to break away, but the promise of sustenance seems to breathe life into Isabella. She sits up, pulling Pierce to her chest. She fastens her jaws on the doctor's neck and begins to drink.

I hate what Pierce has turned Isabella into, but there are strict laws in the vampire community about when and how a vampire feeds. And killing a well-known doctor and draining her blood might put Isabella in just as much danger from her own kind as she was from Pierce.

Zack grabs hold of Isabella's hair in an effort to pull her free from Pierce's body.

Isabella easily throws him off, jaws snapping at Zack's throat.

"Find blood," he shouts. "There's got to be some around here."

I'm already headed for the door across the way. When I push it open, there's only one bed inside. It's an operating suite, complete with monitors and an oxygen supply. The table is empty. My heart is pounding as I run for the second door. It also leads to a patient room. Again with one bed. This time occupied. Dexter is still and pale under the blanket tucked around him. Intravenous tubes in his arms connect to two overhead infusion bags—one containing blood, the other a clear liquid that I assume is keeping Dexter hydrated—and sedated. In this room, there is a refrigerator. When I open it, I find the blood bags. I grab several and race back to Zack.

He's moved in again. This time instead of trying to grab Isabella, he goes for the coffin. Its silver lining burns his hands. He pulls away with a hiss, shaking them both. Then his expression turns resolute and he grabs the side using only his left. I smell his flesh burn, watch as smoke curls up between his fingers.

"Zack!"

Sweat beads on his forehead. He grits his teeth and growls in rage, not backing down. Before I can reach him to help, the coffin tips. Zack is pinned beneath it along with Pierce and Isabella. I catch a glimpse of his blistered hand as I move to help lift the coffin. I needn't have bothered. Isabella, now stronger from the blood, arches her back and throws it off, then turns her rage on Zack.

With lightning-fast reflexes he's on his feet, poised and ready. Isabella rushes toward him, pushing him through the open door, out into the lab, and they fall to the floor.

I lower the shields and try to get into Isabella's mind—to plant a calming seed. But she's too far gone to listen to rational thought. Half mad from silver poisoning, her mind is broken. She's capable only of acting on instinct, acting to ease the pain of starvation and to fight for survival.

She's forgotten Pierce now, turning her snapping jaws to Zack. Even with Zack's damaged hand, he's able to fend off her attacks, holding her at arm's length. Under normal circumstances, a Were would be no match for a vampire's strength. But Zack is powerful and Isabella is young, weak, and her need to feed is paramount.

I grab a scalpel from a nearby tray and slice open one of the bag's ports. At the smell of blood, Isabella whirls toward me. I hold it out and she snatches it from my hands, latching on to it like a babe sucking at its mother's breast. By the time she's finished with the first, I have another open and ready for her. "Get more, Zack," I yell.

When Isabella accepts the blood, there's the dawning of recognition and wonder in her eyes. I catch a glimpse of myself in the window and am reminded that the shields are still down. I glance around for Zack. His back is to me, heading into the laboratory. I realize this may be my only chance to get into her head.

"Isabella, listen to me. We're here to help you, but you have to trust us. We're friends of Michael's."

"Michael?"

"He's never given up on you." I hand her the third blood bag. "Cooperate with us."

Zack is coming back toward us, a handful of blood bags and a clean white sheet in his hands. I pull up the shields, wait for him to join us. Isabella is still looking at me, a puzzled frown pulling at the corners of her mouth. But she says nothing, accepting the sheet Zack holds out to her.

She wraps the sheet around her nude body.

"Trust us," Zack says, offering her another blood bag. "We'll get you home. Safe and sound."

He goes to Pierce, lying still under Isabella's coffin, blood pooling beneath her head. He feels for a pulse, looks up at me, shakes his head.

I sigh and look around the room. The five remaining coffins are closed. While Zack stays with Isabella, I open them, one by one, throwing off the silver blankets that cover the vampires trapped inside and pulling needles from arms, stopping the flow of anesthesia rendering them immobile.

Only one opens his eyes immediately upon being freed.

Evan.

CHAPTER 21

Evan sits up in the coffin, shaking his head as if to clear his thoughts. He looks at me, narrows his eyes, and growls. "Emma? What are you doing here? What am *I* doing here?" He looks around. "Where am I?" He glances down. "Shit. Why the fuck am I naked?"

Questions fired machine-gun-style, not pausing for reply or comment. Eyes now burrowing into my skull.

"It's a long story."

"Emma." Zack has pulled another sheet off the shelf and he tosses it to me.

I hold it up and Evan climbs out of the coffin, still glaring at me. Once on his own two feet, he folds the sheet in two, then wraps it around his waist like a towel. He turns back to examine the tomb that held him prisoner, fingering the plastic coil and then yanking it from the canister. Where a drop of liquid touches his skin, a blister erupts. He peers at it. "Silver."

He glares at me. "What happened?"

"You were kidnapped."

Alarm darkens Evan's face as if he's searching for the meaning of my words, searching for some memory of how he got here, searching for the clue that will snap the pieces of the puzzle together. He moves to peer into the coffins on either side of the one that held him. The vampires inside haven't opened their eyes. Two men, their skin wrinkled and black, lie in a dark, viscous fluid that weeps from scars like Isabella's. It pools at the bottom of the coffin. The smell is acrid and tinged with decay.

When I join him, Evan's head is bowed. "They've been exposed too long." He says it softly and matter-of-factly. "Look at their skin. The silver poisoning is bone deep. Even if we could revive them, they would remain mad. We can't bring them back."

"You've seen this kind of thing before?" I ask. My memory slips back to a terrible period when the Inquisition ran rampant and torture became an art.

He nods. "Wrapping a vampire in silver was a favorite torment during the Middle Ages."

"Middle Ages?" Zack has joined us, catching Evan's last remark. "How old are you?"

Evan ignores the question, his eyes searching the room.

I can guess what he's looking for. What he intends to do. What he must do.

There is a small desk in the back of the room with a wooden folding chair beside it. He crosses the room with quick strides, sweeps up the chair, and smashes it against the floor. He lifts a leg of the chair, broken off at the base and splintered into a sharp point.

Then he's back at the coffins. With no hesitation, he drives the stake through the hearts of the two vampires. First one, then the other. There is a long sigh from each, like a release of both breath and life. A cloud rises as their bodies disintegrate and then they are gone. Only a fine red ash remains, coating the bottom of the caskets, coagulating in the fluid like a grisly scab.

Evan remains motionless for a moment, his eyes closed, his shoulders slumped.

Pierce may have thought vampires were inhuman, but this is a most human reaction. The reaction of having taken life . . . of coming face-to-face with the finality of real death.

Evan straightens and turns to look at me again. "How long have I been gone?"

"About two days."

He grimaces. "Liz must be frantic. I need to call her."

I hand him my cell and step away to allow him a moment of privacy. Zack has moved to the next coffin and freed Amy. I can't help smiling. Although she's weak, she's able to stand on her own. She's safe. Our case solved.

Evan rejoins me, hands me back my cell with a smile of thanks. "I've got to get home. Preferably with my clothes." He glances around again. "Then I'm going to have a lot of questions."

Zack has offered Amy a blood bag. Now he turns to Evan. "Do you need blood?"

He shakes his head. "I can wait."

Isabella had been quietly listening to the exchange between Evan and me. Now she's turned her attention to the bag in Zack's hand. Minutes ago she would have killed for blood. I glance over at Pierce's body, battered and broken. She did kill for it. Now that she's fed, the transformation is astounding. Color and texture have returned to her skin and hair. She looks once again like the picture Dexter gave the police when she went missing. She joins Evan as he beats Zack to the last closed coffin, opens it, and peers inside.

There's a flick of recognition and something else—a

shadow of guilt? Evan says gruffly, "This one's got to have blood."

"I'll get it." Isabella plucks one from the pile Zack left on a nearby table and opens it.

"You know him." It's not a question. Evan's expression tells me it's true.

"His name is Owen Cooper." Evan jerks the sheet wrapped around his waist tighter. His expression is filled with both frustration and anger. "Where the fuck are my clothes?" His voice rises, giving vent to anger the only way he can.

I lay a hand on his arm. "I'll see if I can find them." I head for the single closed door I haven't yet opened. "Let's see what's behind door number four." When I open it, there's only an empty bed inside and a closet, also empty.

On my way back to the lab, I notice a trash can marked HAZARDOUS WASTE pushed underneath the sink against the back wall. Incineration would be a neat and tidy way to dispose of evidence. I lift the lid. There's a suit lying right on top. I pull it out and shake it. Shirt, tie, and shoes are bunched inside and fall to the floor. The suit is well tailored, looks to be the right size. Probably Evan's. Under the suit in the trash can are other men's clothing, black jeans, black T-shirt, leather jacket. Owen's maybe? I quickly gather them up. The women's clothes are nowhere to be found. Pierce must have already disposed of them. I make a side trip into the lab and grab two sets of scrubs from the shelf. Not exactly designer duds, but somehow I don't think the vampires will complain.

"What were they going to do with us?" Evan asks when I reenter the room.

I realize the others have all quieted, awaiting my response. "Dr. Pierce discovered that vampire organs could universally be transplanted into humans. And because a vampire's organs regenerate—"

"She could do it over and over again." Isabella, still wrapped in a sheet, places a hand over her abdomen where I saw the web of scars.

I wonder if even now the scars are becoming fainter, skin knitting itself whole.

Zack is speaking. "Until the silver poisoning made it impossible."

Evan's eyes are hard as he accepts his clothes from me. They are focused on Pierce's body. "Is she the one who did this to us?"

I nod.

"Who killed her?"

I gesture toward Isabella. She and Amy are standing together, talking softly. "When Isabella awoke, she was mad from starvation. It was pure reflex."

Evan looks me in the eye. "If she hadn't killed the bitch, I would have." He drops the sheet and quickly steps into his clothes.

I approach the women and hand them the scrubs. Neither looks uncomfortable as they both drop their sheets, too, and slip them on. Vampires have low inhibitions. I'm the one who turns away. Accepting sheets to cover themselves was obviously for my benefit. Certainly not Zack's. He's quietly speaking with a naked Owen as if it's the most natural thing in the world. The only creature less modest than a vampire is a shifter.

Zack's handed Owen four bags of blood.

"Thanks, man."

The vampire still hasn't made an attempt to sit up. He

gulps the offered blood eagerly, draining the first bag in seconds. He seems to be fumbling with the second, and without hesitation, Zack breaks it open and hands it to him. This time, he drinks more slowly. Within minutes of finishing the second bag, he's able to climb out of the coffin. Some of the wounds on his body where the silver blanket came in contact with his flesh have already started to heal. Owen stretches. He looks to have been in his midtwenties when he was turned. He has light brown hair and a sinewy build, which at the moment is prominently on display.

I toss the remaining clothes I have to Zack so he can give them to the vampire, then turn to Evan, who has been staring at Owen. "Does he need more blood?"

Evan doesn't answer. He's fully dressed now, down to the knotted tie and polished shoes, clothes wrinkled but presentable.

He heads toward Owen. "You still look like shit, my friend," Evan tells him. Then to me, "He's going to need one, maybe two more bags."

"How do you two know each other?" Zack asks.

But Evan's eyes don't flicker from the younger vampire. "You were taken with me?"

Owen nods.

I leave to fetch more blood. When I return, Owen's on his fourth. He finishes it off and tosses it to the side, wiping the blood from his chin with his forearm.

Then he sees the clothes in Zack's hand. He grins and reaches over to grab the leather jacket. "I thought for sure this was toast," he says. He pulls on the jeans, ignores the T-shirt, zips on the jacket. "I feel better already."

Evan breaks into bag number five and offers it to him.

His hand goes to Owen's shoulder and gives it an encouraging squeeze. "You're going to be fine."

Zack looks from one to the other. "If you two were taken at the same time, why does he look so much worse?"

Evan doesn't answer, his expression calm, expectant. I get the impression he knows, but considers this Owen's tale to tell.

"I'd been detoxing . . . again . . . trying to kick drinking straight from the tap . . . again." Owen tosses the empty blood bag onto the floor. "I hadn't fed in seventy-two hours."

Evan holds up the last full bag, a questioning look on his face.

Owen shakes his head. "I'm good." Then to Zack, "Evan is my sponsor. He was going to take me to an Emporium. I was due to start back on the bagged stuff." He turns back to Evan. "Dude, who the fuck did you piss off?"

"You saw what happened? You tell me," Evan says. "I don't remember anything except leaving the office two nights ago. I was on my way out when you pulled up." He passes a hand over his face. "I never sensed anyone near me. The next thing I knew, I woke up in a coffin."

"You were walking. There was a pop and you dropped, like a fly. I got out of my car and headed toward you. That's the last thing I remember."

"You didn't see anyone?" I ask.

"Not a fucking soul," Owen replies.

"When did you last see Barbara Pierce?" I ask Evan.

His eyes flick to her body. "At my office, when she visited the afternoon before the benefit. It was the only time I'd ever met her. I usually dealt with Alan directly. We had a lunch meeting scheduled and he was going to hand-deliver my tickets for the benefit. But he got stuck dealing with some last-minute details. So his mother stopped by to drop them off instead."

"That's the day you disappeared." From Zack.

"Did you serve anything to eat or drink while she was there?" I ask.

"We all had tea."

"Maybe she slipped some slow-working drug into your tea. Then waited for you to leave the building," I suggest, saying it to calm Evan. To try to contain this. It's Mager who brought the vampires down. I'm sure of it. But it's not up to Evan or anyone else in the vampire community to exact justice upon him. Mager may be a despicable criminal, but he's also human.

Unfortunately, Evan isn't buying it. "Too much left to chance. Based on what Owen saw, I'd say she had help." Evan's jaw tightens as he looks around. "An operation of this size? She had to have help. Is Barakov in on this? Or Alan?"

He tone is sharp. He *wants* someone else to be involved. Someone alive on whom he can exact revenge.

I can't blame him. But I can't let him.

"No," I reply. "Alan told us Barakov didn't know anything about what his wife was doing. His only involvement was to give her the idea about silver's effect on vampires." I sweep my hand around. "This was all her own idea."

"And you believe him?" Isabella asks.

"He couldn't have lied," I reply simply. "I know."

"And yet Alan knew something, because here you are," Evan says.

"He only recently found out what his mother was doing."

"And he sent you here?"

"Yes."

"Why?"

My thoughts turn to Dexter. Is this the time to tell them, to tell Isabella, why she is here?

"Wait a minute," Amy interrupts before I can speak. "Barakov? I know that name."

"So do I," adds Isabella. "And I know Alan Pierce. Are you sure they aren't all in on this together?"

Zack steps forward. "We're positive. She had help, obviously." He's choosing his words carefully. "But her husband wasn't involved in your kidnappings. Neither was Alan."

"You will find out who was, though, right?" Amy asks Zack, her green eyes flashing.

"We'll do what we can. Now that you're safe, that's the priority," he replies. He hears the threat in Amy's tone, too. And he's already seen Isabella in action.

Amy and Isabella seem to have recovered completely. Recovered enough in fact for Amy to fix Zack and me with a steely gaze and ask, "Who are you?"

Zack extends a hand. "I'm Special Agent Zack Armstrong. This is Special Agent Emma Monroe. FBI."

She shakes both of our hands in turn, then looks at us from beneath lowered eyebrows. "What are you? Agents of the FBI's X-Files Bureau?"

"I didn't know they let the furry into the Bureau these days," snorts Owen.

Zack glares at the vampire he's just saved. "Even a young pup knows not to bite the hand that feeds it," he growls.

Owen looks appropriately contrite. "Sorry, Agent Armstrong. That was out of line. I owe you both. Big-time."

Evan looks around the lab. "Is anyone else here?"

Zack and I exchange a quick look. His neutral expression and small shrug throw the question to me. He's going to let me decide if we should tell them about Dexter. Tell Isabella that she was to be his donor. I don't know if she was aware that he was sick. Or if Dexter is aware of anything that happened since Alan drugged him the night before. I don't know how to begin.

Zack picks up on my hesitation and comes to my rescue, smoothly waving away Evan's question by a skillful change of subject.

"Amy, Ms. Haskell is going to be very relieved to see you. She's been worried sick."

Amy's eyes widen in surprise. "How long have I been gone?"

"A little over two weeks."

She passes a hand over her face. "My show in New York . . ."

Zack and I look at each other. That's the least of it. We have to come up with explanations—cover stories—for Amy, Isabella, and Owen.

And for our superiors. We certainly can't report any of *this* to the Bureau.

I look from Amy to Isabella. "You two need to come up with a story to explain why you've been gone. Particularly you, Amy. Your disappearance hit the papers and there's been a lot of speculation, especially since you missed the opening of your own show. Haskell has done a good job deflecting the press, but you're going to have to come up with an explanation the public will buy."

Amy nods. She shoots the others a look of resignation. "I'll have to give it some thought. You'd think as a vampire, I'd be used to lying, wouldn't you?"

There's a general murmur of agreement.

I turn to Isabella. "Any ideas? You've been gone the longest, a little over two months."

"Two months!" Her expression darkens. "That bitch stole two months of my life? How on earth am I going to catch up with school? Never mind my internship."

She's on the verge of tears, so I give her a minute. "You should know, Michael never gave up hope."

Isabella's face clears and her eyes brighten. "He wouldn't. No matter what, Michael always seems to be there for me."

"He knows you best," I say. "He'll be wanting an explanation and could be the hardest to convince."

Isabella nods. "I'll tell him I had to get away to clear my head. He knows how conflicted I've been about this whole vampire thing. He'll yell and carry on, but he'll accept it. That's what best friends do." She frowns. "What am I going to say to the people at school? They've probably dropped me by now."

"I can pay the dean an unofficial visit and explain you were under our protection," Zack says. "A witness to something we can't discuss, but that it's over now. I'll flash my badge, be vague but officious. I can be very convincing."

Isabella's eyes sweep Zack, head to feet. "I'm sure you can be. Especially since the dean's a she." Isabella is smiling again. "I'm confident you'll wrap her around your finger in no time flat."

"I'm not sure I can do anything about your internship, though," he continues. "Michael mentioned they couldn't hold the position."

She sighs, then steps closer to me, lowers her voice. "How is Michael?"

Her question jolts me back into facing the predicament I dodged before.

Her friend is in the next room, awaiting a transplant that isn't going to happen. Should I tell her? How will she feel knowing her freedom may be his death warrant?

She's wringing her hands. "His health had been failing."

Once again, I'm torn between telling her the truth—all of it—and leaving it to Dexter to explain the gravity of his condition when they're together.

I shrug noncommittally. "You'll see him soon enough. He'll be thrilled to have you home."

Owen's laugh makes Isabella turn away from me. Another reprieve. Zack has been questioning Owen, asking if he has a story ready. Owen's response is a burst of laughter.

"I don't need a story," he says, grinning. "I've never been part of the mainstream. I'm forever disappearing, going off on binges. My sire seems to have infinite patience for my bullshit and accepts my comings and goings. I've only been gone a couple of days, right? I doubt anyone's missed me. Evan, if you give me a lift to the nearest Emporium, I can take it from there. If I'm going to stay on the wagon, I'm going to need a good supply."

Amy glances down at the scrubs. "There's one problem. I can't go home like this."

"Me, either," chimes in Isabella. "We'll need clothes to make our stories stick."

Evan holds out a hand to me. "Can I borrow your car? I'll bring Amy and Isabella to Liz. She'll be able to take care of the clothes."

I drop my keys in his hand. "Leave the car in your guest spot and the keys in the glove box. I have a spare.

When we're finished here, Zack will drive me over to get it." I lower my voice. "Don't rush to get Isabella and Amy home. We'll need some time to sort this mess out."

"No kidding." Evan smiles in sympathy, looking around. "I'll drop Owen off first. You know Liz. She'll want to know every detail of what happened. That should buy you a couple of hours at least." His voice softens. "I can't thank you enough, Emma. You've gone above and beyond. I hope you don't get in trouble with your boss. I'm not sure how you're going to explain—"

I interrupt with a wave of a hand. "Don't worry about that, just get home. Liz has some news I think you'll like." I cast my own skeptical eye around the room. "But you're right, Zack and I have a lot of cleaning up to do."

Evan shepherds everyone out, the vampires leaving with repeated offerings of thanks.

Then Zack and I are alone. I take stock of the mess we're in. We have a secret lab in downtown San Diego filled with custom-made silver-lined coffins. We have one very dead transplant surgeon. And last, but not least, we have a sedated and critically ill famous artist. I walk over to where Dr. Barbara Pierce's body is lying on the floor. She's looking up at me, her face drained of color, her eyes empty, her neck grotesquely twisted, mangled by a dozen frenzied bite marks.

It's one thing for Isabella and Amy to come up with plausible cover stories. How are Zack and I ever going to come up with ours? I look over at Zack. "Got any bright ideas, Mr. Handyman?"

He's at the sink. He's just finished rinsing off his burned hands and is wrapping gauze around them. "Now that we have a body to get rid of, she appreciates me."

"We don't have much time. We can't leave Alan sitting

in his office forever. Somebody from the foundation might come in and find him."

Zack joins me. We're now standing across from each other, Pierce's body on the floor between us. "Fast, fool-proof, or free," he says. "Pick two. You can't have all three."

"You're going to charge me?" I ask.

Zack frowns. "Don't be ridiculous. I can do free and foolproof, but it's going to take some time. Or free and fast, but—"

I cut him off. I get it. "We need a cleaner."

He nods. "I know someone in the area," he says. "I can call in a favor."

The tone of his voice tells me he will, but he doesn't really want to. I understand. He's trying to leave his old life, his old contacts, behind.

Still, what choice do we have? I can't see any way out of the situation we find ourselves in.

I open my mouth to respond, but before I can make a sound, Zack holds up his hand to silence me.

I freeze.

He cocks his head slightly to the side and listens, his expression intent.

I listen, too, but I don't hear a thing.

In short order Zack points to his ear, holds up three fingers. I nod. There are three people outside. He points to me, to himself, then with both hands to the walls on either side of the entrance. I already have my gun out. Together, we move, swiftly, silently. My back is flush against the left side of the door, Zack is on the right. I'm acutely aware I'm not wearing Kevlar and try to remember the last time I discharged my weapon at the firing range. It's been a while.

I slowly release a breath and try to relax. My eyes connect with Zack's. He appears calm, confident. His stance is relaxed. He holds his weapon as if it were a natural extension of his body. He senses what's coming. Reflexively, his nose lifts, his nostrils flare, his eyes widen. I see the change in him, but not in enough time to react.

Next thing I know, I'm pinned to the wall. My feet are barely touching the floor. My arms are being held high above my head.

By an extremely old and pissed-off vampire.

CHAPTER 22

This vampire's strength is like none I've ever encountered. The Glock falls from my hand and clatters to the floor. Before I can get a good look at him, his face is buried in the crook of my neck. His nose travels from the spot just behind my ear, to the top of my shoulder, skimming along the surface of my skin. He hesitates for a fraction of a second along the way, and I shudder. The involuntary response, a testament to his power and my fear, pleases him. I feel him smile against my collarbone.

He slowly pulls back, his face just inches from mine.

I realize I've seen him before. Twice.

First at Liz's.

Then going into the Blood Eemporium in the Gaslamp District.

The man in black.

"A Siren. Remarkable," he whispers, a quiet reverence to his tone.

That voice. A rumbling baritone. Familiar. Unmistakable. Simon's "boss."

He's as tall as Zack, maybe slightly taller. His muscles are leaner, his face thinner, the cheekbones are more defined. Shoulder-length black hair hangs loose in waves framing his oval-shaped face and clear blue eyes.

My mouth is dry. He sees through the glamour. I swallow. "You know what I am?"

Behind me I hear Zack growling in frustration. Sounds of scuffling, as if he's fighting to be released. But I can't see him. My view is blocked by an expanse of chest covered in a very expensive black dress shirt under a leather jacket. The top two buttons of the shirt are open, hinting at the smooth, flawless chest beneath.

The vampire's smile is bittersweet. "A sister of yours made me happy once. But that was many, many years ago . . . and before I was turned. I am Kallistos."

Behind him, the struggling ceases. For a fraction of a second, everything is completely still. The name means nothing to me. Evidently it means something to Zack.

"Kallistos Kouros, Sovereign of the Western Territory?" he asks.

"The one and only." The smile turns so bright it could light up a room. He exudes the kind of easy confidence possessed only by one comfortable with his power. "Release him." Kallistos is speaking to someone else, but all of his attention is focused on me. His grip loosens on my hands and he gently lowers my arms to my side and takes a step back.

He tries to slip into my mind. I feel the long-reaching tendrils of his will searching for an opening. He's very strong and very skilled, but a vampire's thrall is no match for my own powers. He may be a tad over a thousand years old, but I'm older and I've had many years of practice. I deftly and unceremoniously push him out.

The force of my rejection is so strong it must feel like a slap in the face. I could have been gentler, kinder, used more finesse. But Kallistos needs to know when it comes to this, *I* have the upper hand, and always will. He doesn't try to push back. Not even a little. He accepts the boundary that I've drawn. It's almost as if he's longed for it, for someone he can't readily control.

"A wondrous and worthy opponent." His voice is low and deep. "I love a woman who knows what she wants. Have dinner with me."

Well, that was unexpected.

Suddenly Zack and I are shoulder to shoulder. He hands me my gun and puts his arm possessively around my waist. "My partner has plans."

"Plans," Kallistos repeats. The word rolls off his tongue as if it's foreign to him and he's testing it out. Men like Kallistos don't have to make plans. The world is at their disposal. He's used to getting what he wants, when he wants it.

"That's right," Zack answers.

A slow, sardonic smile forms on Kallistos' lips. "Look at you, trying to mark your territory."

Zack doesn't rise to the bait. "I don't consider Agent Monroe territory."

Kallistos leans in. The smile fades. "Trust me, you'd be better off if you did."

"Which sister?" I ask, moving so that I am between Zack and Kallistos. Which sister doesn't matter. Whether it was my older sister or my younger, I can guess the story. They fell in love. It didn't end happily ever after. I just want to put distance between him and Zack. I feel Zack's rage mounting.

"I'm not here to dredge up the past." Kallistos steps back, now flanked by the two other vampires he'd brought with him.

"Why are you here?" I ask him.

"The witch called me. She asked for my help. Her

story piqued my interest, so I went to see her. We've had a rash of missing vampires lately. While I was there, one of her spells kicked in. She was able to pinpoint Evan's location. Here. She wanted to come with me but—" He looks around the room. "I didn't know what we'd find. I convinced her to wait."

Convinced? Compelled, most likely. "You just missed Evan," I say. "He should be home shortly."

Kallistos turns and surveys the room, taking in the disarray. "There were others."

"Six." Zack gestures to the coffins on the far side of the room. "Two were completely desiccated. Evan said they were beyond help."

Kallistos crosses to one of the silver-lined tombs, opens the lid, then places his hands on the side and peers in. Smoke rises between his fingers. I smell his flesh burn, yet he doesn't flinch. "She kept them in here?"

"Yes," Zack replies. "Evan released them."

"What they must have endured. And some say we are the monsters." His expression is a mixture of bewilderment and disgust.

His gaze sweeps the room. "The ones Evan released, who were they?"

Zack's crosses his arms. He's being cooperative, but he isn't happy about the interrogation. "No idea."

Kallistos walks over to Barbara Pierce. "This one was responsible for their capture and containment?"

Zack nods.

"What happened to her?"

"Isabella Mancini killed her. When she woke, she was half mad from starvation and torture," I explain. "There were two others we were able to save, an Amy Patterson and some kid named Owen Cooper." His expression changes ever so slightly when I mention the last name. Is it relief? I can't tell. "No missing person's report on Cooper as far as I know. That name wasn't familiar."

"That's because he doesn't quite live in the mainstream. Amy Patterson. Isn't she the artist who's been missing?" he asks.

I nod.

Kallistos points to the door Zack is standing in front of. Zack has his arms crossed over his chest, his expression stern.

"Who's in there? I detected four heartbeats in the building—three on this floor, one on the main floor. From the way you're guarding the door, I'm going to guess human."

Zack looks surprised that Kallistos was able to detect the number of heartbeats before even entering the room. I have heard that only the oldest and most powerful of vampires acquire the skill, but in my immortal life span, I've never met one. No wonder Zack hasn't, either.

Before today.

I wonder what other tricks Kallistos has up his sleeve.

"He had nothing to do with this," I say. "Like the others, he was kidnapped and brought here against his will. He's sick, dying, and he's come to peace with that. His lover hadn't. We need to get him to a hospital."

Kallistos' eyes narrow. "But what is he doing *here*, in this lab? Why were any of them here?"

I realize he doesn't know about Pierce's organ factory. I tell him, quickly, succinctly. How she was blackmailed and forced to harvest organs from humans for a black market transplant operation. How she came up with the idea of using vampires since, to her way of thinking, they were already dead. I relayed her discoveries. Vampires are universal donors, possessing organs that won't be rejected. They're capable of donating repeatedly, potentially endlessly. And then, finally, I told him about the silver, how she used it to subdue, restrain, and anesthetize her captives during surgery. How prolonged exposure to the silver appeared to be what caused the severe desiccation, the madness, the need for absolute death.

I expect an explosion of revulsion and rage. Instead his eyes are clouded with sadness. "This is why we hide ourselves, our powers, our gift," he says. "Perhaps someday when humans learn *humanity*, things will be different."

Kallistos removes his jacket, then begins to roll up his sleeves. "We can avoid the hospital for this human. Out of my way."

I cross to stand beside Zack.

"He's not going to be turned," Zack tells him.

Kallistos isn't used to being told anything. That much is obvious. He doesn't react with anger, though. Instead his gaze turns to me.

"I can help him. Surely, a soul as old as you, a creature with your amount of . . . experience . . . knows this."

I do know. That's what makes this entire debacle even more tragic. I nod.

Kallistos turns to Zack. "Move aside, dog."

"Make me."

Kallistos grins and takes one step closer. I reach out, planting a hand firmly in the middle of his chest. "This is unnecessary. Explain to him."

Several seconds pass. I hold my breath.

"I have no intention of turning him," the vampire assures Zack.

Only he doesn't buy it. He continues to stand his ground.

I reach for Zack's arm. "Trust him. The blood of an old one has the power to heal. A few sips of Kallistos' blood and Michael will be cured."

"I've never heard—"

"Trust me."

His lips press into a thin line. "You're *certain*?" His hand is now poised on the doorknob. He looks at me expectantly. I know what's he's asking. His intent telegraphs itself as clearly as if he'd spoken it aloud. He wants to know if I can read Kallistos, if it's safe.

"Yes," I say. "I'm sure. Absolutely sure."

The door opens. Kallistos pushes past. I turn to follow, sense Zack at my back. I turn, shake my head. "No, you have to stay here."

Confusion clouds his face.

"Please," I add. "I don't want you caught in the wake of my powers. I need to read him alone. You need to trust me. I can't deal with both of you at the same time."

He looks ready to argue, but he holds his tongue.

"I'm sorry."

Zack takes my hand in his. I feel something cool and round press into it. His expression gives away nothing.

"Be careful."

I give him a reassuring smile as I discreetly slide my hand into my pocket. "Always."

Zack closes the door once I pass through and I lock it between us, leaning my head against it for an instant before a voice at my ear whispers in silky smoothness, "If you wanted to be alone with me, all you had to do is ask."

Kallistos.

He's behind me. Right behind me. So close, I feel the pulse of his breath against my neck.

The man has no respect for personal space. My spine

stiffens. I turn to face him, push him away. The door is now at my back.

He steps close again, leans over me, one arm poised over my head. "That door won't hold him. He can hear us, you know. Are you trying to purposefully drive your wolf wild?"

"What I'm trying to do is find out how honest you are. How noble your intentions." I keep my voice steady, the tone professional.

Kallistos lowers his hand, draws a finger along the contours of my face, my lips, as if he's going to touch them. But he doesn't. "My intentions are quite dishonorable, I can assure you."

He's not talking about Dexter and we both know it.

"What I wouldn't give to possess this mouth," he whispers, finger still poised over my lips. "Along with the rest of you."

I push the finger away. "You presume far too much, Mr. Kouros. You have nothing I want."

"Oh no? I can give you what you crave, what you need. Anything you desire, save my heart. I made that mistake once. I can guarantee you, I will never make it again. We could have decades, centuries of pure, uncomplicated pleasure. No. Strings. Attached."

"I've been alive long enough to know there are always strings." I duck under his arm, moving away.

Kallistos smiles. "I make you nervous."

"Actually, you're making me impatient. We're wasting time." I gesture to Dexter, still and pale on the bed. "If you aren't going to help him, we need to get him to a hospital."

He spreads his arms wide. "Let's get on with it, then. You're here to ensure that I'm not going to harm the human. Use your power to test me. You'll find you can trust me. You'll taste the truth in my statement."

We move to stand on opposite sides of the room, the bed containing an unconscious Michael Dexter between us. Suddenly my conviction wavers. I have never tested the powers of one so powerful. Am I about to test Kallistos, or is he about to test me? Is he counting on me to walk away rather than to risk our mutual exposure, or is he goading me into giving him what he wants, a glimpse of the real me? He knew a Siren once, my sister. He knows the danger, yet he invites me in. Why?

Kallistos' gaze is haughty, as if he knows the battle I'm fighting, as if he expects me to back down. I draw myself up, remember that I bested him just minutes before, and let the walls fall away, the doors to my power fly open. It happens in a rush, fast and furious. The heat rises around us, the wind that comes with it rages. It would knock a lesser vampire off his feet. Kallistos stands tall, feet firmly planted on the floor. The hem of his leather coat whips out behind him.

"What do you plan to do to him?" I shout out over the din of the storm I've created.

"I'm going to give him blood. To stabilize him. To cure him. He will no longer need a hospital."

"Why would you do this for a human you do not know?"

I imagine he finds me impertinent, perhaps even insulting. So be it. There are things at stake that are more important than smoothing the feathers of a self-appointed sovereign.

But if he's insulted, he doesn't show it. "Because I gave you my word. You said he wasn't at fault and . . . you're attached to him. Yes?"

I tilt my head, narrowing my eyes. "And when he is cured? What happens then?"

"My men will see him safely home. He'll remember none of this. I have no more desire than you to risk exposure." His tone is surprisingly calm and measured, with no hint of deceit.

Then he's right in front of me, his hands on my shoulders, his eyes boring into mine. "Why hide who you are?" he whispers. "You could rule the world with your beauty, possess anything in it, anything but me."

"That's convenient," I mutter with a roll of my eyes. "Since I don't want you. Now, getting back to Dexter—"

My breath catches midsentence. Kallistos' movements are a blur. One hand behind my neck, the other moves to cup the side of my face. For an instant our eyes lock. I feel my heart beat faster.

Then his mouth is on mine. Hard, hot, and demanding. His lips part, his tongue slides inside my mouth. Something ignites. I feel myself relent, feel my heart beat faster, feel my blood turn to fire. I want to return the kiss and for the briefest moment, before I come back to my senses, I do. Wantonly. Wickedly. With uncontrolled abandon.

"Stop." I wrench control back, reeling in my power more swiftly than ever before. I swear the air is momentarily sucked out of the room. The surge is so strong I'm caught in it. I feel myself stagger back, light-headed, dizzy.

Kallistos doesn't move.

I raise my hand, intent on slapping the smug look right off his face.

He thwarts me, grabbing hold of my wrist.

"Emma? Are you all right?" Zack's voice through the door seems far away, distant.

I shake my head to clear it. Kallistos releases me. He makes no move to stop me as I turn to the door and fumble with the lock. But before I can open it, my legs momentarily give way. A strong arm encircles my waist and holds me steady.

"Breathe," he says.

My cheek is pressed against something hard and cool. Kallistos' chest.

"It's been far too long since you've so fully let it go." His lips graze the top of my head. "You've grown unused to it. Just ride it out. You'll be right as rain in a minute. Assure your wolfhound."

"I'm fine, Zack." The words fall unbidden from my lips. Kallistos is in my head. How can this be?

I move away, put distance between the vampire and myself until my head stops spinning. This time when I speak, it's on my own. I face Kallistos. "Take care of Dexter."

Then I turn my back on him, step again to the door. My hands are shaking, but when I try this time, the door opens. There's a blast of cool air. Then Zack's arms are around me. I lean into him.

"What happened?" Zack asks.

"He told the truth. He won't harm Dexter." My words sound hollow. I can't meet Zack's eyes.

Zack lifts my chin. "I meant what happened to you."

One of Dexter's monitors begins to beep. It's been disconnected. His IV lines have also been pulled out. They're draped over the bedside pole, contents from the bags drip onto the floor.

Kallistos holds his wrist to Dexter's mouth. The smear of blood on his lower lip tells me he punctured his wrist with his own fangs. Dexter sucks hungrily at the blood, a reflex action over which he has no control. Kallistos strokes Dexter's hair as he feeds, watching me.

When color returns to Dexter's face, Kallistos calls out, "Tony!"

One of the two who came in with him comes to the door. "Yes, sir?"

"The data?" Kallistos asks.

"It's all backed up on a server. Peter has control of it. There are a few handwritten notes. I have them boxed and ready to go."

Dexter's eyes are closed, but his throat is still working. Kallistos gently disengages Dexter's mouth from his wrist, then passes a hand over Dexter's face. Dexter falls back onto the pillows, his face relaxed in sleep. Kallistos' wounds close instantly, but not before leaving several bright red dots on the clean white bedsheets.

Kallistos turns to Tony. "Use the van to take him home. Wait for him to come to, then make him forget what happened here."

The minion nods and steps toward the bed.

Kallistos exits and walks past Zack and me. He stops in front of the sink Zack used earlier and washes the remnants of blood from his wrist. He's talking over his shoulder. "Make sure you take the notes with you, Tony. Security is the priority. We don't want any loose ends."

"Understood," Tony answers.

Tony and his crony go to work, following orders like good little soldiers. Within seconds they are heading out, one with Dexter wrapped in a sheet and thrown over his shoulder like a sack of potatoes, the other carrying a box.

Kallistos approaches, the paper towels he used to dry his hands now wadded into a tight little ball. Without breaking his stride he lobs it across the room and into a trash can. "We'll clean the rest of this up. You've done enough." He offers Zack his hand. Any animosity he felt toward Zack seems forgotten.

Zack's animosity obviously isn't.

"His intentions are honorable," I tell Zack. I'd tasted the truth of Kallistos' statement. And his power. The effect lingers like a shot of adrenaline. I try to push it out of my head. I look around. "We could use the help, Zack."

Zack peers at me, but he knows how limited our options are. He's frowning reluctantly, but he nods. The two men shake.

Then Kallistos kisses my hand.

The sensation of his mouth on my hand lingers, warm and wet.

Revulsion tightens the lines around Zack's mouth. He takes a step forward.

I stay him with a look that conveys Kallistos isn't worth it. We have our own loose ends to wrap up. Alan Pierce and Davis Mager. Mager can wait a bit, but Alan is still handcuffed to the radiator in his office. We need to get back and release him.

"We should get out of here," I say.

"Go. I will deal with this," Kallistos assures us.

Zack isn't ready to let go of his anger. "How are you—"

But Kallistos has Zack locked in his gaze. "Go."

Zack backs away. A rush of anger sends blood to my face. Kallistos is compelling Zack and he is powerless against it. At the same time, I know it's useless to object. We have to get back to Alan.

We leave Kallistos kneeling by Dr. Pierce's body.

Once outside, I breathe in the fresh air. It clears my

head and stops the pounding of a heart still racing from the encounter with Kallistos. I may be the stronger one when it comes to mind games, but he left an imprint of his power etched deep in my psyche.

"Are you sure about him?" Zack asks me as we slide into the car.

"Yes," I say. There's no hesitation. Still . . .

Zack fires up the engine.

Before he can pull away, I put out a hand to stop him. "Wait a second." Someone is emerging from the building, coughing and sputtering. A man I've never seen before. He's heavyset, in his forties, maybe fifties, and dressed in a uniform. The logo on his collar is the same as the one on the sign out front. He's on his cell phone "Look." I point him out to Zack. "Must be the security guard. Can you hear what he's saying?"

Zack lowers his window and listens.

Just then, Kallistos strolls out. His car is waiting for him across the street. He ignores the man on the sidewalk, walks right past him, just as the man ignores him. But then he nods toward the guard and winks before crossing to his car.

"Son of a bitch," Zack growls.

He reaches for the door handle.

I reach for him. "What is it?"

Zack points to the man on the phone. "He's saying there's a gas leak. Kallistos is going to blow up the goddamned lab."

The man takes off at a slow run and starts jogging down the street, away from the building.

Kallistos' car pulls away. If the speed in which he is making his departure is any indication, we don't have much time.

I tighten my grip on Zack's arm. Kallistos' wink as he passed the guard suddenly makes sense. "You can't go in there!"

"People could get hurt. Humans, Emma."

"He said there were only four heartbeats. Yours, mine, Dexter's, and that guy must be the fourth. The building's clear."

Zack points to the adjacent ones on either side. "Those may not be. This is far from foolproof. There's going to be collateral damage."

He's right, of course. I look around. The entire area is a blend of new and old construction. An explosion and fire down here could quickly get out of control. But there's no way we can stop it now.

"We need to put some distance between us and the building fast," I say.

Zack is shaking with fury. "Letting him handle the cleanup was a bad call. What the hell were we thinking? Call 911. Tell them to get an emergency crew here. Jesus, Emma. We're going to need a good story."

Zack throws the car into gear and steps on the gas. The car lurches forward.

I grab my cell and dial.

It rings once.

We drive past the security guard, huffing and puffing.

It rings again. The emergency operator answers. I give her my name and badge number. "We're in front of a medical building on the corner of Fourth and Hawthorn. Send emergency vehicles right away. The building's about to—"

An explosion drowns out the rest. The force of it pushes us forward. I feel the rear tires of the Suburban lift off the ground. The cell phone flies out of my hand

and onto the floor. We spin. Somehow Zack prevents us from flipping. When the car comes to a stop, we're facing the building. Car alarms are going off all around us, and rooftops are covered with the glass that rained down upon them from the nearby buildings. A fire hydrant in front of the building is spewing water into the street. The man who called in the "gas leak" is lying facedown on the blacktop. Zack takes off at a full run in his direction. I search frantically for the cell phone, find it. I'm still connected to the emergency operator.

"There are people injured. Send help right away," I shout. Then I disconnect and race to follow Zack.

The man is unconscious, and there's a small pool of blood under his head. Zack's crouched alongside him.

"Is he alive?"

Zack nods, but his expression is murderous. "No thanks to Kallistos. Fucking vampire."

I turn in a circle, take in the devastation around us. There are sirens in the background. They're getting closer.

Zack reaches for my hand. He pulls me forward. Plucks a piece of glass out of my forehead that I didn't even notice was there. "You okay? Your head hit the side window pretty hard."

My knees buckle. The adrenaline surge is wearing off. He steadies me.

"I'm okay," I say.

He lifts my chin until my eyes connect with his. "Listen to me. This may be the only opportunity we have to get our story straight. We were introduced to Barbara Pierce at the fund-raiser. She seemed off. Toward the end of the night she approached, told us she had something important for the FBI, begged us to come to her office.

There was a paranoid flavor about her, a sense of desperation. Then she disappeared into the crowd. We tried to follow her, but couldn't. Are you with me?"

I nod. "Yes."

"We got her address this morning, went to her office. She was completely unraveled. Said she couldn't live with what she was doing any longer. She confessed to killing Charlotte, gave up Davis Mager and his scheme, admitted to harvesting organs from dozens of homeless. She said she wanted to show us. She opened the panel leading to her lab. She went ahead of us, slipping through a door and locking us out. You can describe the lab just as it was."

"We would have tried to go after her," I say.

"We did. She knew exactly what she was doing. Along one wall were rows of tanks. Some were clearly labeled oxygen. Others were marked with unfamiliar letters and symbols. Pierce opened the valves on all of them. Then she held up a lighter."

The sirens are getting closer. Zack's voice is sounding farther and farther away.

He continues. I'm desperately trying to follow. "She yelled for us to go. To get Mager. To tell people that in the end she did the right thing. I started to break the glass, to try to get to her. But she was determined. It was save ourselves or die in the blast. We ran and called for help."

I can barely hear him now. Darkness is closing in from all sides.

Zack is shaking me. "Emma? Emma?"

It's the last thing I remember.

CHAPTER 23

My head spins. I feel Zack's arms around me as he lowers me to the ground and calls for help. By the time the paramedic is at my side, the darkness has receded and I've shaken myself back to full consciousness. I sit up, waving the guy away. "I'm fine. Tend to the guard."

Zack is protesting that I get checked out. But the paramedic shines a light in first one eye and then the other and stands up. "Someone's with the guard." He's speaking to Zack about me. "Her pupils are equal in size and reacting to light. Still, she lost consciousness. We should get her to a hospital."

"I'm not going to a hospital. The guard, he's going to make it?"

"Looks like it. We're lucky he was the only one seriously hurt." He looks down at me, then up at Zack again. "If she gets nauseated, dizzy, get her to an ER, okay?"

But his words barely register as I try to get my head around all that's happened.

I can't believe the mess this case has turned into. I've worked missing persons in the San Diego FBI office for six years now. This isn't the first time I've come across a supernatural element in need of containment. In those other rare instances, justice was served and the fantastical easily buried. Yes, the link to the vampires needed to be covered up. But for Kallistos to blow up the place? I think of the guard, lying injured in the street. What the hell was he thinking?

"We should take you to a hospital," Zack is still insisting.

My head is pounding; my shoulders and neck muscles are clenched so tight that it hurts to turn toward him. Still, I do, even managing to shake my head—carefully. "No hospital. I'll be fine." And I will be. Whatever injuries I might have, I won't die from them. Thousands of years and more than a few bumps and bruises testify that I know my body. Besides, there's something more urgent we need to do than take what would be a wasted trip to a hospital. "We've got to get back to Alan. It's been close to two and a half hours."

"Could be two and a half years. I'm telling you, he'll be right where we left him."

"Unless someone showed up at Green Leaf and freed him. Alan's recollection won't corroborate our story. We need a vampire to wipe his memory, and I'd much rather ask Evan to do it than try to reach Kallistos."

"We are not asking Kallistos," Zack says, his tone and expression thunderous. "He's helped us enough for one day. If we can't get Evan, I'll make a call or two."

He helps me to my feet. A couple of Bureau representatives are already on the scene and taking charge of the joint investigation with SDPD, freeing us to take our leave and return to headquarters. One of the Suburbans they arrived in is at our disposal, and we head for it now.

Only we're going to make a quick stop before reporting in.

A fifteen-minute drive never seemed so long.

When we finally arrive at Green Leaf, I have to climb carefully out of the SUV. I stretch to loosen the knots, slowly, and take a deep breath.

"Emma?"

Zack's pointing to the front gate. It's open. His gun is already out.

"You're still feeling the effects of the explosion," he says. "You should stay here."

Like hell. "Yeah, yeah." I pull my gun, look around. There are no cars parked in front except ours. Nerves tingling, I walk through the gate, then quickly move up the steps to approach the front entrance. My back is flat against the front of the house. Zack's is, too. We form mirror images on each side of the door, which is ajar. It's cracked just enough to give me a glimpse of inside.

Zack points to his ear, shakes his head, then tilts it toward the door. He's not hearing anything inside.

I give the door a push, calling out, "Hello? Agent Monroe here."

No answer.

I slip inside the entryway, leading with my gun to sweep the area.

It's so quiet I hear the beat of my heart.

"Alan?"

No answer. No noise at all.

Zack comes in, gun at the ready. He moves past me, through the waiting room. I see his shoulders relax. He lowers his weapon.

"Damn it!"

"What?"

I take a step closer, then see what he does. Across the way the door to Alan's office is standing wide open.

Zack's cuffs are still attached to the radiator.

But Alan is gone.

"Shit." I holster my gun. He couldn't have left of his own accord.

A kernel of suspicion takes root in my stomach. But someone could have taken him. I don't like what I'm thinking.

I release a breath, holster the Glock. "Fucker."

"Sums it up nicely." I watch as he walks to the radiator, unhooks his cuffs, and pockets them. He turns and frowns. "This has Kallistos written all over it."

He begins rummaging around on Alan's desk. The spreadsheets have been disturbed, and a file that wasn't here earlier is thrown haphazardly on top of them. He picks up the folder, opens it. Without a word, he pulls out a sheet of paper and after perusing it, hands it to me. It's a computer printout, a list of surgeries Dr. Pierce performed in her hidden clinic.

"Why would Alan have this?" I ask.

"He shouldn't have it," is Zack's curt reply. "It's Pierce's personal log, a record of the illegal organ transplants. She names Mager as her accomplice. The names of their human victims are listed, too, as well as the names of the organ recipients. She even notes dates, how much they paid for the surgery, and how much she earned from each." He looks up at me. "It's all here. Up to a point."

I release a breath. "Up to the point where she started using vampires. Either those surgeries weren't logged—"

"Or Kallistos omitted those pages in order to protect his own."

"Still, he's given us evidence," I say. "Evidence we can use against Mager."

Zack's expression doesn't soften. "Frankly, I'd rather he'd left Alan." He holds another scrap of paper out to me. "Besides, he has an ulterior motive—you. This was clipped to the spreadsheet."

It's a note addressed to me. Precise, old-world cursive. *Emma. You owe me. If you don't get Mager, I will. Until next time. Kallistos.*

I scrunch the paper up into a tiny little ball. "Is this a game to him?" I feel as if my head's about to explode. I pull my phone out and start to dial once more. "I'm calling Liz. She'll know how to reach Kallistos. Ask him if he took Alan."

"If?" Zack stays my hand. "Wait. How did Kallistos know about Alan?"

"Maybe he was following us earlier? Or had someone else following us? He knew about the investigation. About the missing vampires."

Zack thinks about the possibility for a moment, then rejects it. "I don't think anyone's been following us. Checking for tails? It's a hard habit to break."

I have another idea. This one chills my blood.

How did he know about Alan? Maybe he divined it from my head when I was so cleverly testing him. Or when he was kissing me.

"You think maybe he just wiped Alan's memory and sent him home?"

Zack gives me a look that tells me I don't want to know what he's thinking.

"Spit it out," I say.

"I don't think Kallistos is that forgiving. He didn't bat cleanup to help us. He did it to make sure we didn't get our hands on evidence involving his vamps." He points to the spreadsheet in my hand. "He left what he wanted us to have. If we don't move quickly to see that Mager is brought in, that note says he'll exact his own brand of justice." He jabs at the spreadsheet. "He played us."

"He played me, you mean." I stuff the note he left for me in my pocket. When I do, my fingers brush against the object Zack placed in my hand earlier. I pull it out. It's a smooth, polished stone the size of a quarter. "What is this?"

Zack plucks it from my outstretched palm. "No, I mean he played *us*." He palms the stone. "It's an old talisman. It's supposed to offer protection. It didn't. Kallistos used thrall. Either he's exceptionally strong or the power's faded." He slips it into his pocket.

"Well, my power is perfectly intact. In thousands of years I've never been wrong when reading someone. Whatever he's done with Alan, he decided to do it after we left him. I'm sure of it. Unless . . ."

"Unless?"

"Unless I didn't probe deep enough, push hard enough." *Unless I was as caught up in Kallistos' spell as he was in mine.* I find myself thinking of his kiss, the heat that infused my body, the same heat sending color to my cheeks now. I give myself a mental shake. Concentrate on what is real. Tally up what we were able to accomplish. We saved Isabella, Amy, Evan, and Owen. We lost two other vampires, possibly more, depending on how long Pierce has been running her clinic from hell. Possibly one human—Alan. Shit. I look hard at Zack. "Well, at least we have something to give Johnson. With the spreadsheet we can link Mager to Pierce."

"We can tell him Pierce gave it to us." Zack looks around the office once more. "I don't see anything else here that's out of place. Do you?"

Before I have a chance to reply, my cell phone rings. I turn to answer it. "Hello?"

"Agent Monroe?"

It's Michael Dexter. He sounds almost euphoric.

"Yes, Michael. How are you?"

"Never been better. You aren't going to believe this. Isabella is home!"

"Wait a minute, Michael. Zack is here. I'm putting you on speaker."

We listen as Michael explains how Isabella had fallen off the wagon and fed from a human. The shame drove her into isolation. "She just needed to get her head on straight. Do some soul searching."

"That's wonderful." I pause. "How are you feeling?"

I can hear his breathing through the phone. "Better, now. But we had a bit of a scare last night. You know I'd been working really hard on that piece so it would be ready for the auction? I guess it all finally caught up with me. Alan says I literally passed out on him once we got home. I scared you to death, didn't I?"

There's a murmur of response in the background.

I look up at Zack. Alan's with Dexter?

Zack moves closer, listening.

"I remember him pouring us both a nightcap," he continues. "I must have gone out like a light. But damned if I don't feel better than I have in weeks. I slept for an unbelievably long time. I feel like a new man."

Thanks to Kallistos.

I feel a hitch in my chest. Alan is alive. I take a breath. "I'm so glad Isabella is home safe and sound. Take care of each other."

"We will. Thank you. For everything."

We say good-bye and disconnect. I look up at Zack.

His mouth is pressed in a thin, hard line. "What's wrong? Alan is home and evidently none the worse for wear. Michael doesn't even remember how sick he was. I'd say that's some good news at least."

"Kallistos surprised me." His tone is grudging. "I'm not easily surprised."

"Or often wrong?"

"I didn't say that," Zack says. "Amy will be home shortly. In fact, she could already be there. Are you sure Dexter's all right?"

"Better than all right. He'll get a surprise at his next checkup. Kallistos cured him. I'm certain of it."

"Be careful." Zack's expression hardens. "Don't make Kallistos out to be a hero. He still blew up a building, almost killed that security guard, and endangered God knows how many others." He passes a hand over his face, a gesture of resignation and weariness. "Enough about him. We've got a shitload of paperwork and Johnson waiting for us at headquarters."

He reaches into his pocket for his car keys. When he pulls them out, the talisman falls to the floor.

"Still want to get it checked out?"

He sticks it back into his pocket. "With you as my partner, I'd better."

I smile. "I'll give you Liz's number."

Johnson is waiting for us when we get back to headquarters. He motions us into his office. He has a grin on his face and a note in his hand. "Message from the DA. Bernadette Haskell called him to say Amy Patterson is home. She'll hold a press conference tomorrow in New York explaining her absence and apologizing for causing so much worry. Looks like case closed."

Zack and I exchange looks. Johnson thinks the case is over.

He closes the door, then crosses his arms in front of his chest. "Now, what the hell were you doing in that building downtown?"

Or maybe not.

"We uncovered something unexpected there," Zack begins. "It's big."

Johnson motions for us to take seats. He walks around his desk and does the same. "I'm listening."

"A direct link between Dr. Barbara Pierce and the murder of several homeless people used as donors in a black market cash-for-organs scheme," Zack explains, taking the lead. "She confessed it all to us before setting off the blast and committing suicide."

Johnson holds up a hand. "Stop. You're telling me this Dr. Pierce died in the lab that blew up today?"

I nod. "Yes. That's where she'd been doing the transplants."

"Why confess and then destroy all of the evidence?" he asks.

Zack blows out a breath. "She wasn't doing the transplants voluntarily. She was being blackmailed. And she wasn't the only one. These operations were far too complicated for her to do alone. There were other medical personnel, not to mention organ recipients who had no idea they were involved in anything illegal—some of them children. She was trying, in her own way, to minimize the damage."

"Christ." Johnson leans back in his chair and waves encouragement. "Let's hear all of it."

Zack relays the story—the concocted story. How, while we were following up on a lead for the Patterson case last night, Dr. Pierce approached us. She was nervous, seemed off. She knew we were from the FBI and insisted we come to her office today, that she had something important to tell us, to give to us. How when we tracked her down this morning she was waiting for us. Said she was tired of the deception. Ashamed of what she'd done. Couldn't live with the guilt. How she took her own life and very nearly took ours.

Finally he pauses.

Johnson shakes his head. "You're lucky you weren't killed."

"That wasn't her intention," I say. "She wanted to give us this." I hand him the spreadsheet. "She slipped it under the door to the lab after locking herself inside."

He takes the sheet of paper in hand. "A list of the recipients and donors?"

Zack leans forward. "More than that, sir. She also gave us a name, Davis Mager. The man supplying the organs. My guess is that Mager is just the beginning, a small cog in a very large illegal transplant scheme."

"A donated organ always reflects the DNA of the donor," I add. "Pierce said most of Mager's 'donors' were homeless. Forensics should be able to match up the transplanted organs to that string of missing homeless cases Garner's been working on."

"Right," Zack agrees, then connects the last dot. "Garner builds a case against Mager for the string of murders *and* exposes them as being part of a large operation that stretches who knows how far."

Johnson jumps up and makes a beeline for the door. "Garner?" he shouts.

"Yes, sir?"

"Get your ass in here. Armstrong and Monroe are about to make your day."

It's three hours before the paperwork is complete and we've finished briefing Johnson and Garner, who was more than happy to take over the investigation. A BOLO is issued for Davis Mager. Turns out he has a vast and colorful criminal record. The only thing Zack and I fear is that the weasel might try to cut himself a deal to get out of doing significant time. On the other hand, if he manages to elude the law, he certainly won't elude Kallistos.

"Are you ready to get out of here?" Zack asks once Johnson's dismissed us.

I nod, gathering my bag and jacket. "Hell of a first case, huh?"

Zack smiles but doesn't say anything until we're outside and approaching his car. Then he reaches out. The back of his hand barely brushes mine, a feather touch. "Your place or mine?"

"Yours. I could use a walk on the beach." I climb inside and rest my head back on the seat. "But let's swing by Evan's first, so I can get my car."

He pulls out of the office parking lot and heads for the freeway. I close my eyes. I know Barbara Pierce's death was justified. Thanks to her notes, Davis Mager will be made to answer for his crimes, too. And a dozen cold cases solved. But all the same, I don't have the feeling of satisfaction I usually have at the end of a case. We've saved four kidnap victims whose stories will never be told. We lost two vampires whose names we never knew. Someone may be searching for them, too. And then there are the patients whose lives were saved by

Pierce. Others, like Mager's daughter and Michael Dexter, were likely unsuspecting and as much victims of Mager and Pierce as the homeless who lost their lives.

I glance over at Zack. His expression is once again calm, composed. He's a good partner. This was a bad case.

"Sorry you transferred?" I ask.

A smile tips the corners of his mouth. "Are you kidding? How could I be sorry? What kind of man would pass up the opportunity to work with a real honest-to-God Siren?"

I turn away from him and stare out the side window. His attempt to bring some levity to the situation just makes my heart heavier. When he reaches over to take my hand, my stomach knots, my heart wrenches.

What the hell am I doing? Why did I suggest going to his house?

Zack and I both know we aren't going there just to walk on the beach.

Liz's face is stark and rigid in my head. Disapproving. Her words of warning and wisdom ring in my ear. I know she means well. I know she's right. I know that if I really, truly care for Zack, I need to protect him.

I need to end things with him.

Soon.

CHAPTER 24

I'd hoped the walk on the beach would clear my head, and for a while it does. Zack and I stroll in silence, watching the water, listening to the pounding of the surf. Our pace is leisurely. Clouds are beginning to roll in from the horizon. A stiff breeze batters the waves.

Explains why we have the beach to ourselves.

Still, I don't complain. The chill in the air is a balm to my troubled spirit.

My head is spinning. There's what to do about Zack, of course. But Sarah and Kallistos are also weighing on my mind.

Kallistos. I led him to Alan. He read me during that kiss, when I thought I was reading him. I'm sure of it now. It's the only explanation I can think of. The memory of his kiss lingers in my head. I keep replaying it over and over, trying to pinpoint the moment of my monumental failure. I've grown too out of touch with the supernatural community. I'm out of practice. It would be wise to reacquaint myself with those in control as well as their politics. There is a certain amount of safety in anonymity, but knowledge is power, and the lack of it I possessed today about Kallistos Kouros has cost others and me. I can't let him take me by surprise again. I need to find out all I can about Kallistos, and I know where I'm going to start.

Liz.

Then there's Sarah. Did she and Zack really sleep together the other night? Does it matter? Either way, I know I should tell him she confronted me. Why am I so hesitant? Because part of me is afraid. Not for myself, for Zack. I know about werewolves and pack dynamics. Politics and power in their community, unlike that of the vampires, is constantly shifting. Some pack leaders rule with an iron fist and they can be brutal in their dealings with those over whom they have authority. I don't know if Zack's told me everything about why he left South Carolina. I don't know if his going back would place him in danger. I do know the way he feels about me would. It could be Sarah isn't all that bad. Perhaps she'd even be good for Zack, make him happy. Maybe if she was to stick around, and I was out of the picture, whatever they had could be rekindled.

Zack's arm is suddenly draped over my shoulders. "What are you thinking about?" he asks.

"I'm thinking maybe it's time we start back?" Not true, but safe.

His grip tightens. "Are you cold? You can have my jacket."

I shake my head. "No. Just a little tired. The events of the week are catching up to me."

"How's the headache?"

"Better. I think the fresh air did the trick."

We swing around and retrace our footsteps, still outlined in the damp sand.

"Do you think our version of what happened is going to hold?" I ask after a moment.

"Yes."

I give his arm a playful swat. "You spin a pretty convincing tale."

He shrugs. "Well, Amy's home, so that case is closed. And we just handed Garner the evidence to close the case that everyone will be talking about tomorrow. We stick to the story. Mager will go down and pay for the crimes he's committed." He gives me a sideways glance. "How are you at lying?"

I grin. "I'm betting not as good as you!"

"We'll practice."

Then another troublesome thought occurs to me. I've seen thrall wear off on occasion. "What happens if Alan starts to remember what really happened? It's going to be a shock when his mother's body is discovered in that burned-out clinic and the story hits the papers. How do you think Kallistos will react then? I want to believe that Alan's safe and that no more humans will be hurt. I want to believe it's over, but maybe it's not."

Zack squeezes my shoulders. "You're worrying too much. Kallistos is ancient. He's a king. His thrall will hold."

"Maybe he had one of his henchmen do it."

Zack shakes his head. "A vampire as old as he is has to be an expert at tying off loose ends. He left the note for you in Alan's office, so we know he was there. No. He wouldn't have left the task to anyone else. He knows Alan poses a threat. He would have tied off that loose end himself, too."

I feel a shudder pass through my body. Zack has nailed it. That's what Alan would be to Kallistos, nothing but a loose end.

Zack feels the tremor. "There's something else on your mind. What is it?"

I hesitate a moment before answering, "I'm thinking about how all this will affect the organ recipients on Pierce's log. Do you think they'll escape prosecution?"

"Don't know," Zack replies with a shrug. "My guess is they'll cooperate. Mager will go down. He's a three-time loser. One more conviction and he'll be put away for life."

I let my head rest on Zack's shoulder as we walk. "I hope so. I'd hate to see someone in Michael's situation dragged through the media and punished. If we'd arrive just a few hours later, his name would have been on that list."

I think of all the people—friends—I lost before organ transplants were available. I shake my head. "It's not so black-and-white to me. If you were dying, or a friend was dying, and someone came to you with the way to save him, wouldn't you take it? Regardless of whether it was breaking the law?"

Zack's arm tightens around my shoulder. "I don't know. But I have a feeling I know what your answer would be."

To my relief, his tone is neither judgmental nor condescending.

He stops and draws me into his arms. "Let's stop talking about work and start thinking about something much more pleasant."

I smile up at him. "And what would that be?"

He's leaning down, his lips now a whisper away. "This."

And then we're kissing and all misgivings about Kallistos and Alan and Sarah and the complications of the case are chased from my mind. Right now there's only Zack.

Our case is closed. And for the moment, being in his arms feels wonderful. I try to focus on the sensation and block out everything else.

Tomorrow will be a new day. With it will come a new case.

But I don't want to think about what's to come tomorrow. I'm tired of sacrificing my present because of my past.

Right now I just want to live. And I can. At least for one night.

Tonight will be about Zack and me.

Tomorrow will come soon enough.

CHAPTER 25

I really need to have a talk with Zack about leaving his door unlocked. Maybe it's still safe to do on the beach in South Carolina. It most definitely isn't in San Diego. Especially with Stalker Sarah around. I close and lock the door before setting the brown paper bag filled to the brim with cartons of Thai food on his countertop.

After our short walk on the beach, I was starving. Zack, however, was a ball of pent-up energy. So I suggested he go for a run while I foraged for food. The ease with which the domestic simplicity of our arrangement fell into place is bittersweet. I know our arrangement is neither simple nor secure. While I should be thinking with my head, the heart wants what the heart wants. And I'm tired of being denied. So very tired.

My cell phone chimes. There's a new text message from an unknown number: *Dinner tonight? K.*

K? Kallistos? How the hell did he get my number?

Of course, Liz.

The shower is running overhead. My eyes drift to the ceiling.

The phone chimes again. Another message: *I'll make it worth your while.*

This has to be Liz's doing. Probably with the best of

intentions. I know what I might be interrupting, but I dial anyway.

"You gave him my number?"

"Who?" Liz's breathless voice and a groan from Evan in the background confirm my suspicions.

Too bad. "Kallistos! He's texting me."

"That's why you called me?"

"How could you give him my number?" I ask.

"It was for your own good," Liz replies. "You know my views on rebound sex. Nothing heals a broken heart faster."

"My heart is not broken."

"Yet."

"Call him off, Liz. I mean it."

"You've met Kallistos. I couldn't call him off if I wanted to. He gets what he goes after."

"Not this time." I disconnect before she has a chance to argue. Immediately my cell phone rings and the call indicator shows it's Liz. I power off the phone and try to push my anger aside. I understand what Liz is trying to do. But no one ever really knows what the future will hold. This curse may seem eternal, but it's not. It can't be. Someday, it will be lifted. Zack and I may not have a promising future. But we are here. This minute. Together.

And right now Zack is still in the shower.

Suddenly I'm no longer feeling hungry. What I'm feeling is very, very dirty.

I pop the cartons of food in a warming oven and race up the stairs to join him.

The bathroom door is cracked open. Steam from the shower billows out into the bedroom, warm, wet, and inviting. The familiar scent of citrus and spice that I'm beginning to associate with Zack hangs in the air. I want to wrap myself in it, drown in it, drown in him. And for the next few hours, I will.

I push the door open with my arm and step inside. He must have heard me coming. He's waiting for me.

"Took you long enough to get up here."

He's inside the shower stall, heat rising around him. His hair is slicked straight back. His hands grip the top of the glass door, making his biceps bulge. He's hard and ready.

I let my eyes drift over his body, appreciating every spectacular inch. "Been thinking about me?" I ask him.

He glances down at his erection. "Can't seem to stop."

"Food's in the oven," I tell him, moving closer until only the glass separates us.

"It's not food I'm hungry for at the moment."

I see the predator in his eyes. His naked desire sends a chill up my spine.

"I've missed you," he says.

The confession makes me smile. "We practically spent the entire day together."

"Wearing far too many clothes."

Before our walk on the beach, I'd stopped by the house to exchange my work clothes for something more comfortable, a white peasant blouse, my most comfortable blue jeans, and a pair of brown leather sandals.

I reach back and pull the band from my hair, letting it fall around my shoulders. "Maybe I should take some of these off?"

"Unless you want them to get wet."

The sandals are already gone. The jeans and blouse come off next, leaving only the white lace bra and panties.

"God, I could just eat you up," Zack growls, his voice

rough with desire. He reaches down with one hand and strokes himself from tip to base and back up again. I remember the feel of him, the taste of him.

"Would you like me to do that for you?" I unfasten the back of my bra, then turn around, slip off the straps, and let it fall onto the growing pile of clothes on the floor.

"What I want you to do is get your ass in here."

I hear the shower door open behind me, feel a rush of heat and moisture roll out. He's anxious. I can tell. Yet I take my time. This is the fun part, the buildup, the seduction. I pull down my panties slowly, with a sway of my hips. As they fall to my ankles, Zack scoops me up. One arm is wrapped around my waist, his hand cupping the opposite breast. His other reaches forward, his palm covers my sex, his fingers deftly separate and slide inside.

"Tell me you want me," Zack murmurs.

I push back against him, providing friction where he needs it the most. The words tumble out. "I want you. Desperately. Completely. Recklessly." I don't think I've ever spoken with such honesty to a man.

In the blink of an eye we're in the shower. The speed at which he's moved leaves me breathless. I'm pinned facing the side wall, hands above my head, feet spread apart. I feel his breath on my back between my shoulders, feel the low rumble of a growl forming in his chest and belly. Teeth graze my neck. I freeze. The beast is close to the surface. I feel it.

"Zack?" I hear a tinge of panic in my voice.

"Shh. It's okay. No need to be afraid," he assures me. "I control the wolf. It doesn't control me. Except for those three nights a month, but I'm even getting better at that. You can trust me. I *want* you to trust me."

He releases my arms, letting his hands skim down the length of them, then over my shoulders before settling on my hips. He turns me around and tilts my chin up so that I can look him in the eye. The light above the shower enhances the gold in them.

I don't have to use my powers to feel the truth and sincerity of Zack's statement.

I place my hand on his chest and swallow down the lump in my throat. Zack and I are alike in so many ways. Living lives shrouded in secrets and built on too many lies. It's impossible to connect with anyone when you can't be real. And at the end of the day, whether human, Were, or Siren, that's what we crave, what we truly yearn for—a connection.

"I wouldn't be here, Zack, if I didn't trust you."

It's almost as if he was waiting for permission, for assurance. Zack cups my face in the palms of his hands. His mouth covers mine and he kisses me deeply. Our tongues curl around each other, languidly exploring. Time stands still for me. I focus on the moment, on the sensation. On the taste and feel and smell of the man before me.

His hand leaves my hip. He lifts one of my legs onto the bench in the back of the shower, leaving me open and so wanting. Two fingers slip inside.

I gasp. My eyes widen and my head snaps back.

My reaction evokes a grin. His pumping is slow and steady, the rhythm old and familiar. After one night together, he already knows my body. He knows how to touch me and how to make me respond.

My hands reach for his biceps. I feel his power and strength as I run my hand over them, wanting, needing to hold on to something. I'm climbing. Higher and higher.

Zack adds another finger. His thumb is working, too. I want more. I want him with me, in me.

"Please." My body is strung as tight as a bow. I'm breathing too fast.

"Tell me what you need, baby."

One hand guides him, the other moves to still his movements. "You," I manage to say before my knees start to buckle.

I needn't worry.

Zack is there to catch me, more than catch me. He lifts me up.

My arms and legs wrap around him. The cool tile presses into my back as I slide down, letting him fill me to the hilt. He eases out, and then back in, deeper this time. My stomach is a mass of coils, tight, ready to explode.

"I'm all yours," he whispers into my ear.

My heart wrenches.

It's too much.

It's not enough.

"Give it all to me, then." I reach back and grab a fistful of his hair. "Don't. Hold. Back."

He doesn't. He tilts his hips and picks up the pace, making me appreciate just how much Zack Armstrong has to give.

CHAPTER 26

"You'll be very relieved to know that my legs are working again. And I found chopsticks." I tilt my head toward the breast pocket of the shirt I'm wearing. It's Zack's. I commandeered it from his closet.

He's kneeling in front of the fireplace, dressed only in sweats. The fire is roaring and he's lit the gas heaters on the upstairs deck. There's a love seat and chair out there along with a coffee table. I have the bag of Thai in one hand and two beers in the other. Zack promptly relieves me of one of the beers and the bag of food.

"Smells great!"

I follow him outside. "I worked very hard heating it up in the microwave."

Zack's arranging the cartons, but he pauses to pull me into his arms. His hand curls around the same spot where Sarah grabbed me this morning at the elevator. Without thinking, I wince.

"Did I hurt you in the shower?" The alarm in his voice makes me realize I can't pass this off as something he did. It would cut him to the quick.

"No, it happened earlier today."

He's pushing up the sleeve and inspecting my arm. There's already a bruise. Several. With a gentle finger, he traces the outline of the handprint. "Did Kallistos do this to you when you were locked in that room with him?"

"No. It wasn't Kallistos." The last thing I need is for Zack to have one more reason to go gunning for Kallistos. I tell him the truth. "It was Sarah."

"Sarah?" From the expression on his face I can tell it wasn't the answer he was expecting.

"She showed up at the office."

"Looking for me?"

"Me, actually."

He frowns. "I have a feeling I'm not going to like your answer, but what for?"

"To give me the stay-away-from-my-man speech."

"I'm not her—"

"Did the two of you sleep together the other night? Just tell me the truth, Zack. I'm ancient. I haven't the heart for games and betrayal."

To his credit, Zack doesn't skip a beat. "Yes. Slept. She showed up here after you left. She had no place to stay. She knew I wouldn't turn her away. I couldn't. We shared the cage."

"That's it?"

"That's it. I meant it when I told you it was over between the two of us." He reaches into his pocket and pulls out his phone. "I've got to put an end to this. It isn't Sarah's fault. Without meaning to, I've put her in a bad spot. She's desperate and feeling cornered. That's a dangerous combination."

He pushes a button on his cell and listens intently before leaving a message. "J.C., it's Zack. Look, I know what you're trying to do. I can even understand it. But it's not going to work. I told you before, I'm done. I'm not coming back. This isn't my fight and Sarah isn't going to convince me otherwise. She has no sway over me. None. If you don't set this right, I'll have to."

Zack tosses the phone onto the coffee table, then walks over to the rail and stares out at the ocean. The nerve in his jaw is ticking. I give him a moment to collect his thoughts before asking, "So, who's J.C.?"

He turns back to face me. "J. C. Hewitt, he's the current beta of my old pack. He's wilder than a June bug and dumber than a doornail. Before I left there was an upset, a turnover in leadership. The new alpha, Asa Wade, is a heartless bully. He's ruthless. He's also smart and ambitious. He started to develop alliances. The culture began to shift in a direction I couldn't abide."

"And that's why you left?"

Zack nods. "People were getting hurt. Everyone was afraid. Some, including J.C., were looking to me to put a stop to it all."

I hand Zack his beer. "They were pressuring you to take on this Wade character?"

He drinks down half of it before answering, "I've spent too much time on my own. Too much time dealing with brutal killers and cold-blooded sociopaths who will do anything to hold on to power. I joined the pack because I wanted to be a part of something, not because I wanted to be in charge or responsible." Sadness washes over him, clouding his features. "Power has a way of changing a man. I'm not fit to be a leader. I've made too many mistakes." He finishes off the rest of his beer.

I hand him mine. "I bet it wasn't an easy decision, walking away."

Zack reaches for my hand and leads me to the love seat. "Easy, no. But I'd walked away from bigger and badder than Asa Wade. I was lost once. I promised myself I'd never go down that road again. Some of the pack members evidently think they can still persuade me to come back, J.C. for one. Apparently Wade has his eye on Sarah and he scared the shit out of her. It didn't take much persuading. J.C. planted the seed and—"

"Sarah came here to talk you into going back and getting rid of Wade."

"Only in doing that, she put herself in a tight spot. She can't really go back. Not without betraying her agenda or submitting to Wade. That pack, that place, it's all she's ever known."

"Is it the only pack you've known?"

Zack nods, his expression grave. "It didn't take long, after walking away from my old life, to realize that walking away wasn't enough. I needed to walk toward something. I needed to find meaning."

"And you found it with them?"

"For a while. It felt like home." Zack shakes his head and with it the melancholy seems to lift, replaced by something else. Resolve. Determination. "Wade is the worst kind of wolf. Sarah can't go back there."

I feel a flush of compassion for Sarah. "What are you going to do?"

Zack kisses me on the forehead and plucks two of the chopsticks from my pocket. "Eat. Worship every inch of you. Figure out the Sarah problem tomorrow." He dives into the shrimp pad Thai.

His ease with casual affection is enviable. I'm out of practice. For good reason, I remind myself. I pop open the container of drunken noodles and give the contents a pensive stir. My perspective concerning Sarah is shifting. She's desperate and afraid, torn away from all she's known and facing life alone in a strange place. Something I've experienced a thousand times. Perhaps—

"Emma?"

Zack's voice pulls me back. He's said something and I've totally missed it. I try for a smile. "Sorry. It's been a long day."

He tilts his head to the side and studies me. "Something else is on your mind. Out with it."

I bite back the urge to deny and deflect and go for the truth. "I don't want to see anyone get hurt. You or Sarah."

It's the truth. But I'm also thinking of more than pack politics. I'm thinking of Demeter. I blow into the container. It gives me a place to focus.

Zack turns sideways in the love seat. "I know how to take care of myself. I was trained by the best. But I also know my limitations, when to walk away, when to get out." He reaches out and gives my hand a squeeze. "I did the right thing leaving South Carolina. I'm glad I did."

"I don't want to lose you," I tell him in a rare moment of candor, even though I know I will, know it's inevitable.

"You won't," he assures me. "Listen, Emma. I get it. You've been in a relationship that ended badly—am I right?"

The intuitiveness of his unexpected observation cuts me to the quick. But it also makes me realize I have to stop pretending that *our* relationship can end any way but badly. Our fate's sealed. Still, I nod, slowly.

"That guy, whoever he was . . . he's not me. That relationship is not this relationship."

"I don't *do* relationships. Not anymore. I've been on

my own for more years than you can possibly imagine. I've grown used to being on my own and—"

Zack cuts me off. "Isn't it the guy the one who's supposed to be commitment-phobic?"

He looks amused. He has no idea how serious this is and I have no idea how to explain it without placing him further in harm's way. His statement about knowing when to walk away doesn't reassure me. Zack Armstrong is not the kind of man who backs down when the stakes are high. He's a lover *and* a fighter.

I don't want to have this conversation. I want to get lost in Zack. I want him to explore my body with his mouth, to fuck me fiercely, to bring me to the edge of blissful oblivion, to that place where there's no need for penance and no fear of punishment. Where I don't have to come to terms with how selfish and reckless I'm being for just a few more hours of happiness. I blink back tears.

Zack's brow furrows. "I understand your hesitation. I can't blame you. I'm a man with a dangerous past. I have a lot of regrets. I've made mistakes. So many that I sometimes wonder if I'll ever be able to make up for them. Maybe we should go back to pretending, play it safe. Is that what you want?" He doesn't wait for an answer. He reaches out and cups my face in the palm of his hand. "I just don't think I can. I don't want to. This thing that's building between us, I want to see it through. Don't you?"

I kiss the inside palm of his hand. "More than anything." I'm speaking purely from my heart because the decision's been made. It's as if the weight of the world has lifted from my shoulders. Demeter can't—won't—deny me these last moments of pleasure. "Make love to me."

Zack leans over me and covers my mouth with his, drinking me in and enveloping me in his arms. The kiss is leisurely. He takes his time and I savor every second, letting the passion build until my heart is pounding.

He pulls back. "Say please," he murmurs, his tone light, teasing.

A Siren never begs. I can have any man at any time. I've conquered kings, seduced holy men and rakes, driven the famous and infamous to desperation with want. I've fallen in lust and I've fallen in love. But I've always been in control.

I swing one long leg across Zack's lap. Rising onto my knees, I straddle his hips and slowly unbutton the shirt I'm wearing. His erection grows under me and I wantonly begin to ride it. Seeing the desire build in his eyes emboldens me, giving me the confidence to try something I'd never done before.

"Please, Zack. Please—" The rest of my sentence is swallowed in a gasp.

I'm standing in the living room, staring out the patio doors. The ocean looms black and restless under a star-filled sky. The pounding of the waves crashes down on me, as relentless as my eternal despair.

Zack is right, this case may not have gone the way we anticipated, but Amy, Isabella, and the others are home safe. That counts for something, but not enough.

"Will it ever be enough?" The sound of my voice is swallowed by the wind. But I know she hears it. She hears everything. I don't expect an answer. Nothing has changed; I feel it to the core of my very being. The words Demeter uttered thousands of years ago hold the same power over me today as they did then.

"You will live as mortal, but love will be denied to you, and you will rescue girls until I, Demeter, think you have

done your penance. I will be watching. Always watching. Cross me, your lovers will die, and your penance will increase tenfold. All because you didn't save my daughter."

Her words, crushing, brutal, echo in my head. I feel empty. I'm so immersed in my unhappiness I don't know Zack has come up behind me until I feel his arms slip around my waist. I want nothing more than to turn around, bury my face in his chest and remain forever locked in his embrace.

But that's not going to happen.

That can't happen. I've already seen to it.

After we'd made love, after Zack drifted off to sleep, I got up, showered, and dressed. I scrubbed out the shower and sink, rinsing away any trace of me, of my scent, of my perfume. Then I raced down to the kitchen to clean the dishes, toss away the empty food containers. As soon as I heard the shower running upstairs, I went back up and stripped the bed, put on fresh sheets. The ones that smell like me are now spinning in the washer.

I'm prepared for questions.

Questions that he'll soon forget asking.

He nuzzles my neck, sending shivers racing up my spine.

When I don't move, don't respond to his touch, Zack puts his hands on my shoulders and turns me to face him.

"Are you all right?" he asks. "You're dressed. And the bed's made." He waves a hand toward the house. "You cleaned up the kitchen. Are you leaving? I was hoping you'd stay."

I look into his face, press my palms into my thighs to keep from reaching up and pulling it closer, to keep from kissing him. Instead I release a sigh. "I think I'd better be getting home. The week is finally catching up with me."

His head tilts to the side, his gaze intent. "Are you sure nothing's wrong? We're okay?"

"Absolutely," I say, my voice full of reassurance. "I could sure use a cup of coffee before I go, though. I hope you don't mind, I made some."

He smiles, a slow, sweet smile. "Running low on caffeine? Come on. Sit down. I'll pour you a cup."

I reach out and take his hand. "Let me get it."

He takes a seat at the dining room table. I feel his eyes on me while I gather cups, spoons, creamer from the refrigerator, and the sugar bowl. I place them on the table, then make the trek back into the kitchen for the coffeepot. The pot feels unbearably heavy in my hand. I pour the bitter brew into his cup and watch the steam rise and dissipate.

He adds the sugar and cream to his coffee and gives it a stir. "Are you sure you're all right?"

"Never been better." I force a smile, then on impulse, lean in and cover his mouth with mine. The kiss is soft and sweet and takes my breath away. "This is real, isn't it?"

Zack cups the side of my face in the palm of his hand and traces my lips with the pad of his thumb. "Yes. Are you positive I can't persuade you to stay?"

The certainty in his voice, the tenderness in his touch makes my heart ache. If I let him persuade me to stay, we'll both be lost. There is no denying it. I can't pretend. I've fallen in love with Zachary Armstrong. What's worse, I fear he's falling in love with me. Liz is right. I need to fix this. I can't let it continue.

I won't let it continue.

I wait and watch as he takes a few contented sips of his coffee.

Then, because I can't bear the thought of watching

the transformation, I leave the table and wander back outside.

The moon, although not full, is still high and bright in the sky. The ocean sparkles beneath it. The air smells of salt. Some things never change. Tears sting my eyes, but I stubbornly wipe them away. I did what I had to do.

Zack's chair scrapes back from the table. I steel myself for what I know is coming. He comes outside and joins me at the wall that separates the back deck from the beach. We are side by side, arms folded on the wall, not touching. He's brought his coffee with him.

"Beautiful morning," he says.

I close my eyes for the briefest of moments. I can hear the difference in his voice already. No intimacy, no closing of the space between us except for a friendly shoulder bump. "Quite a week, huh?"

"Yes. It's been quite a week," I say, trying to keep the emotion out of my voice. "It's late. I think I'd better get home."

Zack smiles. "Past your bedtime?"

"I didn't get much sleep last night."

I glance over at him. Neither did Zack. But he doesn't remember. His memory of what happened between us last night is gone. Like so many others, it's been replaced by new ones. Safe ones. I wonder what scene is playing in his mind right now.

He takes a last pull of his coffee, sweetened with sugar and a spell to guarantee his security. Zack sets the cup on the sea wall. He drapes an arm casually over my shoulder. "I'll walk you out."

When we're at the car, he opens the door. "See you at the office on Monday."

He waits until I've secured my seat belt and started

the engine to turn back to the house. Then, with a wave, he's gone, disappearing through the front door and pulling it closed behind him without a parting glance my way.

I sit for a moment, staring after him. The empty envelope in my jacket pocket crackles when I lean forward to release the emergency brake. I take it out, crumple it, and toss it on the passenger seat. Loneliness like the cut of a razor slashes at my gut. I wish Liz could cast a spell that would make me forget these last few days. But she can't. I tried using magic before, to forget other tragic losses, or as Demeter would call them, mistakes. Remembering is part of my punishment, the penance Demeter exacts. I can feel the goddess watching, feel the chill of her smile of satisfaction that I will remember every moment Zack and I spent together. That I will remember how Zack felt inside me and how my body responded to his touch. But worse, I will remember how good we were together. I will think of it every time I look into his eyes and see reflected there not love, but the casual concern of one coworker for another. Mirroring that indifference will be torture. Suddenly I can't breathe. I roll down my window.

Air rushes in, so cold it burns my skin. I close my eyes. I know what this means. Demeter is here. Her voice comes to me as frigid as the web of ice that now covers my windshield.

"You did the right thing, Ligea."

Demeter stands on a sheet of ice between Zack's front door and the car. As she walks toward me, frost spreads across the ground, following her like death's shadow. Her cobalt eyes are as unforgiving as ever, but her sword is sheathed.

"How many more? How many more will I have to save?"

"Until I am satisfied. And I will be watching you, watching you with this man."

"It's over between us."

Demeter smiles. "For now. He's different. You and I both know it."

My phone buzzes. There's a text message coming in. But the tears clouding my vision prevent me from reading it. When I look up, Demeter is gone. I squeeze my eyes shut, count to ten, then look again at my phone. The message is from Johnson.

Sorry to interrupt your weekend, I read. *But there's a girl missing. We need you to come in.*

I get ready to reply when Zack's front door opens. He's rushing toward me, coat in one hand, cell phone in the other.

"Glad you haven't left," he says. "Johnson sent me a text."

"Just got one, too. Looks like we've got a new case."

"Never a dull moment or a day off."

"Regretting that transfer yet?"

Zack shakes his head and buckles his seat belt. "Nope. Hey, a little luck, your special skill set, and my combination of strength, guile, and boyish charm, we might even solve this one."

To Zack I say, "Let's go, partner." To myself I repeat the words I always say at the beginning of every case.

Redemption could be one rescue away.

ABOUT THE AUTHOR

S. J. Harper is the pen name for the writing team of **Samantha Sommersby** and **Jeanne C. Stein**, two friends who met at Comic-Con in San Diego and quickly bonded over a mutual love of good wine, edgy urban fantasy, and everything Joss Whedon.

Samantha Sommersby left what she used to call her "real-life" day job in the psychiatric field to pursue writing full-time in 2007. She is the author of more than ten novels and novellas, including the critically acclaimed *Forbidden* series. She currently lives with her husband and cocker spaniel, Buck, in a century-old Southern California Craftsman. Sam happily spends her days immersed in a world where vampires, werewolves, and demons are real, myths and legends are revered, magic is possible, and love still conquers all.

Jeanne Stein is the national bestselling author of *The Anna Strong Vampire Chronicles*. She also has numerous short story credits, including most recently the novella *Blood Debt* from the *New York Times* bestselling anthology *Hexed*. Her series has been picked up in three foreign countries and her short stories published in collections here in the U.S. and the U.K. She lives in Denver, Colorado, where she finds gardening a challenge more daunting than navigating the world of mythical creatures.

Faith Hunter

Blood Trade

The Master of Natchez, Mississippi has a nasty problem
on his hands. Rogue vampires—those who believe that
humans should be nothing more than prey—are
terrorizing his city. Luckily, he knows the perfect
skinwalker to call. But what he doesn't tell Jane
Yellowrock is that there's something different about
these vamps. Something that makes them harder to kill—
even for a pro like Jane. Now, her simple job has turned
into a fight to stay alive...

Also in the series:
Skinwalker
Blood Cross
Mercy Blade
Raven Cursed
Death's Rival

"Smart, sexy, and ruthless."
—*New York Times* bestselling author Kim Harrison

FROM *NEW YORK TIMES* BESTSELLING AUTHOR

Keri Arthur

Darkness Splintered
A Dark Angels Novel

When half-werewolf, half-Aedh Risa Jones loses the
second key to hell, she angers several powerful people.
She's starting to feel the pressure from all sides—even
from her father, who gives her an ultimatum: get back the
key or he will kill her friends.

<u>Also Available</u>
Darkness Unbound
Darkness Rising
Darkness Devours
Darkness Hunts
Darkness Unmasked

**"Keri Arthur's imagination and energy infuse
everything she writes with zest."**

—#1 *New York Times* bestselling author
Charlaine Harris

Available wherever books are sold or at
penguin.com
facebook.com/ProjectParanormalBooks